One Flame Hour

Susana Cory-Wright

© 2021 Susana Cory-Wright

All rights reserved.

ISBN: 9798458455350

In Memory of Henry James

2007 - 2020

ACKNOWLEDGMENTS

This book is dedicated to the memory of one boy whose remarkable creativity, gift for friendship, and courage *will* live on in our hearts.

As ever, I draw strength from my incredible family - Jonathan, Emma, James and Maximilian. This book, as always, is for you.

There are lots of lovely shops in our town filled with wonderful people who kept us going during this extraordinary year, but I would like to commend the staff of our local Winchester M&S branch in particular. As bemused and fearful as the rest of us were in the early days of the pandemic, they were resolutely optimistic in the face of the unknown. Often, indeed, theirs was the *only* face we saw outside our 'bubble.'

Therefore, this book is also dedicated to Gemma, Ian, Kate and Rosanna, with gratitude.

For one brief golden moment rare like wine,
The gracious city swept across the line;
Oblivious of the colour of my skin,
Forgetting that I was an alien guest,
She bent to me, my hostile heart to win,
Caught me in passion to her pillowy breast.
The great, proud city, seized with a strange love,
Bowed down for one flame hour my pride to prove.

Claude McKay

One Flame Hour

1

"What *is* that?" said Seb his tone mildly curious but not so mild that it hadn't woken her.

"What's what?" Carla mumbled. She hadn't heard a thing, so deeply submerged in layers of rich, velvety sleep, that the house could have burned down and she wouldn't have known. Hang on, had it? No, it couldn't have. Surely Seb would be far more alarmed if that were the case. She let herself slip back under…

"That noise? You don't hear it?"

Seb was fully awake now and no longer his kind, mellow self once he realised that it was Carla's phone, not his, vibrating across the oak floorboards - floorboards that meant every sound was amplified. If she dropped a hair clip, Seb heard it. A red light from the travel adaptor (Alfie seemed to have taken all their Samsung connectors to boarding school with him) simultaneously illuminated a corner of the room.

"Mmmn?" Carla turned in her sleep.

Since the start of the pandemic, Carla's sleep patterns had altered. At the beginning, these had been exaggerated; jumbled dreams that were always just on the brink of turning into nightmares. Now they were just disturbed. She would invariably fall asleep while they watched a film only to wake a couple of hours later, quite refreshed, head whizzing with regret at all the things she had failed to accomplish. She would be awake for hours mournful for lost opportunities; of having prized straight hair over a dip in the sea, rushing a lunch, not having kept more of the twins' artwork when they

One Flame Hour

were small (they were now in their twenties), before falling asleep again in the early hours and just as the alarm was about to go off.

She was in such a sleep now and her turn to feel resentful at having been woken. She was confident that Seb would resolve whatever emergency presented itself. They weren't *both* needed, surely. Not even the intermittently flashing light could keep her from sinking back into slumber. The bed was so lovely and warm... the house so deliciously *quiet;* no creaks emanating from Alfie's bedroom which was right above theirs. No vibration as *his* phone jumped along the floor. At last, after so many months of lockdown, they had the house to themselves. And after a few uncertain months when they wondered if schools would re-open at all, Alfie was safely ensconced in his boarding house. No need to get up just yet...

"Definitely yours," said Seb grumpily.

"M-mine?" she murmured incomprehensively. Sleep was pulling her deeper still, at last, into the waiting, welcome pool of oblivion. Her body was folded into the foetal position, away from his. Her side was cool and smooth. Not *too* cool, though, just the right temperature. There was no-

"It's yours!" said Seb loudly. "Answer it!"

Carla's eyes flew open. Without her contact lenses, the room was familiar only through memory, tepid shadows fleshing out the empty spaces: the Victorian button chair in the corner, the linen-covered stool in a Canova fabric she'd always loved - huge white peonies on a pale green background. She tracked the pulsating light. Maybe it would just peter out. Seb gave her a gentle kick. Without actually getting out of bed, Carla wedged a corner of the duvet between her knees and stretched as far as she could inching the phone towards her

One Flame Hour

by its cord, in just the way Seb always advised against. She held the screen to her face... which very clearly read: 'Sunday: two a.m.' Oh, dear, a call at that time had to be bad news. The bad news being that it was *only* 2 a.m...She wriggled back up the bed. Seb yanked the covers to his side none too gently.

"It's brother Roger," mouthed Carla as the familiar number rolled across the screen. Relief that something hadn't happened to one of the twins or Alfie, was quickly replaced by a different anxiety. If the urgency didn't concern their children, then what?

"Yes? Everything OK?" she said in one breath. *Quick! Just say what it is! No matter what it is. Just say it.*

"*Camarada!*"

Brother Roger's greeting was always effusive but for some unexplained reason, it was also nearly always in Portuguese. Occasionally he addressed her in Basque or Gallego. Although they were neither. Their father was born in Barcelona, so a Catalan. Very different. There was the familiar drag of a cigarette.

"Are you *smoking?*" Even at two in the morning she reverted to being big sister. Seb sighed loudly and tugged the duvet. She hunkered further down the covers, hoping her body would blot out light from her phone.

"*No!* Well, yes. God, Carl."

"OK, so what is it?" whispered Carla. "Has something happened?"

Carla was used to her younger brother's Sunday calls, but this was late/early, even for him.

"The police are here," he stage-whispered back.

"What do you mean, the *police*?" she squeaked hoping that Seb overhearing the word 'police' would be empathetic. A final peeved wrench of the bedsheets, that left her without any covers at all, persuaded her otherwise. She swung her legs over the side of the bed, fumbling for her dressing gown. "Hang on Rog, having to move."

Their bedroom was the coldest room in the house and she padded through to her walk-in closet to sit on the thick rug by the window. A streetlight illuminated rails of clothing, a recent Mother's Day card from Alfie on the mantlepiece of the tiny fireplace, the Walt Disney ash tray her father had brought back from California when she was little, promising to take her when she was older which he never had, and the houses opposite.

"They've come for the big E."

"At *this* time?" Carla was incredulous. Their mother, Eugenia, was a hyper (some time psychotic) eighty-eight-year- old, (*and* a COVID survivor) but what on earth could she have possibly done to warrant a police visit?

"A bit hacked off, actually." There was another sharp intake of tobacco.

"Both of you, I should imagine."

There was a delayed lag as her brother let out a mouthful of smoke. Or so Carla imagined. Roger seemed prepared to chat as though it were the middle of the day. By now, Carla was wide awake anyway so it might as well have been. "I've been sleeping on the sofa for two weeks but knowing that Eugenia was leaving later today, I had the best sleep I've had in months."

"Until now."

"What?"

"Until being woken up." Carla hugged her knees under a Missoni lurex gold gown. Would she ever wear such a garment again? And the shoes? A sliver of light spot lit a pair of strappy suede Jimmy Choos: slender heels, thin laces. Certainly, those were highly impractical to wear tramping down the cobbled streets of her medieval town. Never mind the mud. Torrential rain recently had rendered the surrounding fields and walkways a river of mire.

"Yeah. Good, I can hear you better."

"So, why the police?"

"Well." Another drag. "They've said Eugenia can't travel. They're here to prevent it."

"At two a.m.?"

Carla could imagine her brother swiping the air in front of him. The dog started barking.

"*Calla te!*" He pronounced the 'te' with particular emphasis. "Shut up! Not you, Carl. *Hendricks*. No, I'm not bloody walking now."

"Roger," said Carla. "As much as I'm enjoying this little chat."

"Yeah, so basically what happened is: Eugenia used the same taxi firm that took her from the doctor's when she was

One Flame Hour

confirmed as having COVID two weeks ago. They couldn't believe a woman of her age was travelling so soon after having had the virus."

"Let alone *surviving*."

"Precisely."

"I mean what is the likelihood - one kidney, asthma, her *age…*"

There was a small silence.

"Anyway, the taxi firm called the police. And here they are."

"But they can't *really* prevent her leaving?"

"Nah, she's good. Just thought you'd like to share in the entertainment."

The cathedral clock struck the hour.

"Kind of you," she said.

"Not at all."

Carla pondered absent-mindedly how it was that they'd never called Eugenia (who had a Spanish name although she was Canadian) anything other than by her first name. She'd never been a 'mummy' or a 'mum' or a 'mother'. As if subconsciously, linking the notion of softness and mothers, Carla buried her face against the dewy velvet of an emerald-green trouser leg. All these clothes for occasions that seemed as fanciful as something out of a fairy tale. All the little beaded bags, tortoiseshell clutches, including the Louis Vuitton mink-edged, embroidered tiny evening minaudière that was no bigger than a Christmas tree bauble.

One Flame Hour

"Did you know?" said Carla. "That the minaudière was invented in the '30's by Charles Arpel when he saw a wealthy socialite toss her lipstick and change into a tin box?"

"I did not." The wonderful thing about brother Roger was that you could tell him any random bit of trivia and he'd be interested. In fact, he *collected* trivia for his pub quizzes.

Another sharp intake of tobacco. Men smoking was something Carla had grown up with. That highly evocative (provocative in Roger's case) click, a sound that was part of her DNA. It was probably the very first thing she'd ever heard. It was definitely the first thing she remembered *seeing*, her father's face hanging over her cot, a cigarette dangling from his mouth. No cute wind-up cuddly music clowns for her.

"What does the word come from?"

Carla fingered another exquisite evening box - Gucci this time, rose gold with tiny interlocking 'g's, a jewelled firefly on the front. There was a central amethyst for a belly, while its wings, a patchwork of semi-precious stones, were edged with diamonds. Utterly useless. It couldn't hold a phone, lip gloss or even a credit card - on second thoughts it might just hold a mask (if there was anywhere, they could go to that would require such a pointless article) but it was very beautiful all the same. If it wasn't so heavy, she could have worn it as a pendant. Another example of her maths not being quite up to it as she'd not understood the dimensions.

"A minaudière is a coquettish woman - from the French - 'to flirt'."

"Which is not the word best used to describe Eugenia at this moment."

One Flame Hour

As if on cue, Carla could hear their mother's shrill voice- her North American accent more pronounced as she got older - telling the police exactly what she intended doing, when and to whom.

"Well, that's a waste of police time if ever there was one. Let alone tax-payer's money," sighed Carla setting down aside her toys.

There was another silence- the all-enveloping, unearthly silence of early morning - at having a house to oneself. She never knew the exact time the streetlight switched off.

"Yup. She's definitely not going quietly." Another hurl of abuse. "Ouch. Actually, she's not going at all."

"You've been amazing, Roger," added Carla warmly. Which was true. Their mother had been visiting from Gibraltar (where she currently resided) when she had fallen ill and had spent the past fortnight being nursed by Roger and his wife. No mean feat in a small, two-bedroomed, one-bathroom house.

"Yeah, well, you'd have done the same."

Carla let the ensuing silence do the answering. She unfurled, feeling stiff. The dawn was breaking, the streetlight finally dimming or was it simply being cancelled out by the emerging sunrise?

"But you're all feeling OK, you haven't succumbed to the dreaded *beeruus*?"

Roger laughed behind his cigarette, reminded of the way their Spanish father had pronounced the word. He'd always enjoyed a good virus (which had let him off household tasks and preparations for any big family event or gathering, *especially* Christmas) long before this present pandemic made itself known. There was another silence as they both, in their separate ways, remembered their father. It was coming up to the seventh anniversary of his death.

"No."

"Amazing if you think about it. Makes me wonder how contagious it really is."

"Oh, it's real and it's contagious. But we know there are so many variables, so many factors. Like obesity - apparently if you have an BMI greater than 40, it increases the risk of dying by 90%."

"Really?" Carla didn't like to remind Roger of his ever-expanding girth. Like Cyril Connolly, her brother liked to joke that inside him, there was an even fatter man trying to get out. In fact, he was looking forward to meeting him.

"Yeah, it's reached epidemic proportions," said Roger comfortably, clearly believing that he didn't fall into any 'at risk' category despite drinking, smoking and eating too much. "What do you think he'd have made of all this?"

Hendricks let out a yelp. Carla jumped.

"What was that?"

"Think I might have stepped on the damn dog. God, he's a nuisance. What do I think who would have made of it? Pa?"

Carla nodded into the phone. "Yes, Pa."

"Don't think he'd have noticed. Pa was pretty anti-social at the best of times."

One Flame Hour

Carla frowned. "Was he?"

She could picture their father clearly, his form springing up before her eyes as immediate and defined had he been a NCP in one of Alfie's far too realistic computer games: tall, languid always a cigarette and coffee in hand. They could never pass a café without him having to stop. A simple errand could take hours by the time he'd satisfied sweet tooth cravings and a caffeine or tobacco hit. In fact, the last time she'd taken him out, it had.

"Remember the incident with the barber?"

"I was just thinking about it. But that's not a fair example. I mean there were extenuating circumstances."

"There always were."

"Mmmn."

Suddenly cold, Carla pulled down a blush-coloured cashmere wrap from one of the hangers. Trimmed in fox, she'd bought it at the Max Mara boutique at the airport in Sydney while flying to see Tom in New Zealand. Tom had been on his gap year and it was the first time that he'd been properly separated from his twin, Sophie. He'd been vulnerable as had she. Reminded of that trip and of their father, Carla snuggled into its comforting lushness, fatigue pulling at her eyelids. She hugged her ankles, resting her head on her knees. Papa. That last time in London…

*

One Flame Hour

Alfredo - but always called 'Papa.' If they never called Eugenia 'Mum' it would never have occurred to Carla, or her siblings Christophe and Roger, to call Alfredo anything other than 'Papa.' Older than Eugenia by a mere decade, Alfredo was like someone out of another century in terms of manners and behaviour. He kissed women's hands - or rather raised a woman's hand half-way to his lips claiming it was vulgar to actually kiss it - obsessed over the correct way of addressing clerical aristocracy and spent his spare time compiling obscure (unintelligible) idioms for dictionaries that much to the family's amazement were published and did well.

By the time Alfredo had experienced his first stroke he wasn't so much diminished as rabid with rage and frustration. There was nothing docile about Papa's twilight years and although somewhat incapacitated, he'd become adept at slipping the constraints placed on him by his minders - namely Eugenia. But the effort of exerting any sort of will contrary to Alfredo's had become too much even for their mother (which was saying something) and increasingly, within reason, he was left to his own devices. Carla often wondered what exactly his ablutions constituted of as his appearance grew more and more unkempt. Taking matters into her own hands, Carla booked an appointment at the barber's, called The Green Man, in Harrods. Located in the basement or demi-floor below ground, it was a place she had always thought, if she were a man, she might enjoy. She'd occasionally glanced down the stairwell on her way out through the Hans Place exit and seen men, sitting immobile, their faces wrapped in hot towels, steam floating halo-like around their shrouded faces.

On the day in question, Carla had arrived to take Papa (wheelchair and all) to his appointment. But things had gone wrong from the get-go. Unusually for a Spaniard, Papa wasn't particularly tactile. In fact, too late, Carla recalled how he didn't like being touched at all and especially not by

One Flame Hour

strangers. She'd never for a moment considered that an old-fashioned shave might not be welcome. She glanced at his fingernails. A manicure wouldn't go amiss either.

As a cheerful Moroccan spun towards them on mirrored slippers, Carla felt the first twinges of misgiving. Unjustly, Moroccans were still maligned in Spain - in fact there was an expression *'no seas tan moro'* (don't be such a Moor) that conveyed the low esteem in which they were held. There was also the unfortunate fact that Papa still referred to Morocco as 'Spanish Sahara', considered Gibraltar to be in his country's domain and held no truck with the Arab-Berbers' claim to Ceuta and Melilla - Spanish cities in Africa. Even before they descended into the wood-panelled green carpeted man cave, Papa had begun patting his pockets, shifting in his chair, groping for a cigarette, her *'You can't smoke here Daddy!'* dying on her lips.

"Sir, sir," the attendant had begun, rolling his 'r's.

Her father's chin lifted haughtily, his eyes narrowing dangerously. "Don't you 'sir' me, sir!" he said half-rising out of his chair.

"He's the barber," said Carla smoothly.

"He's a *Berber*," said Papa turning his face away petulantly.

"Berber barber, that's me," said the Moroccan unperturbed and with a jovial grin, adding, "We're a little …tired, perhaps? No problem. You're going to leave a new man! Ha! Ha! Not a *green* man but *a new* man!"

Alfredo looked at him with utter contempt.

"Just leave him to me," the barber addressed Carla seeing her doubtful expression. Performing a neat deadlift, he released

One Flame Hour

the brake on her father's chair. As he straightened, his hand rested lightly on Papa's shoulder. "We'll get on just fine, won't we?"

Papa leapt from his chair as if electrocuted. "*No me toque!*" he shouted, using the formal mode of address. 'Don't you *touch* me!' He swotted the man's hand from his shoulder as if it were a fly, an insolent insect who had dared penetrate Papa's rarefied ether.

Carla closed her eyes. *Please, if you have any sense, just respond in the informal 'usted!'* If the Moroccan let slip a *'tu'*, they were done for. Had a leper stepped forward to touch him, Papa couldn't have been more appalled, his entire body recoiling with repugnance.

"Don't you want your face shaved, sirrr? You'll feel so much better."

"I feel perfectly fine as it is, thank you," snapped Papa, repeating a '*No me toque!*' before flicking away the Moroccan's hand.

"Go!" the barber hissed. "Take a break, God knows you must need one. Leave him to me."

Which Carla had, returning an hour or so later. She'd had a most delicious wander by herself visiting the first-floor coat department where they'd called her 'Madam' probably remembering (although hopefully not mistaking her for) Carla's mother Eugenia, who'd practically lived in the department store when they were young. She'd returned to The Green Man, her equilibrium restored and refreshed for the journey home. But the Moroccan was with another customer. He'd swung around practically spitting, waving a cut-throat razor in the air. Carla noted absent-mindedly that

One Flame Hour

it had a pretty, carved handle. "Never again!" he'd hissed without a trace of his former good humour. "*Jamás!*"

The manager appeared from behind his desk not an inappropriate whisker in sight. His name tag said 'Jude.'

"Jude," Carla said glancing at the badge. "Hi. Um - wh-where is my father?"

"Oh, he left," said the manager sombrely, with, Carla had the impression, barely contained fury.

"*Left*?" Carla had echoed incredulous. "How 'left'? He's in a wheelchair!"

"We took him through the staff exit so he wouldn't have to use the lift."

Her murmured "how kind" silenced with an "Oh, it wasn't kind, believe me. We didn't want our other customers overhearing his torrent of abuse. He seems fixated on 'Spanish Sahara.' Never heard of the place. Where is it by the way? Oh, never mind. Look," he said relenting slightly. "It was safer taking him through the staff exit. That way he wouldn't have to walk at all, and the exit goes straight on to the street. He said he'd be fine then."

Carla's eyes overflowed with thick, mutinous tears. "Did you actually *see* him leave?" she said her voice warbling. She dug her fingers into the palms of her hand. *Come on, Carla! Keep it together! Don't be so pathetic!* "I mean is there a possibility that he's still here in the building, *somewhere?*"

There was one thing for certain: there wasn't a man alive, happier in his skin, *provided* he could smoke, and Carla should be comforted by the fact. And, although she might be fretting on his behalf, Papa wouldn't be. There was even an outside chance he was curled up in an armchair somewhere or had crawled into one of the display gazebos on the fourth floor. Perhaps, she should also check out the furniture department to make sure that he wasn't lying star fish on a Hypnos Dream Cloud mattress having his requisite siesta. The escalators were also close to the exit Jude had described.

Maybe Papa had simply turned left (rather than go straight out) and was at this very moment having a well-deserved rest after the trauma he'd been subjected to. She recalled a time when they'd been on holiday and Papa had locked himself out of his hotel room. He'd wandered up and down the corridor trying the door handle of various rooms. Of course, this only being possible in the days before electronic keys. And, as luck would have it, one room was indeed unlocked. Papa had let himself in, stretching contentedly on the nicely made bed. There'd even been an *amuse bouche* on the pillow which he'd popped in his mouth before helping himself to a book left splayed on the bedside table. He'd had a little read, dozed and on waking, padded to the coffee machine to make himself an espresso just the way he liked it: black with three sugars. Ignoring the 'no smoking policy', he'd lit up a Peter Stuyvesant before setting off to find the rest of the family.

Jude shook his head and then did one of those inhale/exhale exercises, pushing his tongue to the back of his teeth and counting to six, with which Carla was very familiar. Except that she never got beyond five without snorting unattractively. "Oh, he left," said Jude curtly. "Believe me, we made sure he did. You can rest assured your father is no longer *anywhere* on the premises."

Carla nodded, feeling her chin tremble and her heart lurch uncomfortably. Papa was a man comfortable in his skin but these days, he was also an angry man in a wheelchair. Realistically, how far *could* he have gone? Unlike other disabled, her father had no upper body strength. He'd never

One Flame Hour

worked out in his life. He'd never had to *pick up* anything in his life. In fact, he'd never even played a game of tennis where ball boys weren't included. And since his stroke, he'd refused point blank to do any form of physio. She couldn't imagine he had the energy to push a feather. She wiped away a tear.

"What I *can* do," said Jude more gently, "is take you out through the staff exit. That way you'll be at door six. It's where your father would have left from."

Carla nodded speechless, thoughts whirring. When was a good time to alert her brothers, her mother? Tell them that she had lost their father?

Silently, she followed the man in his rubber-soled shoes, feeling the sweat pour down her back. It was winter, the store over-heated as it was. They covered what seemed like acres of underground corridor, endless locked doors with the impregnable word 'Staff.' Before emerging into the sunshine, she'd glimpsed the grotesque statue of Princess Diana and Dodi Fayed. Carla mumbled her thanks and stood discombobulated on the pavement under the green Harrods awning. She then circled the building asking every door man if they'd seen an elderly man in a wheelchair. "*Alone?*" Oh, God, Carla had thought, panicking. *Yes, alone.* Where oh, where had he got to?

Setting aside her innate shyness, Carla circled the store several times more, asking strangers if they'd seen an elderly man pushing his own wheelchair. Yes, she knew it sounded bizarre. Yes, and careless. She'd tried to imagine herself in her father's wheels, wondering where he might have gone, what might have sparked enough interest or curiosity to set him off in any given direction. And then she'd found herself back at door six, faint with cold and fear herself, and utter despair. What if he'd been knocked over by a car? What if he'd hit his

One Flame Hour

head and was lying unconscious just waiting to be run over by a lorry? What if he had fallen down the steps to one of those chi-chi Chelsea basement flats and wasn't discovered for days because the Filipino maid was in Manila on her annual leave? What if -

What the hell?

Because something had caught her eye. Casting a glance across the street to the little Italian delicatessen that had replaced a former Starbucks, Carla was attracted by the sight of an animated older gentleman. Because there, for all the world as though he had just hopped off a yacht in Portofino, happily conversing with strangers, oblivious to the cold, drinking coffee and eating a chocolate éclair in between smoking a cigarette, was her father.

"Funny," said Carla now. "I don't remember Papa being anti-social at all."

2

"So, what happened in the end? Did your mother get away?" asked Seb blearily coming into the kitchen a few hours later. Carla hadn't been able to go back to sleep after Roger's phone call. Despite the fact that their thirteen-year-old son Alfie was finally back at school and they could have a lie in, they habitually woke at the same early time. It was just ironic that now they were free again, that lockdown had lifted, there was nowhere *to* go. Nowhere that is, that didn't require quarantining on their return and besides, they had to be home in time for Alfie's half term. One boy in Alfie's class hadn't seen his parents since mid-August. That would be tough, Carla thought. Even Alfie, whom they saw from time to time - a few hours snatched here and there if he passed by the house on his way to rowing on the river or in between classes, seemed distant. After spending such concentrated amounts of time, the whole of lockdown living together 24/7, he had adapted to boarding school life astonishingly quickly. Of course, it helped that his school was literally yards away as the crow flew. And even so, he had grown apart. He was no longer 'theirs'. As much as children ever were…

"'*Your children are not your children…*'" Carla mumbled to herself. *They are the sons and daughters of life's yearning for itself…*

"Come again?"

Seb opened the tap at full throttle, the sound of gushing water drowning the rest of her words. His pained expression indicated that it was too early for esoteric references.

One Flame Hour

"Kahil Gibran." She made a mournful face. "The poet."

"I know who you mean."

He ran a hand through his hair - hair that appeared darker (and a good deal thicker than hers despite the trials of the past year) and leant against the range waiting for his coffee to brew.

"Oh, you've already had breakfast," he said glancing at her empty bowl.

She gave an apologetic shrug. "I was up half the night, remember. Yes, my mother got away. Or at least, I'm assuming she did. I've not heard anything to the contrary." She pulled her knees up on the chair and leaned her head on her forearms. "Don't you feel though, that Alfie has really gone this time?"

Seb reached behind him for a mug. "All of 0.8 of a mile away, sure."

Carla felt her eyes well. She knew she was tired. She cleared a space at the table pushing aside her laptop. "It's the end of boyhood though and it seems to have come so quickly."

"Yeah, well that was COVID for you. He'll be home soon enough. Trust me. I'm enjoying him being back at school. I really am. It's you and me, babe."

There was a small pause.

"Exactly."

Seb raised an eyebrow but was wise enough not to comment. He poured himself a cup of coffee setting it to one side and tossing the spoon into the butler's sink. Carla winced as she imagined it scraping the fragile enamel. She'd never have admitted it before but maybe she was just a teeny bit on the spectrum? Increasingly, that kind of thing bothered her. Just as did a cluttered work surface, the mess in the utility room, his office. She glanced uneasily at a damp dish cloth, a pile of papers and the desiccated leaves of the flower arrangement. Her project for the day would be to tidy the house from top to bottom. And now that Alfie was back at school, she would sort out his attic lair as well. The last time she'd looked, books and photograph frames were covered in dust. His electric guitar (the one he'd begged for in March and promised would replace gaming - *yeah right*) lying abandoned next to its sound amplifier, together with copies of the *Beano*. There was a chess set made of Lego, playing cards, sets of protractors and dozens of pencils and coloured pens they seemed to have purchased on a weekly basis to encourage study. Not to mention the streams of connectors and plugs and extension cords and phone chargers. Except they never seemed to be the right ones.

"It's better for him, I agree," she said slowly. "Of course, it is. It seems such a short time since the summer term. Do you remember how quickly he went downhill? How depressed he was? Well, now it would seem the boot's on the other foot. Some mothers hang out in the passage by the music school hoping to catch glimpses of their boys."

Seb blinked. "Why would they do that?"

Why? Because they desperately miss their sons. Because this is such a weird time. Because it's far from over and most of us feel pretty hacked off that the boys are being quarantined...

"And please tell me you're not one of them," Seb added sternly.

One Flame Hour

Carla crossed her fingers under the table, rolling her eyes. *Please…*

"But I do get it. We've gone from one extreme to the other. Lockdown at home followed by lockdown at school. It's just too weird. It's not what we bought into."

Seb tightened the cord around his dressing gown.

"Of course, it's not," he sniffed. "But whoever 'buys' into anything. I've never liked the expression. We have to go with the flow."

"And I've never liked that one," said Carla examining her bare toes. She needed a pedicure. She flexed her foot. She would book herself in soon for the lot, manicure, face threading, root touch up. Because you never knew what was round the corner. There was increasing talk of a 'firebreak' before Christmas, just as Wales had experienced recently: three weeks of a mini lockdown with all but essential shops closing. Boris Johnson was already hinting that he was doing his utmost to 'save Christmas'. Carla hadn't appreciated it was in jeopardy. Except that they already knew there'd be none of the Christmas market or skating rink this year for which their city had garnered a reputation. Here in the South of England they were in a bit of a bubble as it was, but she knew that the North had, and was, suffering severe restrictions with MPs writing to the Prime Minister asking him to show them 'the way out.' Deaths (within twenty-eight days of testing positive) stood at 44, 745. United in an approach as a country, this time around, they were not.

"I just wish I knew what the 'flow' was. What the *strategy* was. I want to know where the evidence is for the measures being imposed on us."

One Flame Hour

Carla challenged him with a look that begged the question, that was just waiting for him to say *'well, if you understood the science…'* as he was generally so fond of saying.

Instead, he smiled calmly.

"I agree with you - I'm not sure there is one anymore. Strategy, that is. I've no idea where this rule of six came from or the ten p.m. pub curfew. It all does seem rather arbitrary especially now that the rule of six has segued into being confined to one's support bubble. Supposedly we're only allowed to have dinner in a restaurant with members of our household."

"Member," said Carla grimly.

"Sorry?"

"Member. Singular. Meaning me. Your support bubble is just me. I'm not sure it even includes Alfie anymore," she said sadly. "He's formed his own with his boarding house. It's just us remember."

Seb smiled artlessly. "How could I forget."

Carla thought of something that would wipe the smirk off his face. She pointed her right foot. She'd always had high arches and in ballet class - en pointe - was able to execute a neat turn. She could almost hear the soft thwack of block shoes as she landed. Maybe taking up ballet again for exercise was something to consider.

Carla fluttered her eyelashes.

One Flame Hour

"Do you know I've a good mind to join the anti-lockdown protestors in Oxford Street on the weekend. It would be a distraction if nothing else." *And boy could we do with that...*

Seb paused coffee mug half-way to his mouth. "You're joking."

Carla considered her pretty toes - they'd be prettier still in Bloodline Red. She'd make an appointment later.

"Of course, I'm joking! But it's all got so boring! At least it would be something to do."

Seb took out a pan and poured in a cup of oats - they had to be Flahavan's 100% Organic Jumbo Oats, not the smaller kind. He was always ultra-patient and careful in preparing his signature dish, allowing the mix to simmer gently before covering it and setting it to one side. Carla never failed to have dipped her spoon in the bowl, before Seb declared the dish ready.

"Do you want some?" he said now. "I know you've had breakfast."

The warming smell of oats wafted towards her as her stomach rumbled obediently.

"Go on then," she said. After all, it felt like hours since she'd eaten. That was the problem with not sleeping, the following day Carla wouldn't *stop* eating. But she could tell Seb was pleased as he carefully spooned the steaming porridge into a fresh bowl and brought her another pot of tea.

"*Are* you bored?" he said setting down his spoon. He always finished in half the time she did.

One Flame Hour

"Not bored, bored," she said carefully. "It's the lack of choice. Just knowing I can't do something makes me want to do it even more. Just human nature. And travel." Carla took a mouthful of porridge letting the warm, creamy baby-type food sooth her digestion. "It feels somehow wrong to indulge in it when so many people are having a bad time, but it's really been my everything. I draw my inspiration, my pleasure, my escape from travelling."

"Escape?" said Seb frowning.

"You know what I mean," she said lightly.

He took her hand.

"OK, so would a trip to London to hear some music cover that base?"

Because, as they both knew, there were still a couple of venues offering music and admitting up to thirty people, thereby complying with government directives. Desperately chasing music, they'd been up to London twice recently. Once, to the Boas' that wonderfully generous couple, purveyor of good taste and benefactor of the arts, whose beautiful neoclassical home was a mecca for musical talent. Before COVID, Bob Boas and his wife had hosted up to three concerts a week but now smaller soirées were held in their first-floor drawing room. Adhering to their household 'bubbles' the audience was seated socially distanced which meant in their case, Carla and Seb had a sofa to themselves. And to emphasise that these were not 'social' events there were no drinks or supper or canapés afterwards.

Carla had been ready mid-afternoon in her excitement at having the chance to get dressed up and having somewhere to go for the first time in months. She'd worn a claret velvet pant suit (Christmas decorations were going up, so she didn't think it was too early to wear it) teamed with Roger Vivier patent flats. Which lead her to recalling one (of the several) retail regrets of recent years - *not* purchasing the velvet rock stud Valentino pumps in the exact same colour she'd seen on sale in Terminal 5 the winter before when they'd been on their way to ski in Austria. Still the RV flats were probably more practical especially as they'd ended up traipsing up and down Marylebone High Street in the search of a cup of tea and a snack. Usually, they were spoilt for choice with the nearby hub of small bistros, fashionable shops, and the Chiltern Firehouse just around the corner. But the place was completely deserted, the only venue open was a Tesco's where they'd bought a bag of mango to nibble on as they wondered down the forlorn streets.

Carla could hardly remember a time that even on a cold autumnal evening, the streets weren't buzzing with people gathered under outdoor heaters, men crowding the pavements of corner pubs, teenager girls in skimpy clothing on a night out. But everything was deadly quiet and the worst thing about it was that they were all becoming used to it. Used to cleaving to one's partner as though he or she was a buoyancy aid, scurrying past strangers in the aisle and constantly, constantly turning one's face away from people, rather towards them. When they'd finally arrived at the concert, tummy rumbling, Carla had sunk gratefully among damask cushions under walls which were a veritable RA of contemporary art. The programme of Renaissance music played on the harpsichord wouldn't normally have been her first choice but *any* live music was better than none at all. Soon her foot was jigging in time to the music and she was able to pretend, if only for a short time that life was back to normal, that the world outside was its usual cacophony of sound and colour and above all, of people.

One Flame Hour

The second time was to the equally, though very different Fidelio Café (*'creating worthwhile experiences through classical music'*) to hear a friend of theirs, the soprano Katerina Mina give her one-artist show and first performance in a year. If they missed hearing music, musicians missed performing for a live audience even more so. Here the white-washed walls were softened in the pink glow of tea lights tucked into every nook and cranny. Spider plants - the kind Carla had grown as a student because all you had to do was plop a cutting on a saucer of water for it to sprout instantly- hung over low shelves and the minstrel's gallery. Men in suits and trainers, bright coloured glasses, women in shapeless linen shifts with oversized beads and geometric haircuts were draped over the tiny bistro style tables. Katerina Mina sang in a backless, red gown and accompanied herself on the piano. Overcome with emotion on more than one occasion, she'd had to wipe the tears from her face. As the strains of *Laschia ch'iu pianga*, reverberated round the small restaurant, Carla groped for Seb's hand, feeling her backbone unhinge.

Would it! Never had trips to London taken on such hedonistic proportions. Yes, another musical evening would be delectable. And the food at Fidelio was exactly that and more. A London café dedicated to, as its blurb put it, 'the promotion and dissemination of classical music' there was none other quite like it. For the price of the ticket, a three-course dinner was included cooked by the incredible Alain Rosenthal an artist himself, combining the exotic flavours of different cultures. Her mouth watered at the thought of the menu they'd enjoyed on their last visit: chilled beetroot velouté, lemon and mint arancini followed by braised duck in anise, orange and ginger. There'd been celeriac purée (Carla loved celeriac) and asparagus. Pudding was elderflower mousse with lavender shortbread.

One Flame Hour

"Yes, oh *yes!*" she exclaimed joyfully. "Do you remember when we tried making our own lavender shortbread?"

Seb snorted. "Don't remind me."

Seb had picked at virtually a whole bowl of raw batter until there was nothing left to bake and Carla had decided the lavender was too precious to use in cooking and splashed it on herself and their laundry until the downstairs smelled of Provence. Not such a bad thing. Mmmn.... Perhaps she should try sprinkling lavender on their pillows again just to test that they retained their sense of smell. Although Seb kept reminding her losing it wasn't always a symptom of Corona. Carla unfurled, feeling cramp in one leg from sitting on it during breakfast. She'd have to get going if they were going to go up to London. She could wear the new silk print skirt - gold ocelots leaping across a mad background of foliage and stars and noughts and crosses. Accents of red and blue and green gave the whole a rich opulent almost Byzantine feel. Or she could wear the dress version. She'd liked the pattern so much she'd bought that too. For just an occasion such as this. A night in London! Just getting in the car and driving to London would be enough...*Oh, to be in traffic now that all are there!*

Carla beamed a smile just as her phone pinged. She had lots to do now. The cleaning could wait. Too boring by far. She'd read her messages later. But the buzzing persisted.

"Maybe you should get it," said Seb. "What if it's the school?"

Reluctantly Carla reached for her phone. But it wasn't Alfie's present school. The message was from their son's year group - the year group that *was* last year. The boys had all moved on to Year 9, to different schools, their 'big' schools. All but one.

One Flame Hour

"Carla?"

Carla tried to speak and then just shook her head, sliding the phone across the table to Seb.

I'm sorry to say that Mylo died peacefully in his sleep…

3

"Do we tell him?"

"No,"

"But what if he finds out - not if," she corrected herself, "*when*. Because he will. The boys in Alfie's house all knew Mylo. I'm not sure Alfie has his phone with him all that much but some of his friends have theirs. They will talk."

Seb frowned. "Alfie has been doing so well though. He's loving boarding." He jutted out his chin. "This will throw him."

"I agree. But how can we *not* tell him."

And so, they went round in circles, sick with grief for Mylo's parents and stunned with shock. Mylo and Alfie's year 9 were a particularly tight-knit group, many of the boys having known each other since nursery. On the last day of term some hadn't been too old to shed a tear. Alfie certainly hadn't been- he'd openly wept on the way home, fat tears rolling unchecked down his flushed cheeks. His older friends had been silent, thoughtful, wistful. Whatever their thoughts on the day, all were cognisant that they had shared and would continue to share, something very special. The boys' parents often tried to analyse why theirs had been such a strong bond. Some said it was by virtue of attending an all-boys' prep school, some that COVID had accentuated these feelings, or then again that it was simply down to luck.

One Flame Hour

Caught up as they'd all been in the turmoil of the pandemic year, with not much thought for the future, the boys were now suddenly aware that they were moving on to the next phase of their lives and were apprehensive. But then they were fortunate to even be, moving on. The summer before, Mylo had suddenly taken ill with a suspected appendicitis. And then the summer had passed and Mylo hadn't gone back to school until the end of term when it was almost Christmas. When he did appear, he'd sported a rather dashing bandana, not that the boys noticed such things. During the February half term, a mother had organized a 'social' introducing girls for the first time. Alfie was buoyant with his own success. From then on, he'd had a circle of girls who were *absolutely* not girlfriends. *Of course not!* And what about Mylo, how had he got on? Carla had asked at the time. Alfie had been quick to reply. *'Oh, the girls really liked him. They liked his head gear. He was funny.'* And then it was March and Carla and Seb had flown off to South America and flown back into the storm of a national lockdown and the beginning of the past year's COVID journey. No one for a moment imagined…

"I thought he had more time," said Carla sadly. She felt cold in her thin dressing gown, planting her feet on the stone floor to absorb some of its underfloor heating. But it did little to warm her. "Do you think it's too early for brandy?"

"It's never too early for brandy."

Seb went into the dining room and brought back a decanter and two glasses. They sat huddled round the kitchen table, the debris of porridge and coffee pushed aside to make room for their drinks as messages pinged backwards and forwards from the year group, everyone expressing dismay, empathy and helplessness in the wake of such a tragedy. It was every parent's secret terror that such a thing could happen to a child; the yearning to hug and hold their own all the greater.

But they couldn't hold Alfie. He was at school. Locked in at school.

"This damn COVID," said Carla fiercely.

Seb's own eyes were moist. "Poor lad," he said. "Poor lad."

"And his parents."

"And his brother."

"And the boys."

"Oh, this is ridiculous!" said Carla a giggle mixed with a sob. "So, how do we tell him?"

"We don't," said Seb firmly. "We let the housemaster do the job."

"Poor housemaster."

Carla's phone lit up as the messages gathered momentum. There was overwhelming, heart-warming support for Mylo's parents followed, just as quickly by frustration at not being able to gather as they would ordinarily have done, at being prohibited from rushing the 200 yards to the school where the boys had all been pupils. All anyone wanted was to get together, to see and hug one another. And how to help? What was best? How to maintain a sense of decorum, to respect the family's wish for privacy and balance that with the more exuberant parent's genuine desire to comfort? One mother suggested the boys, once they'd been told, could write to Magda, Mylo's mother, with memories of Mylo. Which still brought them back to the more immediate and pressing issue of notifying their sons.

One Flame Hour

"It has to be done," said Carla switching her phone to silent mode. It was enough to process the news without the additional stress of reading the messages. "I'll email Alfie's house master now. It's such a small community we don't want the boys hearing the news casually."

She got up from the table, all thoughts of Roger's earlier phone call, her mother, even Alfredo wiped from her mind. She didn't remember losing a close friend till she was much much older. There'd been a girl, she'd been at school with, who'd died in her sleep from an undetected heart condition but even that woman had been in her forties. More recently, a newer but dear friend had died of cancer, but Carla had not lost a school friend when she was Alfie's age. Her heart wept for Alfie and for Magda. And now she reached for her phone incapable of staying silent.

May perpetual light shine on his soul... she wrote.

Magda sent the image of a black heart by return.

Carla gazed through the French doors allowing herself to be distracted by their patio garden and anaesthetising her emotions just a little longer. She couldn't begin to imagine what it must be like to lose a child. Leaves scurried along the guttering which had become glutinous with water-logged soil and the last petals of summer blossom. Despite the monthly visit of a gardener, she had failed to cut back enough shrubbery and in the unforgiving morning light, its drabness was stark and unforgiving. How was it already autumn? The past months had been subsumed by the pandemic, the gorgeous sunshine of the spring when the country, no, the *world* had pulled together in the belief that they could fight the virus, seemed equally as incredulous as the inception of

COVID itself. Naively, they had blindly followed government directives, trusting SAGE, trusting this or that so-called expert. But as far as Carla could see that was precisely the problem - not one of these specialists had a total view. And even more naïve was the idea that lockdown could be short-lived. Anyway, what did it matter? Scientists no one had ever heard about prior to the start of the pandemic were being rolled out from godforsaken parts of the country to preach more gloom and doom. Would it never end?

Carla's thoughts anchored on the summer before, when things had been normal when they'd not the remotest idea of what lay ahead. She wished there was a way of preserving that feeling of total abandon, of blitheness as they sailed from Split to Dubrovnik. Having grown up with boats all his life, Seb was a competent sailor; more importantly for Carla and in contrast to other boatowners she'd known, he was also a relaxed one. She remembered the scorching heat as they'd set sail out of the port, Seb steering nonchalantly with one hand, his phone in the other. She'd giggled as Alfie, agile as a mountain goat, zig-zagged across the deck, hopping on one foot to try and avoid the metal cleats that had become poker hot in the midday sun. Desperate to cool off, Seb had moored the boat in a small cove off Komiza bay.

While Seb and Alfie had fun diving off the side of the yacht, Carla swam to shore. Shaking herself dry, she'd been surprised to find a tiny church dedicated to Mary the Piratess. She'd swum back to tell Seb and Alfie about the painting of the Virgin Mary, to tell them the story. *'Do we have to?'* Alfie hadn't been keen but she'd insisted. There were pirates here once, she'd said. Pirates that had robbed the church of this painting. *'So'?* So…when the pirates got back to their boat and tried to set sail, the boat wouldn't move, wouldn't budge. Carla had made puffing sounds, tickled her soon-to-be a teenager son, made him laugh. It was only when they

One Flame Hour

returned the picture, she said, that the boat had finally moved. *'Oh.'* Oh? She'd echoed in mock disappointment. Yeah, good story, he'd conceded and Seb had punched the air. *One to the parents...*

In Split, they'd visited the stunning Diocletian's palace with its defaced sphinx. In the old town, they'd negotiated crowds (was there a time when there actually *were* crowds?) and the stultifying, breath-sucking, smothering, sweltering heat, hugging cool stone walls like slow salamanders loath to emerge from their shadow. Beyond Sponza palace, they'd marvelled at the medieval quarantine district which remarkably, in the 14th century, had been the first place in the world to introduce a quarantine system as a protective measure against infectious diseases - namely the Black Death. But what did Alfie really care? As they walked in the charring heat, their footsteps becoming ever slower, until they were practically creeping along, pandemics and disease were consigned to history. Alfie had a board game called *Pandemic*, and as they stood in the long stone Lazaretti complex, with its paprika coloured tiles, purpose built to house newcomers off the ships for forty days, Carla tried to draw a connection. It was known as *'quaranta giorni'* in Italian - she told him, hence the name.

Carla shivered, a sharp cold blast vaulting her to the present. Surly now was the first time in history that the *healthy*, were being quarantined? Little had they known then that the word 'quarantine' would become part of their daily parlance. But then little did anyone ever know what the future held in store. And thank providence they didn't. How could Carla's friend have possibly imagined that one year on, her life would be turned upside down, never ever to be the same again? And while Carla had struggled in her own way over the past year, overcoming a bout of depression, Alfie's 'disappearance', an attack by Rottweilers (as if on cue Carla's

One Flame Hour

leg began to throb), an encounter with Naked Man by the water meadows, not to mention the bombshell of discovering that Seb's apparently gay brother hadn't always been gay and fathered a love child who was not so much older than Alfie, not one bit of any of that either separately or together could possibly compare with what Magda had experienced.

Carla thought with a guilty pang that while she snapped photos of her sun-kissed, freckly, boy, Magda had captured hers in the various stages of an illness that would soon destroy him. There had been the short-lived, one-time elation when the disease was thought to be in remission. Carla recalled visiting Mylo in hospital on that occasion. The bed had been strewn with brightly coloured beads the size of the wooden sewing 'eggs' Carla's Spanish grandmother had used to darn socks. Mylo was propped up on pillows, beaming, proudly displaying the necklace he had strung together - colours in no particular sequence but each representing a successful course completed. And survived. That unspoken caveat haunted every finished piece like a phantom bead. But while Carla could hurry back home to sit in the sun and listen to Alfie complain about being bored, Magda's respite was nonexistent. Hospital stays were punctuated by ever shorter visits home while Magda and her husband juggled care of Mylo's younger brother. Magda must have known unspeakable exhaustion, underpinned by unspeakable despair.

Carla poured herself another brandy, its warming effect, steadying her nerves, making everything seem even more disconnected but she also knew that come a poignant aria on Classic FM, she'd be weeping again within seconds. And within seconds the various channels of communication set up at the beginning of the pandemic (but latterly dormant as the boys moved on to their new schools), were up and running once again. The old year group WhatsApp was in full swing

One Flame Hour

and Carla's phone showed call after missed call. Everyone was eager to help the family and commiserate in their grief. Mylo's mother was suddenly the centre of attention in a way she had never been when her son was alive.

Carla remembered when a friend had died many years before. At his funeral there was almost a tug of war over who had loved and known him best. 'As he said to me on his deathbed,' said the priest. 'As he said moments before he died,' said the man's best friend. 'Ah, but it was as he drew his very *last* breath…' countered the priest. Until it got to the point where Carla half expected the best friend to claim that the spirit of the dead man had spoken to *him* moments before they entered the church. And so, it was now. The lucky few who had been with Mylo before he died, on the very day before he died so suddenly in his sleep, having tea and cake with him in the garden on a warm balmy afternoon, were suddenly held in a rarefied, unassailable position.

For the moment, the boys were shielded because they were still in class, but it was only a matter of hours before Alfie heard about Mylo unless Carla was able to get in touch with his house master first. She pinged him an email informing him of the news and within a short time the master replied with the suggestion that he and the house matron together, inform Alfie and the one other boy in Alfie's house who had also known Mylo. Much relieved, Carla readily agreed.

Have you told Alfie? The other boy's mother texted her as if reading her mind.

Not yet.

Have you told Kit?

Not yet.

One Flame Hour

By the end of the day, the boys did know but Alfie was still silent. There were no demands for tuck, no 'love u' or 'miss you moreee.' Carla had reassured the house master that Alfie would probably take the news in his stride, might not show much emotion, appear calm, preternaturally composed. But he hadn't. Apparently, Alfie had burst into tears covering his face and Carla was powerless to go and comfort him, to hold him in her arms, to keep him safe.

4

Seb got up suddenly from the table, taking half his place setting with him. "Was that the doorbell?"

"Dunno," said Carla. "Was it?" Often neither could hear above the din being made by next door's builders. If three quarters of the street was deadly quiet - Carla wondered if all the neighbours had second homes - the builders more than made up for the absence of *their* noise. Building renovation had begun in March, just as the world went into a national lockdown and hadn't yet let up. Sometimes, when the drilling began, it felt as though even her teeth were vibrating.

"Yeah, definitely think so." Seb padded down the hall returning moments later half sliding, half pushing a square package along the stone floor.

"Looks too heavy to be another helmet," she said trying to keep her tone light while wiping tears from her cheek. She'd thought of nothing but Mylo ever since she heard the news and started most days with a little weep. But she pounced on the *idea* of this new delivery with relish - any diversion welcome. Seb had recently begun playing polo again for which he'd had to update his antiquated equipment. New regs made it impossible not to. "So?" she added as he made no attempt to open the package. Carla, on the other hand, felt rather smug at not having succumbed recently to any retail therapy.

"It's just a bit of fun," said Seb sheepishly. "An experiment. If it doesn't work, it can always go back."

One Flame Hour

"Sure," said Carla doubtfully. She told herself the same thing all the time, but invariably ended up keeping the item in question. It was such a faff returning things and in these COVID times, doubly so with post offices closing early. "But what is it?"

Seb reached for the bread knife and began slicing cardboard and masking tape as though he were clearing a path through the jungle. Breathless, but triumphant he pulled a large wheel shape from bubble wrap.

Carla blanched. It was all too reminiscent of Papa's wheelchair. Was Seb ill? Was he trying to tell her something? Had she been so preoccupied (more like frustrated) by lockdown and its restrictions that she'd missed something? She eyed him closely. He certainly *looked* OK, but who could tell with these things, these hidden killers, these lurking *beeruuses*? But then again, Seb had been on a diet recently to try and get as fit as possible just in case he *did* contract COVID, not wishing to give the deadly bacilli any chance at all. But was weight loss due to an *illness* rather than merely cutting down on bread and cake? *Oh...* a thought sliced through her too now, more acute than the steel feel of his blade. How would Seb ever deal with not being able to play polo?

She stood up. "Seb, *amo*r," she began and then remembering that she was only 14% Spanish, switched to English. "Darling- is -?"

Seb stood up, pushing the hair out of his eyes. "Is what?"

"N-nothing."

"Then grab one end, will you?" Seb straddled a long plank of polished wood and reaching deep into the box began

One Flame Hour

extracting pullies and smaller wheels. By the time the bolts and chain were spread out on the kitchen floor, they resembled a medieval torture device.

Carla sat back on her heels. Did Seb have a *brain* tumour? Was he planning on (incredulous thought but you never knew with Seb) putting her in *stocks*?

"What is this?" she whispered.

Seb stopped. He was looking, not reading (he didn't believe in following instructions) the accompanying information pack.

"This?" Seb pushed the cylinder with his foot. "Why, this is the means to a new sexier me and you-" he added smiling impishly. "I mean not that there's anything wrong obviously - nothing needs improvement."

"Seb. What is. It."

"Oh," said Seb bolting a handle to two vertical sides of wood. "This is a water rower. See and it can be folded up very neatly."

"I do see," said Carla. It still looked like a hideous torture machine: *The rack* or *Spanish Wheel* at the very least.

"It won't bother you at all."

Carla could tell Seb was angling to have it assembled there and then in the kitchen for them all to trip over.

"Great," said Carla crisply. "It can go in the cellar."

She picked up the accompanying insert.

One Flame Hour

"'*The most realistic simulator of on-water rowing,*'" she read.

"Well, I *could* have had a vegan treadmill," Seb interrupted a tad defensively.

"Ah, yes, but this is made from hardwood from the Appalachian Mountains," continued Carla placidly. "Good heavens! Given the price tag you could have *bought* the mountains!" She flipped the page. "*And* you can get all kinds of stuff to go with it. You've got the *Performance Ergometer*, right?" She looked up. "You could have the phone and arm tablet too. That's extra - fifty quid extra but that way you can chat and row at the same time."

"Or *you* can."

"Funny. And talking of phones." She let the booklet glide to the floor. Alfie was texting her in his twice daily 'secret' language. 'A book for collection' meant he needed more tuck.

"The usual?" said Seb.

Carla nodded. Seb enjoyed shopping for his boy - buying him bars of chocolate to be shared with the rest of his school mates. He'd wrap them up in a Sainsbury's bag and leave it on the porch. Another 'secret' message and Alfie would slip down to retrieve it rather than have the bag go through the usual COVID procedure which meant it had to be left on the doorstep, untouched for seventy-two hours. So far, neither had been caught. And no one had died from COVID.

"He also wants a book."

"What a book, book?"

"Yup, a real book."

"Can't he order it."

"Nope, wants you to get it."

"On his kindle.?"

"Seb," said Carla patiently. "You know it's got nothing to do with any of that. It's a hoop. He wants you to order the book and deliver it. It's part of the little game. Measuring how much you care."

Seb had assembled the bare bones of the structure.

"I wouldn't do too much more," said Carla. "It's got to go downstairs remember. You'll just have to dismantle it."

"I know," said Seb. "I just want to see it working. What's the book?"

"What?"

"The book Alfie wants."

"Oh, yes." She'd lost the original message and scanning through Alfie's ever-shorter missives was appalled by his spelling. It was riddled with acronyms she didn't recognise and lots of 'pls', 'rlly' and 'lemme's. "It's called *The Science of Boredom.*"

Seb began filling the cylinder with water. "Just want to see how it works," he said excitedly. "And sounds." He flexed a muscle. "This could be the making of me." He sniffed. "What does Alfie want with a book like that? He shouldn't have time to be bored or even know the meaning of the word."

Carla agreed but tell that to their son, not her. "I'll tell him you'll get it for him in a bit."

Can you pls bring the food?

Carla read the message aloud.

"He also wants wafers, brownies and chocolate."

"I'll go in the morning. He'll have to wait." Seb ran his hand along the smooth wood, head to one side. "Do you think I should go for the digital heart rate monitor? It has a transmission distance of 1.5 metres."

Carla had no idea what that even meant. "Why not?"

"It includes a chest belt and uses ANT + wireless technology."

"Go for it."

There was a ping.

Wot date is half term?

Carla moved to flick through the calendar open on the counter before replying. She gave up trying to get Alfie to write in complete words, let alone sentences. Seb had positioned himself on the makeshift seat which even to her untrained eye didn't look too secure. Interspersed with the horizontal planks of wood were strips of leather and ironware stained to give an antiquated finish. It recalled the old-fashioned school horses over which Carla could never leap.

One Flame Hour

"Are you sure that's such a good idea?"

Seb rolled his eyes. "It's fine - I just want to see if it really does give off the 'welcoming emotional connection' its inventor claims it will. You know the guy was a Yale engineer when he invented this."

"That explains all the locks."

"Not that kind of Yale."

"Duh." It was Carla's turn to roll her eyes. "Not sure that tomorrow's going to cut it. Your boy," she glanced at her phone, "says can you leave his tuck in the foyer now, please." But Seb was well into his stride, knees hunched against his chest, back flat, head straight. She bent to pick up the brochure she'd thrown on the floor earlier.

"Do you think you should do some warm-up exercises? 'Stretch yourself before you wreck yourself'?"

"Do. You. Think. You. Could. Leave. Me. Be?"

"Oh," said Carla stung. "Of course. I'll get Alfie his tuck." *That'll spur him on* thought Carla. Seb hated missing out on any contact with Alfie even if it only meant walking five minutes to his boarding house. They never actually had to see him, but it was comforting just to know he was nearby, that somewhere behind those curtained windows, he was (hopefully) doing his homework. She thought with a pang of Mylo. Of course, she'd go now. She'd do whatever it took to make Alfie's evenings pass more pleasantly. Maybe they spoiled him but what wouldn't Magda give now, to have the chance to do the same for Mylo?

One Flame Hour

"I'll leave you in peace," she said smoothly stepping over Seb's contraption. But as she did so, she heard a great woosh of water. "Wow, it's realistic!" she said genuinely impressed. Too realistic as it turned out. As her foot caught in an unsecured strap, the cylinder split in two and both she and Seb tumbled to the ground, completely drenched.

5

"Oh, boy,"

"What?"

"I knew we'd chosen the right place when we spent a week on the Isle of Wight."

Seb was flicking through the daily papers as Carla drove. Usually, Seb did the driving but today she needed to concentrate on the road, on anything to keep her mind off the hour ahead of them. Her heart thumped uncomfortably; her stomach muscles cramped. She could hardly breathe.

"What do you mean?"

"'Sixteen members of the Special Boat Service descended from helicopters,'" he read aloud glancing over his shoulder, "'to regain control of an oil tanker after seven Nigerian stowaways showed violence.'"

"Crikey, the Isle of *Wight*? Near to where we were in August?" Carla winced. She knew she sounded over bright.

"Yup and the twenty-two-man crew locked themselves in the ship's citadel."

"What's a citadel?' said Alfie. He was pale but composed, staring blankly out of the window. It was impossible to gauge where his head was. At noon, they'd collected Alfie from his house. An awkward time as it was. She knew he'd be hungry and although she'd brought along some snacks, none of them

One Flame Hour

could eat anything. Parents of the eight boys invited to attend, had been granted permission to leave their 'bubble' provided they complied with COVID rules, were driven to the 'funeral' in separate cars and once there, adhered to social distancing. It was an achingly beautiful day, the sky so bright and cloudless that had it not been for the crispness in the air, it might still have been summer. It was the kind of autumnal day that is always poignant, always nostalgic. Without being told, the boys had opted to wear their old school ties, a further external bond of solidarity in this moment's internal tsunami of sorrow.

"Well, in terms of a *ship*," explained Seb, jumping at the chance to keep the subject neutral, "it's a room where the crew can hide in case of an attack by pirates. In olden days it was a stronghold or fortress if you like, where people could seek shelter in times of battle. But today, it must have a good communication system, proper ventilation and of course supplies of food and water. Can you think of any famous citadels?"

"The Alcázar of Toledo," said Carla automatically.

Seb made a face.

"What?"

"I know *you* know," said Seb. "I was asking Alfie. Eyes on the road, yah?" Only the return of his slight South African accent indicated that Seb was less collected than he made out. *'I hate funerals,' he'd said that morning. 'Who doesn't?' She'd retorted. 'Anyway, you're not ducking out of this one. Besides it's not a funeral, funeral. All you have to do is stand for two minutes. Remember this is about Alfie - we're going to support him and to honour Mylo.'*

"That's OK," said Alfie gallantly.

"No," insisted Seb. "Try and think of one. Closer to home maybe."

"Can't."

"Yes, you can."

"Think beheadings," said Carla chirpily.

"Wow," said Seb.

"Tower of London," said Alfie eyes beginning to cloud over.

"Yes!" Seb was triumphant. "And did you know that more than 7,400 migrants have reached England this year in small boats?"

"Were any of them pirates?" said Alfie, his voice warbling.

"Er…not sure."

"Alfie," began Carla looking at him through the mirror. His eyes had filled with tears.

"I'm fine," he said fiercely. "I'm fine."

"We're here," said Seb motioning to the small car park where a couple of Alfie's friends were waiting.

Carla parked beside Clodagh, mother of one of the boys' classmates. It had been Clodagh's idea to form a guard of honour. Carla wished she'd thought of it herself. It was such a lovely thing to do. But of course, it had to be run past Magda first and to Carla's delight, she had agreed. To one side of the car park there was a wood and a pond, to the other, was the village green. It was there that the boys and their parents would spread out, well-spaced naturally, quietly, silently so as not to attract undue attention and in so doing cause any further distress to Mylo's family.

Carla pulled the hand break rather more vigorously than she intended and turned to Alfie her heart full but the words of wisdom and comfort she so wanted to speak, completely eluding her. It was at times like these that she yearned for her Spanish family. Driven, guided, sustained by a profound religious faith, they always knew just what to say. Any funeral in Spain, Carla had ever attended, no matter how sad, tragic, expected, or shocking, had seen her family behave with grace, displaying an enviable strength, an unassailable faith. For Alfie's sake, would that she was able 'to name the unnameable… communicate the unknowable …' Who had said that?

But Alfie was out of the car by the time she'd undone her seat belt and Carla was left staring helplessly at his retreating form.

"Let him go," said Seb reading her mind. "He's with his friends."

"Bernstein," she said.

"What?" Seb did a double take.

"It was Leonard Bernstein who said that we can't 'name the unnameable, communicate the unknowable.'"

Seb pressed her shoulder. For once he knew where she was going with this one. "He said, it about music, yes. And it's a great shame that we can't have any today."

One Flame Hour

Carla nodded. There was so much that was a shame about the day. When they were younger, Carla and her brothers had believed in something, God, a higher power, whatever you wanted to call it. There was no wiggle room, no opportunity to think differently and that in itself had been a comfort. But how to say any of this to Alfie? Yes, the boys were all good boys, they sang their hymns, they probably spent more time in the cathedral than many boys their age given that they went to a cathedral school, but a faith? Did any of them even believe? Did Alfie? But then it was a stretch for any of them to find any sort of meaning in the death of a child.

Clodagh approached the car and Carla rolled down the window.

"You go on," said Seb. "I'll just wait here a bit longer."

Carla nodded. She grabbed her sunglasses.

"Oh, good," said Clodagh for a moment, ignoring social distancing and hooking Carla's arm through hers. She nodded in the direction of the far end of the car park. "There's Mr Trotter."

The boys' former headmaster had arrived and was standing at the furthest end of the park together with a couple of teachers. He had been invited to give the address. Carla half raised a hand in greeting but he turned. Her arm fluttered to her side.

"Maybe he'll speak to the boys," she said. Wouldn't that be a relief! As a man who had retired from teaching to become a priest, surely, he would know what to say? Yes, she'd leave it to him. She felt her shoulders droop, as if she could somehow shift the responsibility.

One Flame Hour

Alfie had joined his friends but they were silent, grouped together, their hands in their suit pockets, kicking the ground. But then she and Clodagh were silent too. Usually, they had so much to chat about, but today they were strangers and ill at ease. It was bitterly cold; a wind whipped their hair. Clodagh was all in black while Carla had chosen a navy Goat dress that she'd purchased for the memorial of a man who had died of COVID and then because of it, the memorial had never taken place. She was glad she'd purchased the 60s-style long-sleeved shift then, not wanting to over think what to wear now, not wanting to appear vain (well no more than usual) and yet out of respect for Magda who was always immaculate, to have been seen to make an effort. All the mothers of the boys in Mylo's class had too. They were all in little black suits, set off by dark sunglasses. And Carla could count the times on her hand that she'd seen Seb in a tie, today being one of them. The sun, steadily rising was bright but frigid. Ducks gathered on the water's shoreline, barely skimming the pond's surface as if they too found it too cold to settle. Conkers crunched underneath. There was an unearthly silence.

"Come," said Clodagh. "Let's stand. The boys will be at the far end."

Instinctively, they'd moved off together in a group, huddled together for warmth, for courage until another boy's mother had gone over to them and told them to spread out. Still, they shuffled towards each other, uncertain as to what to do. Still, Mr Trotter remained in the car park. Seb came to stand beside her, the requisite two metres apart. With the spacing, parents and boys were soon able to form a line the length of the small common. They waited in silence.

"The hearse will arrive at the other end where the boys are," said Clodagh in a stage whisper and then the funeral

One Flame Hour

conductor will alight and walk alone in front." She glanced at her wristwatch. "They won't be long now."

Carla felt her knees tremble with cold. Her dress which had seemed almost too warm when she'd purchased it for the May memorial, wasn't nearly warm enough for a September one. Her stomach leapt to her throat; her heart began to pound.

"Hands out of your pockets!"

The cry, at first undistinguishable from a military command, came from the centre of the line of parents. Carla jolted. At first, she wasn't clear who it was meant for but another, brisk "Hands out of your pockets boys!" and she realised it was directed to the boys, their boys. In fact, it didn't matter what the words meant, what the instruction meant, the tone had the desired effect. It was a call to them all. In the absence of a church gathering, in the absence of the choir for which the boys' school was renowned, in the absence of a roof over their heads, in the absence of the right to touch and hold and comfort one another, it was a call to stand to attention, to ready themselves, to show respect. Carla turned briefly as the funeral director paused under the railway bridge, a grimly bleak person in a top hat, holding a stick. She searched for Alfie, but he was turned away, the first boy in the line-up and closest to the approaching hearse.

She felt her whole body shake violently, uncontrollably, and tears coursed down her face freely. She didn't bother to wipe them away. She set her shoulders, stared ahead but no matter how hard she tried, she couldn't keep her body from shuddering. *'Keep it together, Carla!' she told herself. 'Dig deep. But for goodness' sake, keep it together! Think of something else.'* But she couldn't. All she could think of was Mylo, Alfie's friend, like him, on the brink of the next journey, no longer a

One Flame Hour

child but a youth. And the grief for Magda, for his parents and young brother, would not end today. Today, was the first day in a lifetime without him, of thinking every day of how much he was missed. Every birthday that his friends enjoyed and he would not, every step towards manhood that they took and he did not, would bring fresh anguish. And there would come the day when they became fathers themselves, while Mylo was forever petrified in time; a Peter Pan who had wanted to grow up.

Carla was making odd palpitating sounds, a gurgle at the back of her throat. Her nails pressed deep into the palms of her hand, into the scaphoid. She thought randomly, desperately, *anything* to stop blubbing - of the fourteen bones that make up the fingers of each hand, the eight that create the wrist, plus the other numerous muscles, ligaments, tendons and sheaths so necessary to rendering the limb useful. But what were they called, the ones that are also in the toes - the name that sounded like 'pharaoh'? She frowned. 'Phalanges' that was it. A word, now that she thought about it that also sounded like the Spanish anti-Franco movement *Falange*... that in the 1930s had wanted to re-take Gibraltar. Yes, concentrate on that. She was doing better until her mind drifted yet again and she wondered idly if Mylo's hands were clasped together or by his side. Oh, this would not do! She tried another approach, pulled in her stomach, so that her rib cage protruded and clenched her shoulder blades tight. *'Imagine holding a pencil between them...'* Carla could hear JessicaSmithTV, fitness guru, as clearly as if she were prancing in front of her.

But an imaginary figure wasn't the only thing dancing about.

Patrick!" hissed Clodagh to the stranger, who'd been moving up and down the line of parents taking pictures. "Jesus wept! Not now!"

One Flame Hour

Patrick ... thought Carla. She'd only ever known one other Patrick and she'd not thought about *him*, since Papa died. She began to breathe more easily, more evenly.

I can do this now. I will be calm. For Magda. For Alfie. I won't think of the now but embrace the memory that is floating towards me: outrageous, macabre and completely bonkers.

Just in time...

*

Eugenia's apartment, when Carla finally arrived, having traipsed across the runway in high heels, and then walked for half an hour in blazing sunshine, was buzzing with misplaced activity. It wasn't a place Carla knew well having only visited once before. On that occasion, Carla had found the whole experience unnerving. A small place in the shadow of an ominous black, pointed rock. And the language! Far from being at ease with the locals, Carla was mystified by a people who despite speaking heavily accented English, didn't speak Spanish either. 'Why on earth did your parents move to Gibraltar, anyway, when your father was a *Catalan?*' People invariably asked. A very good question and one she often pondered herself. But truth to tell, Alfredo, for his part seemed unperturbed by the move. It was a question asked one last time towards the end of his illness.

Sitting with him, watching the ebb and flow of his breathing, her hands cupped for some ridiculous reason just in front of his face as if she could somehow catch each breath and spoon it back in, she'd replied to his agency nurse that it no longer mattered where he was, her father wasn't aware. They say hearing is the last sense to go and this certainly seemed to be the case with Alfredo. He'd opened his unseeing eyes and asked calmly. 'Of what, am I not aware?' Carla had taken his hand, his beautiful hand with its long, straight phalanges, their surprisingly youthful skin. 'That you're in Gibraltar, Papa.' She'd pronounced it like a Spaniard would and gently, because after all he was dying and dying a long way from home. Alfredo had sighed and closed his eyes. 'Doesn't matter,' he'd whispered hoarsely but firmly. 'It's Spanish.'

A closet Falange then? Carla hadn't thought about it before. Perhaps. It didn't matter. *Toma ya…* as they say in Spanish. *Put that in your pipe…* Which was funny, because *ceniza* (Spanish for ash) and related topics would be an ongoing theme in the days to come. Alfredo had died and here was Carla having got up at four a.m. to get the Easy flight out to Gib. Her Hermès bag (which the odious flight attendant had initially refused to accept as hand luggage) contained a nightie, cigarette (!) pants and ballerina flats which would do her for the few days she was away. Her mother travelled even more frequently than Carla and her bathrooms were a veritable beauty salon of sample products so there was no need to pack anything other than a toothbrush.

Carla had pressed all the buzzers of the supposedly serviced building (there was no concierge in sight) until brother Roger had finally answered.

"Yeah, Carl. Come on up."

And she had, every step making her feel smaller and younger until by the time she stepped into the antiquated flat with its baby grand piano overflowing with photographs of Carla's first wedding (her mother had never accepted her second), she felt barely of school age. She hated the assault on her feelings that returning 'home' created: as though a giant were trampling up and down the xylophone of her emotions. She recognised furniture from other houses, in the other countries they'd lived - all somehow displaced as though they'd only found temporary purchase, ready to be relocated, re-positioned and lodged in another time, another memory. Eugenia was in bed. Josefa the maid was doing her usual demolition job of perfectly good fish in the kitchen, and her other brother Christophe was standing on the balcony looking towards Africa. Or maybe Africa was the other direction. Towards the yacht club at any rate.

His lips pursed when she tottered over the low step. She'd never felt confident in these high rise- (high rise for Gib that is) buildings, with their paper-thin walls and delicate balconies jutting over the communal swimming pool below, let alone her Louboutins which had seemed like the right choice leaving Eaton Square but were now not quite so appropriate for Main Street.

"Just in time," said Christophe. "The mass is in twenty minutes."

Didn't she know it. Only the fact, that she was dressed as if for a cocktail party at six a.m. had persuaded the Easy attendant that there was no way Carla could put her bag in the hold as every minute counted the other end and she simply had to get to her father's funeral. She was ready if not hot and bothered and upset and more than a little put out that no one had come to meet her. What happened to the theory propagated by Spanish men, that women were considered delicate at funerals and had to be looked after? Her father had just died for god's sake! Where was Eugenia's driver? Where was Josefa's extended family? All the layabouts that usually cluttered Eugenia's flat? But the sight of her brothers brought another lump to her throat: Roger smoking, flicking ash over the balcony and Christophe, the only proper adult amongst them, adjusting his regimental tie with intent.

"We do have a *pequeño problema*," he said in correct but accented Spanish. It was one of those peculiar examples in Spanish of a word with a seemingly feminine ending, being in fact, masculine. He spoke Spanish with an English accent while those in Gib spoke English with a Spanish one.

Carla sighed. "You mean apart from Eugenia being out cold and Josefa Moulinexing everything she can get her hands on? Why didn't you tell me to bring a straw?"

"Oh, Eugenia will be fine," said Roger breezily.

"Well, someone ought to wake her. *Dress* her, even."

"Well, that won't be me," said Roger lighting another cigarette.

"Look kids," said Christophe barely containing his irritation. "Apart, from the fact that I've spent two days getting into the safe, because Eugenia couldn't find the keys and I had to get someone from the M.O.D-"

"Whoa, bro," said Roger holding up his hands, his cigarette bobbing from the corner of his mouth. "You have so lost me."

"And me," said Carla suppressing a giggle and shooting Roger a conspiratorial look. Even though she was technically the oldest and Roger the youngest, Christophe had always seemed much more mature than the two of them put together. As long as they could remember, he'd assumed the mantle of the more stable and therefore more reliable sibling. Neither Roger nor Carla had minded in the least. On the contrary, they'd positively welcomed his efforts at keeping their sketchy family intact. He now went on to explain that Eugenia had initially insisted Papa be cremated, but when she realised that his insurance would pay for his body to be *repatriated*, which in his case meant to Barcelona, had decided on a funeral mass in Gib before escorting Alfredo to Spain. They would fly but Papa would go overland. He'd go straight to his burial and then another mass would be said in the church of his former school. So like Pa, thought Carla, to be absent at his own party - all three of them.

Christophe rattled off plans, timings and itineraries. But there'd been a hitch. Papa was to be interned in the family plot which as the name suggested, necessitated deeds. Which were nowhere to be found. At least not in the flat. Eugenia suggested vaguely that some papers might be in the safe or strong room in the cellar. But it had been some years since she'd looked. Even Christophe's habitual calm was disturbed at this. He'd put it bluntly. Without the deeds, there could be no burial. Barcelona was part of Catalonia, no lazy Spain. Things were done by the book. Which had let Christophe on the circuitous route of gaining or rather breaking entry.

"Thank goodness for you, Chris," said Carla sweetly. She could do with a coffee. Better still a small *ron*. "So, I take it you found them then, the deeds?"

She made the gesture of a small snifter behind his back but in Roger's direction, hoping he might get her a drink but Christophe spinning round, scuppered that idea.

"We found the deeds," he said. "So, we can leave this evening. Eighteen hundred hours as planned. It'll be a long day." Unlike Roger, Christophe was super fit, clean shaven, smartly dressed. His suit might have been a uniform it was as perfectly tailored, his shirt as crisp, tie expertly knotted as if it had been mess kit. Roger's tie was a granny knot rather lower down his sternum.

"Well, that's a relief."

"So, the *problema* you mentioned is… no longer?" Roger, bored now, was pacing the flat looking at silver-framed photographs on the piano. There were several of the three of them as children. Roger and Christopher wore sailor suits, Carla a sailor dress, when Eugenia still dressed them all in identical clothes.

"Yes and no," said Christophe slowly. "I also found this." He turned to the walnut dresser Carla remembered from their grandmother's house, an ornate Louis XV (had it been XVI she'd probably have liked it better) and opened a drawer. He pulled out an El Corte Inglés shopping bag.

"I'm not changing my tie," said Roger defensively. "If that's what you're suggesting. If you don't like this one, I'd rather wear one of Papa's…"

Christophe ignored him, carefully lifting a small yellow Jiffy bag out of the larger one. Arm outstretched, he held it out to them carefully on the palm of his hand as though presenting them with a voucher or other similar prize. '*Patrick's Ashes*' was written in black magic marker on the back. In Papa's handwriting.

Carla stared uncomprehending. Roger took the package turning it round before passing it on to Carla who also held the bag momentarily before handing it back to Christophe.

"I don't understand," she stammered.

One Flame Hour

"What bit? The English?" said Christophe sharply. "Better in Spanish? *Cenizas de Patricio*?

"You're not serious," she blanched. "They're not...really? They can't be?"

"Take a look." Christophe undid the unsealed flap on the yellow bag, pulling out the transparent plastic one inside. Roger shook his head.

"Oh, don't be such a baby," said Christophe virtually shaking the bag until Roger, visibly recoiling opened it with a funny pincer movement using his fingers like chop sticks. It reminded Carla of Tom's graduation, in an odd ceremony that involved the graduates taking holding of the master's index finger and repeating some spiel in Latin. Tom, who hated being touched almost as much as Papa had, was appalled. Carla had giggled to herself from the gallery where she was seated. But she wasn't giggling now. Horrified and curious in equal measure, she'd stared transfixed as Roger slid a smaller transparent plastic bag from its protective sheath. Inside that, were grains of what looked like smooth, white-coloured sand.

"Dang," said Roger.

"But ... Patrick died... years ago," said Carla. She was feeling distinctly woozy due to lack of sleep but this latest was making everything seem even more surreal.

"Correct." Christophe was frowning as though she were simple.

"Sorry, I still don't understand. What was Papa doing with Patrick's ashes?"

One Flame Hour

"I'm just amazed Josefa hasn't chucked them into the blender," said Roger. "We might have been having Patrick for lunch."

"Oh, that's horrible," said Carla. "That's just gross."

Patrick Hyde-Clarke had been their father's best friend ever since they could remember. They'd been astonishing alike in looks and were often mistaken for brothers, if not twins. They were both tall (over six feet) and slim. They both sported goatee beards with their hair parted on one side. They often wore similar clothes - tan-coloured slacks and navy cashmere cardigans along the lines of Professor Higgins in *My Fair Lady*. Once, as a practical joke, Carla had sewn up the pockets on Patrick's. Now staring into the mound of white ash she felt guilty. They smoked the same brand of tobacco and shared the same taste in music and art; the same fascination for linguistics and when it came out, the same scorn for *Doctor Zhivago*. There were two differences: one, unlike their father, Patrick had never married and didn't have any children. And two, Patrick had given up smoking. Too late as it happened and when he was dying of emphysema Papa hadn't hesitated to fly to his side, spending the last two weeks of Patrick's life with him at his villa in the South of Spain. No mean feat for a man who couldn't drive. Papa that is. He'd not taken his driver with him either. When Patrick died, it transpired that he'd left Papa almost all his estate. The caveat being that had Alfredo given up smoking by the time the will was read, the whole estate would be his.

"Never mind that," said Christophe. "Patrick has been dead for twenty years. Why didn't Papa get around to scattering his ashes, complying with his wishes, whatever they were?"

Carla shook her head. "Laziness. You know what Alfredo was like."

One Flame Hour

"Yeah," said Roger. "But the question is what do we do with them now?"

"Precisely."

"Bury them together?"

"Are you joking?" said Carla horrified. "*Qúe diran?* What would people say? They'll think they were gay!"

Christophe pushed the bag carefully into his breast pocket and drew himself up to his full height.

"Would that be so terrible?"

Roger rolled his eyes. "OK, then what? Any better suggestions? We can't take them with us, can we?"

"Of course not."

"Just put them - him - back," said Roger.

"Yes," agreed Carla. "Just put them back. Where you found them. Eugenia can sort it out. It's not our responsibility."

Christophe held her gaze, his eyes grazing every bit of her face.

"Isn't it? Aren't those pretty earrings bought on the back of what Patrick left Papa? And that?" he touched the Hermès bag with his own beautifully shod foot.

Carla fingered her diamond studs - total weight of 3 ½ carats (VS2). Christophe was right. Their father had been generous with Patrick's legacy.

One Flame Hour

"And you had a flat," countered Roger.

"So, did you."

Roger pulled out a lighter from his trouser pocket and lit another cigarette. "OK, so we have to think of something else." He inhaled deeply before blowing out smoke through the corner of his mouth.

Carla shifted from one agonising Louboutin to the other. What had possessed her to wear shoes that even when she wasn't on her feet, equated to Chinese foot binding? The conversation was tiptoeing into dangerous territory.

"We're not walking to the church, are we?"

Christophe stared at her. "Of course, we're walking! The church is only on Main Street. Everyone walks everywhere in Gib."

"Yes, OK, I was just asking. Put him back," she said airily. "Put Patrick back where you found him. We've enough to worry about at this moment."

"Yeah, she's right," said Roger patting their brother on his shoulder, his cigarette dangling dangerously close to Christophe's silk jacket. "Waking Eugenia being one of them. We'll talk about it later, yeah? Best head off. See you guys in church."

Which was typical of their laidback brother Roger. To dodge the bullet. In the end, Carla wasn't sure who was responsible for rousing their mother but entering the church Carla did a double take. Only an hour before, their mother had lain prone in her room. Very Duchess of Windsor now, in a waist-long, black-edged diaphanous veil, Eugenia was the embodiment of grace and extreme piety as she sank on one knee before the bishop to kiss his stubby hand. But the rest of the service was anticlimactic. Given their insistence that she be there (and the reason she'd not gone to bed at all the night before in order to catch the four a.m. flight), Carla had assumed it was to be a requiem mass for the family, but given Alfredo's absence (tucked up in the local morgue being prepared for his journey to Spain) and the crowd of locals, not one, Carla was pretty certain, known to Alfredo, she was left mystified. Prayers were said for Alfredo, but they were also said for half the population of Gibraltar. Complete strangers interrupted Carla as she attempted, if not to pray exactly, then to gather her confused thoughts, until she was bobbing up and down like a Jack in the Box. Until she refused to acknowledge one more person and knelt hunched over in the pew hiding her face in frustration, gulping down tears of anger and grief.

Changing afterwards, back at the apartment, Carla felt part of some weird retro show. Josefa, Eugenia's side kick of a maid who never did anything much more than iron linen napkins or polish silver coffee pots no one used, was suddenly galvanised into action, lowering blinds, throwing dust sheets over furniture and chucking away perfectly good food from the fridge.

"But Eugenia's only going away for a couple of days!" hissed Roger.

Carla only shrugged. It was the 'going away' that made her heart contract with fresh pain. Because it wasn't an ordinary departure at all. They had come together, her mother and her brothers for the first time in a long time, to take Alfredo home. He'd have been happy to be going home too, she thought as they exited the building and headed for the border, yes, he'd have been happy. Given the recent delays and altercations with Spain, it was decided they would all walk across the border and Eugenia's driver who lived in La Linea anyway, would meet them on the Spanish side. He would then drive them to Malaga where they would board a plane for Barcelona. Carla felt calmer now, mostly as her feet were no longer killing her. She'd changed into the pants she'd packed, teaming it with the jacket of the suit/dress she'd worn earlier. She'd now been up for over twenty-four hours and was feeling decidedly sketchy and light-headed.

Eugenia's footsteps tapped ahead of them as Christophe struggled with the four-wheel drive suitcase their mother considered necessary for her stay in Spain. Josefa packed for Eugenia the way Prissy had done for Scarlett in *Gone with the Wind*, hurling everything, china bits included, into the bottomless pit of a vast suitcase and slamming the lid. Carla, at the other end of extreme, had vowed only ever to travel with hand luggage. Which she was slightly regretting. Even empty, a Hermès weighed a ton. Only Roger with his backpack was comfortable and therefore should have been relaxed. Except he wasn't. He had begun to perspire even though the heat from earlier in the day had dissipated and there was a pleasant evening breeze.

"Hey, Rog, what's the matter?" she said catching up with him as they neared the border. Two small booths gave shelter to a couple of policemen - English as it turned out, although you'd never have known it given their peculiar accents.

"I'm fine," snapped the usually unflappable Roger."

"OK," said Carla lowering her bag carefully onto the security tray and glaring at the policeman least he scratch her Hermès. "Anyone would think you had Patrick with you."

One Flame Hour

"For fuck's sake," hissed Roger large beads of sweating plopping from his face and his colour alternating from white to red.

Carla's eyes widened as she retrieved her bag. *Touchy.* But she'd let it go. They were all on edge, suffering in their own way. Eugenia had already identified her driver and was sliding onto the back seat hugging two of her three handbags. Carla squeezed in next, half sitting, half crouching with Christophe beside her. Roger was in the front hunched over his rucksack protectively. Someone's phone pinged. Carla glanced at Eugenia whose eyes were closed and Christophe who was studying the road. It pinged again before she realised it was hers. Lifting her bottom to try and wriggling sideways she was able to prize her mobile from the side flap of her bag. Breathless she glanced down.

He's here.

Carla looked up. The text was from brother Roger although surely it would have been easier just to whisper if he didn't want to disturb the others? She caught his eye in the sunblind's mirror but his dipped to his phone. *OK. So…You don't want to talk.*

What do you mean? Who's here? She texted back

Patrick

Her head jerked up, but Roger wouldn't look at her at all this time.

You're joking

No

One Flame Hour

Don't tell Christophe!

Are you nuts?

But we have to go through proper customs? That security check in Gib was nothing! The Spaniards in Malaga are always on the lookout for drugs and Patrick right now, looks exactly like high grade cocaine!

How would you know?

Funny

Look - even if you said they were a friend's ashes; you'd have to have the right paperwork. It's not like smuggling in a jar of Nesquik!

Well, that's helpful, what do you suggest?

Don't know

It's too late. He's here.

Well, we can't just sprinkle him at Malaga airport

Guess not…

And I absolutely forbid you to slip him in with Papa!

I think we should tell Christophe

No way! He'll be furious. You know what he's like about his work and being squeaky clean

And we shouldn't be?

Not the same

Speak for yourself

One Flame Hour

Yeah, OK. Patrick lived in the South of Spain. He might be very happy on the tarmac

Not funny. He deserved better

Carla touched her earrings.

You're right he did, he must, he will

And hours later they'd arrived somehow, in Barcelona. Arrived home. Carla had been overwhelmed with relief, the relief of being with people who had known her as a child, who accepted her for what she was and loved her, faults and all.

"Is that all of you?" her cousin had asked, greeting them on arrival. "The twins?"

"Coming tomorrow," Carla assured him. "Then that's it. Just the four of you, *verdad*?"

Roger had shot her a warning look.

"Well," said Carla serenely. "Depends on how you look at it."

*

"Hands out of your pockets boys!"

This time the instruction was a drill command with an urgency all of its own, jolting her back to the present. The words were irrelevant but she felt calmer, she also felt her heart crumble. She thought of the friendships that saw people perform simple, extraordinary gestures: these boys wearing their school ties, her father travelling to see Patrick one last time - Patrick whose ashes were eventually scattered above the Monastery at Monjuich on the outskirts of Barcelona. She thought of her father but no matter how she missed him now, Alfredo had lived his life. How much worse it was for a parent to bury a child. That should never be.

The hearse moved slowly, the few cars on the road because of COVID, came to a halt, strangers on the opposite side of the green bowed their heads. Turning she saw that Seb was quietly weeping and embarrassed had moved away from her. She saw the bright, gold helmet of Magda's head, the dignity with which Mylo's father acknowledged the mourners. His face showed awe and some wonder that his son should have commanded such a physical presence, such a demonstration of love. Was surprised by it even. She saw Mylo's little brother, his face, small and white and curious at the people standing watching him, watching them. And if Mylo's parents could show such composure then so must she. Carla crossed herself as Mylo passed. Clodagh did the same. Catholics were always conspicuous by making the sign of the cross. It was an automatic reflex. And then somewhere from the wood behind, in a swirl of leaves, came birdsong.

6

"Sockitto'em?" said Alfie breathlessly from somewhere under a bowed head, his expression hidden by his fringe. Clara made a mental note to take him to a barber the next time he was home from school. And not to the Green Man in Harrods. She wasn't sure that it even existed anymore.

"That's it!" Seb was jubilant. Gone was his tie and his jacket was slung over one shoulder like a matador's. It reminded Carla of their god daughter's christening, when he'd arrived at the church late, kicking snow from his shoes, his coat flapping behind him like the caped crusader. Leaning against their car, one foot propped behind him, Seb looked visibly relieved to be away from the funeral scene. He had drawn Alfie to him, and they were talking in low voices. He'd asked him something to which Alfie, from the way he was chewing his nails, had replied non too confidently.

"Really?" said Carla. "A bit American don't you think?" It always alarmed her when Alfie bit his nails, something he only did when he was stressed. Understandably he was stressed now.

They all were after the harrowing event. When the hearse had finally moved out of sight, under the second bridge and around the corner on its way to the same church in which Mylo had been baptised, the boys so strong moments before, had all in a movement that might have been choreographed, turned to their mothers for a comforting hug. *And we had held them*, thought Carla. *How we had held them*. She would never forget that silence, that cold and in the crisp sunlight the way the boys had moved down the line, wild-eyed and bewildered, wanting only their mothers. Nothing could have

One Flame Hour

prepared the boys to see their friend drive past them in a coffin covered with flowers and the raw shock had registered on their young, anguished faces. One boy had clenched his fists so tightly that he'd punched a hole through his jacket pocket. Still, it had been beautiful and dignified and, in its simplicity, a memory for them all, more powerful than any church service could ever have been. They would remember it always; a day that would stand out clearly, acute and jagged, against the blur of their COVID year.

And now, they were standing in a different place, outside Alfie's boarding house. Alfie kicked the gravel with his toe, alternating feet but Carla didn't have the heart to tell him to stop. She didn't have the heart, for anything nor could she find any appropriate words of solace. Carla had felt helpless before, and she felt even less able to offer the wisdom her Spanish family would have been able to in these circumstances. She couldn't reel off passages of either the poetry or scripture that might have helped articulate such despair. But something had to be said, something more uplifting than an expression of barely disguised aggression. It wasn't worthy of the 'Manners Makyth Man' for which Alfie's school was famous.

"And who," said Carla primly straightening up and flicking back her hair, "who exactly do you want to 'sock it' to?"

Seb frowned and Alfie's head shot up to look her squarely in the eye for the first time since she'd held him in her arms earlier. There was an ocean of unsaid feeling between them as her eyes slid away.

"What are you talking about?" he said rudely.

Seb shot him a warning look, and Carla glared at Seb, but both, aware of his upset, said nothing.

"'Sock it to 'em,'" she repeated patiently. "Who do -"

"*Oh*," said Seb smiling as if she'd said something coded. "You meant SOHCAHTOA!"

"That's what I said," said Carla tersely. She desperately wanted a cup of tea, to get home, to have another cry by herself.

"Sine equals opposite over hypotenuse," said Seb.

Carla glared at him. "I have no idea what you're talking about."

"Didn't you do Math at school?" said Alfie.

"Now Alfie," said Seb.

"Barely," said Carla. "I went to a convent remember. We were taught useful things to help us run our husband's estates. Needlework and how to cook a good toad-in-the-hole."

Alfie looked as bemused as she'd done earlier. "What's 'toad in the hole'?"

"It's a helpful mnemonic-"

"No, it's not, it's a fatty dish with sausages."

"For remembering," continued Seb as though he'd not been interrupted and in that *slightly* patronising tone he sometimes had when he felt he could prove superior intelligence. He sniffed pleased with himself.

One Flame Hour

"I know what a mnemonic is," said Carla wanting to cry all over again. She felt they were ganging up on her.

"The trigonometric functions are sine, cosine, and tangent- the three basic ratios of side lengths in right-angled triangles. Trigonometric comes from the Greek word for triangle measurement. And what do they do Alf?"

"Allow us to find missing sides of a right triangle, as well as missing angles," rattled off Alfie in one drawn breath.

"And why would we want to do that?"

"Yess!" said Seb ignoring her. "Hallelujah! Once you know those off pat, you're away!"

"As we must be," said Carla. She hadn't found the words she'd wanted, had sounded far more petulant than she'd intended and felt that she'd failed miserably as the parent of a grieving child. If there was ever a moment to show courage and grace it was now. And both, in her case were sorely lacking.

"Couldn't I come home?" said Alfie, his eyes suddenly filling with tears. "I don't have to be back until supper time. I can stay out longer. I just have games now-"

"Hey, hey," said Seb springing forward from the car. He folded his son in his arms. "Better just to get back into things, yah? Good man. Promise. It's better this way."

"You were a good friend," added Carla limply. *To Mylo* was the unspoken add on.

Alfie rolled his eyes. Hands in his pockets, he turned away.

One Flame Hour

"Hey, hey baby. My turn." She had to pull his suit sleeve to make him face her. Through his jacket she could feel his spine, taut beneath her touch. How would she be now if there was never another moment like this? What if she could never again hold him? Even when he was being understandably sulky? She kissed his cheek tasting salt and sweat and general boy grubbiness. At least his hands below the wrists were clean. "I know it's been hard, my darling. You should never have had to experience something like this at your age but try and believe in a higher power. Try not to lose faith…" her voice trailed as he shrank from her, the words hanging spiky and pathetic, in the air between them.

"Lose faith in what?"

She made a funny, helpless gesture. *He might well ask*. That this was meant to be? That there was a bigger picture? That God worked in mysterious ways? Not even she believed it. She thought of the anger behind Magda's texts in the days between Mylo's death and his funeral. Or rather the images: a broken crimson heart, followed by a black one and finally this morning, a white one - drained and bleached and blanched of everything when there was nothing left to give. Yet they were the lucky ones. Who knew what the future held but at this moment, she still had all her three children: the twins and Alfie.

"It's fine, Mum," said Alfie. "Gotta go."

Reluctantly she released him. "Do you need any tuck?" She whispered the last conspiratorially.

Alfie shook his head. "It's really fine, Mum."

One Flame Hour

"Text me, yes? Or better still let us know when you're rowing and we'll swing by - accidentally on purpose, wink, wink," said Seb.

At last Alfie smiled. "You know, you're the only parents who do that."

"Well, that's not true!" said Carla indignantly but then refrained from saying more, not wanting to betray any confidences. "Tough," she said. "Seb and I walk along the tow path most afternoons. If I want to see my boy, I will."

"Fair enough," said Alfie but Carla could tell he was pleased.

There was a movement behind the housemaster's study. She saw him stand up and mouth 'you ok?' She shrugged… *'Oh you know…'* then pressed Alfie's shoulder one more time before nudging him in his direction.

*

The setting sun stained the sky in shimmering pinks but the warmth of those hues, belied the drop in air temperature. As they passed other College houses, Carla felt a renewed sense of melancholy and shivered in her thin wool dress. They were yards from home though and she would change then. If only her mood was as easily altered! But it wasn't just Mylo's death that was causing this continued reflection (although of course that was the primary source of her sadness), it seemed that during the course of COVID so much more had changed. And change could be measured by the transition from child to youth in Alfie. He and his friends had all left their former schools as children but were returned as young men. She recalled how excited the boys had been to be going to *any* school at the end of six months of lockdown, desperate to be with young people their own age.

Six months… Carla had been alarmed when she was told Alfie would be home for six *days*. Now any parting seemed unnatural and certainly in the light of what had happened to Mylo, even more poignant. Carla knew that with every step a baby took, he was learning to walk away. She could see that this was the case with Alfie - one foot still at home, the other wiggling its toes, trying to assert itself. But what parent really had the courage, or strength or generosity of spirit to let her children go without even the slightest show of resistance? He was certainly no longer 'theirs.' *'Your children are not your children…'*

But if Carla was feeling maudlin it was nothing to what Magda must be experiencing this evening. Because it was the now that mattered. In the days after Mylo's death, there would have been denial, exhaustion and shock. Anger would replace discombobulating grief, followed swiftly by the adrenaline rush required to orchestrate a funeral in these strange, COVID times. But when Magda most needed them, friends who had interrupted their own lives, discarding the tenets of family life to rally round, would unwittingly abandon her. They would assume if they had not experienced something as terrible themselves, that Magda would 'get over it,' that all that was required was time and in time, she would emerge. Others, who didn't know Magda well, might never mention Mylo to her again. All Carla knew was that as time went on, you missed a person more, not less.

Seb squeezed Carla's hand as they turned into their street, past the immaculate twin bay tress of the corner house with its grey/blue shuttered windows and pretty, perfect rose

One Flame Hour

arbour. The hurricane lamp swinging within its arch had just been illuminated, its faint glow rising steadily. Carla felt an equal surge of warmth towards her neighbours - the young couple with the adorable twins, the older widower who had given them a trout when they moved in, the glamorous rock-star couple who sold antiques in the market (Seb had forbidden her from buying any more chairs) and the musician who baked and delivered gingerbread at Christmas. They were all friendly, cheerful people who somehow always knew when to hold back, when to be sociable. Carla and Seb's black clothes indicated that now might be cause for the former.

Their street might have been quiet, but Carla's phone was not. She could feel it vibrating, positively jumping along the interior of the bag tucked under her arm. Seb opened the front door and they went into the silent house, in silence. She went straight up to her dressing room unzipping her Goat dress as she did so and kicking off her Roger Vivier flats. Snug in leather leggings and an oversize cashmere sweater, she curled up on the window seat, pulling the heavy linen curtains around her. Amazingly, there were sixty-five unread messages - all from Les Girls - that group of friends Carla had been at school with and known for some forty years. Increasingly, Carla valued their measured, sensible responses. They were unfailingly kind, slow to pass judgment, and always, always gracious.

Carla scrolled rapidly through the texts. There was continued advice to take high doses of vitamin D (even if the study had only been carried out on mice) and/or that it should be added to bread and milk (as they did in Sweden, Canada and Australia), comments about inhaled interferon (only available in specialist respiratory units), updates on the AstraZeneca, Oxford-developed vaccine (promised by Christmas), and excitement about the Pfizer and BioNTech vaccine (developed by Turkish immigrants), which worked in an entirely different way, being a mRNA medicine.

Actually, she'd heard a little about that one when Seb first read about it. Barely containing his excitement he'd tried to explain (in layman's terms) that it was just 'basic biology.' Which was all very well but Carla didn't have any. 'mRNA medicines work differently from traditional pharmaceuticals,' Seb had said virtually rubbing his hands with glee but when her expression was still blank, added. 'You *do* know that mRNA is just as critical as DNA or that without it your genetic code would never get used by your body?' Carla didn't. 'They're just sets of instructions,' sighed Seb as though conceding that she was right, she really didn't have even a smattering of basic biology. Carla wrinkled her nose. '*If you say so.*' 'See, proteins are the workhorses of the body.' Seb's tone had lost its lecturing tone and becoming almost sensual, 'And proteins prevent or fight infections.' All very interesting. She waded through to the final message.

"Seb!" squealed Carla leaping up and fumbling with the all-enveloping drapes. Seb's study was adjacent to Carla's dressing room and they could usually hear each other through the wall.

"You don't have to tell me," said Seb grimly. "I've seen the headlines." He was sprawled on his chair, his legs propped on his desk. Two large computer screens dominated its cluttered surface. Carla often thought that Seb would have made an ideal candidate for one of those TV Reality shows where you guessed the occupation and character of a given person: *Through the keyhole* or some such. Shelves over-flowed with books on a myriad of subjects: marine biology, pilot books for sailing in Turkey, Western Diseases, Computer Science. There were a few spy novels and scattered pages of piano music he'd been composing. Alongside bits of pottery and drawings Alfie had made for Seb over the years, was a plaster cast of Beethoven's death mask, sporting a polo helmet and A.I. glasses. It gave the great musician a jaunty, debonair and totally modern look.

"Quick, quick, the idiots are making a statement!" she said moving clean but crumpled clothes off the only other chair. Carla had long given up on doing any ironing. None but essentials… "Switch to live news!"

Boris's face, or more specifically his hair, filled the screen. "T'is the season to be jolly …careful," he announced with a stab at humour.

Seb was just in time to restrain Carla from throwing her phone at the screen. Rather, from throwing Seb's. She'd never dream of damaging her own.

"I suppose there is *some* good news," said Seb pulling her towards him and onto his lap.

Carla glared at him. "Where's the good news in that?"

"I suppose," said Seb hesitantly, "for the first time in a while, at least, all four nations of the UK are in agreement."

"How do you figure that?" said Carla tartly, in no mood to be pleasant.

"Well," said Seb patiently. "All *four* have agreed to allow *three* households to meet indoors during a five-day Christmas."

"Oh, whoopie."

"But no, Hogmanay."

One Flame Hour

"Hogmanay?" echoed Carla. "Since when have we ever called it that?"

"Just quoting the PM."

"Don't you dare joke!" said Carla leaning so far over that she almost toppled them both.

"OK. New Year's Eve, then. Whatever you want to call it. Besides, what's in a name?"

"*'A rose by any name would smell as sweet…'*" she quoted grumpily.

And then, on the back of Boris's announcement, Les Girls pinged a meme. It showed Captain Sir Tom and a balloon above his head.

'Fucks sake - here we go again, where are my trainers?'

7

"So, what are *you* doing today?" asked Seb chirpily when Carla came down to breakfast the next morning. The gentle sounds of Classic FM wafted through the house, the underfloor heating made the kitchen feel nice and toasty and the subdued lighting bathed everything in a cinnamon hue. She could even *smell* cinnamon in the porridge simmering on the range. Returning to an empty house, the night before, Carla had experienced that stomach-wrenching, toe-curling feeling of loss. She knew it wasn't only due to having left Alfie at school but also because of Mylo. By contrast, Seb was energetic and upbeat doing his best, to create a convivial, calm ambience. Everything was tidy, nothing out of place. Even his shoes, which he usually kicked off at the front door, and she invariably relocated (with a sigh) to the cupboard under the stairs, had been tidily stored. Nothing was designed to irk and yet his very perkiness had the reverse effect. How could he move on so quickly from the depressing lockdown news, let alone Mylo?

'Move' being the operative word. Carla, still in her cashmere robe felt heavy, leaden, not at all rested, not wanting to exercise at any rate. Seb, on the other hand, with hair slightly damp from his shower was dressed in shorts and a t-shirt, clearly eager to head down to the cellar for his daily 'row.' After initial teething problems with the water cylinder, the rower seemed to be working out well. Even better, after that first suggestion that she might also enjoy the machine, Seb had not reiterated the offer.

"What *can* we do?" said Carla grumpily now, pulling out a chair which having lost its protective felt, scraped along the stone floor. She winced; that sound together with the ping

One Flame Hour

from a text from Les Girls, felt like stinging nettles spreading through her head. No message, just the picture of a Monopoly board, except that it said 'Monotony.' *Ain't that the truth.* Carla had always hated the game at the best of times. "It's all so *excruciatingly* boring," she said with a sniff. "I can't believe we're in another lockdown when we were told categorically that we wouldn't have one. And *now*, we're going to have a tier system harsher than the law before the *last* lockdown!"

"I know," said Seb soothingly. He brought over her tea pot - green cast iron in a traditional Japanese hobnail design - and laid a comforting hand on her shoulder before turning back to the range. "All these random tiers!"

"Do you realise that there are 30 *million* people now in Tier 2?" Carla raised horrified eyes.

"Could be worse," shrugged Seb. "We could be in the North. Not allowed out at all."

"I s'pose," said Carla doubtfully consulting her phone. She scrolled through her messages. "Phil of Café Monde says that people at the end of *his* road have been put in a completely different tier and he can't mix with them!"

"Yeah, that's what a postcode system will do…"

"He's going to close even for takeaways." A pounding pulse had begun gathering momentum at her temples. The more she thought about any of it, the more enraged she felt; the more she read, the more suffocated, the more helpless. "He says it's not worth keeping his place open when he's already having to furlough staff. How on earth are any of the pubs and restaurants going to survive?"

One Flame Hour

"Well, if you eat a meal, then you can have a drink but that means ordering food even if you're not hungry." He hesitated with a carton of cream in one hand, a Luneville jug in the other, wondering if he could get away with putting the carton straight on the table. One look at her expression persuaded him otherwise.

"So, what constitutes food, anyway? A packet of crisps?"

"Nope, think it's got to be a 'substantial meal.' Cornish pasty and salad - that kind of thing and you can't continue drinking after you've eaten, you have to leave."

Carla took the jug of cream from him. "What a lot of food is going to be wasted! We hardly drink as it is and we don't go to pubs, so not sure why I'm even commenting. It's kind of irrelevant."

"Sure," said Seb. "But I like to think there's choice. Even if *we're* not doing something, I like to think others can."

Carla frowned. She hated when he appeared so much calmer, benign and frankly nicer than she did. Silently she watched him finish cooking, tidy away unused utensils, turn the music down and wipe his hands on a dishcloth.

"You OK, darkling?" Seb said as he dished out porridge. He covered her hand briefly with his before sitting down himself. His form of endearment invariably made her smile and went some way to appease her. "Oh, look," he said catching a movement behind her head on the low stone wall visible through the French doors. "There's a robin!" Seb loved his birds, robins especially.

For a moment she contemplated as he did, the plump little scarlet breast, a flash of colour against grey stone.

One Flame Hour

"Sweet," she said feeling anything but herself. "I'm fine," she added. "Just massively pissed off."

Maybe she just needed to eat her breakfast. And of course, Seb was right to enjoy a little bit of nature. She was being a total cow. They had much to be thankful for. She knew that. Besides, she could be in Magda's place this morning. They had left Alfie at school but… she didn't have to go further. Their boy was alive. At least he could *be* at school. *Just for today…* she thought thinking of one of her self-help books. *Just for today…I will think of all the good things. I will be grateful…* The porridge piled high in her pretty pink bowls for example, giving off a curling spiral of steam. She closed her eyes inhaling orange peel and honey and nutmeg.

"Thought I'd give it a seasonal twist," said Seb. His porridge was an artform. He was always the one to prepare it, never happy if she tried her hand at it.

"Well, it's delicious. Sorry," she said meekly.

Seb shook his head. "Nothing to be sorry about," he said kindly. "It's this lockdown."

As if on cue, Alexa interrupted the music programme with a news update. The weather was turning even colder, deaths worldwide had reached an improbable 1, 385,778 (apparently more people had died in America than during WWII), Rishi Sunak (their very own Wykehamist) had earmarked £4.6 billion to help hundreds of thousands back to work with an extra £3 billion going to the NHS, and the agriculture minister had confused issues further by stating that a Scotch egg probably constituted a 'substantial meal' after all. There followed a reminder that restrictions would end on 2nd December. Non-essential shops, gyms and hairdressers would re-open on Thursday the 3rd. As if they needed reminding. Carla had marked the day in every calendar and diary in the house.

"Just in time for Christmas," said Seb. "You can do your sho-"

"*Christmas!*" exploded Carla. The word was the very match to kindle a kilo of dynamite in the form of imploding thoughts.

"No," said Seb warningly. "No. That subject is closed." He devoured his porridge in record time while she was still toying with hers. "One more cup of coffee and then I'm away. Downstairs. You should try and walk. Do some exercise. Distract yourself." Seb kissed the top of her head, happily disappearing into the cellar, with his mug.

Which was all very well, thought Carla savouring a mouthful of porridge, but Seb had become somewhat proprietorial of his rowing machine, keeping the thing in mint condition and tending to its every need as if it were alive. She was reminded of one of the twins' Tamagotchis - that handheld digital pet that had nearly driven her to distraction. Especially when the wretched toy had 'died' after a week. Seb's was rather more successful. A few days after the rower's arrival, he'd purchased the optional and ridiculously expensive cleaning kit: a bottle of Water Blue dye solution, abrasive pad and individually wrapped wipes for stainless steel surfaces. She'd drawn the line at a dumbbells rack retailing at ('*in the face of increasing demand*', according to the catalogue) £5,749. '*How* much?' 'What, you've never considered buying an item of clothing for that, or a handbag?' Carla crossed her fingers. 'Of, course not.' Except she *had* seen a green suede Khaite coat on the Net-a-Porter website, a snip at £4,900. Still cheaper than the dumbbell rack. And you couldn't *wear* dumbbells. 'Look, it's stunning.' The rack, not the coat. She'd glanced over his shoulder at a stack of shelves that looked like the kind made by schoolboys in carpentry class. 'And it comes in five types of wood: cherry, walnut, oak, club-', 'What's club?' 'Dunno, looks like a mixture of two-' Seb's voice was fever pitch with excitement. 'Are the dumbbells included?' 'Hang on -I'll check.' Seb was chewing a thumbnail. 'I think they are!' He was elated. 'You know, you could probably *buy* a forest in Scotland at that price! Mmmn… but then Scotland is in even stricter lockdown then we are. Why not just have the tablet holder? That's only £150.'

Carla finished her porridge biting into a sliver of orange rind. It was probably the Christmassy taste and smell that was adversely affecting her mood. Already, they knew there was to be no special market, no skating rink, no music, no carols, no shopping, no Advent services, no Evensong, i.e., no fun of any description. Why call it Christmas at all? This wasn't life. And it wasn't living. She wasn't even clear why they were doing it. Cases and the so-called 'R' number were well down in their area. The scare mongering had to stop.

The government was pathetically transparent in its attempts to terrify people half to death and into staying home. She loved that no one bothered to clap for the NHS anymore, no child drawings anywhere and absolutely no decorations in sickly colours. Where had all the personal tributes gone? The exquisite impromptu violin concertos? She had a friend who had stood shivering in a ballgown belting out an aria to anyone who cared to listen. And they had, emerging on their doorsteps to 'ooh' and 'ahh' and then post short recordings on social media. There *had* been a 'THANK YOU NHS' on the door of a funeral director's which had made Carla giggle. Surely, it wasn't, it *couldn't* be deliberate, could it? Either that or someone had a macabre sense of humour. And earlier in the week, she'd seen a tree in an estate agent's window made up of loo paper and disposable masks. It just about summed things up.

One Flame Hour

There was a soft thud as post landed on the hall mat. Carla padded through, enjoying the heat underfoot to scoop up the usual unsolicited catalogues: inserts for bedding plants, mattresses (different kind of bed), estate agent queries (really? *Who* was going anywhere at this time of year? The idea of moving in the glorious spring sunshine of the first lockdown was one thing but now?) Checkatrade (ditto), a clothing brand Carla had never heard of, let alone pronounce, and a pamphlet in pink (*'Helping you decide'*) which had she thought was to do with cremation and finally, a letter inviting Carla for a routine mammogram. Carla sat back down at the kitchen table and poured herself another cup of tea. *'It is your choice whether to have breast screening or not,'* she read. She sat up at that. She liked the tone. An adult tone, treating her like a grown up. Why couldn't the government take the same line in its approach to COVID-19? Let the public decide for itself as how best to manage risk? She homed in on the paragraph beginning, *'Breast screening does have some risks… some women will be offered treatment that they do not need…'* It was the prompt she needed to tear up the letter. She'd never had a mammogram on the NHS before. In the past, she'd chosen to go privately, having a scan in the chi-chi surroundings of a Harley Street practice receiving a result a few hours later. But even that had been…she frowned…a couple of years ago. Or was it three?

"What's the matter?" said Seb catching the look on her face. He emerged head and shoulders at the top of the cellar stairs. A glass partition framed in wood, led down to the basement. Double mirrors above, meant that anyone in the kitchen could see if someone was coming up or down. Seb was coming up. "You've gone darker and brighter than the sketchiness of our usual weather." Seb and Carla had favourite words that they came across (or in their cases remembered) from time to time. 'Sketchy' was the current one ever since they'd reminisced earlier in the month, about having lunch at Sketches in London. Now, they tried to use it as much as possible, competing to be the first each day to incorporate the word, however inaccurately, in conversation.

"Oh, very good," said Carla amiably. "One to you."

Seb flicked her a surprised look. She was frowning but her tone seemed at odds with her expression. She didn't usually concede so easily.

"When were we in Manaus? Can you remember?"

Carla cast her own mind back. She couldn't believe she was even having to be reminded of their trip to Brazil. It wasn't, obviously the visit in itself that was fuzzy in her memory. Every aspect of it had been amazing: Copacabana beach, Paraty (cobbled streets and Colonial buildings, a whitewashed church and houses painted in jewel-like colours) and last but no means least, Iguazu. They'd stayed at the Belmond Das Cataratas, the only hotel located within the national park which meant that when the park closed to other visitors, at dusk and early morning, they had the falls all to themselves. They had wandered hand in hand along pathways drenched in dew and water from the cascades, not another soul in sight. That was something Carla would never forget. But it was the opera house built in the heart of the Amazon rainforest that she'd always wanted to see. Once upon a time, Manaus, thanks to a rubber boom, was one of the wealthiest cities in the world. Necks growing stiff, they'd marvelled at ceilings inlaid with gold and precious stones in a former rubber baron's mansion. The same owner would send his clothes back to Portugal to be laundered not trusting the locals with expensive fabrics. The wood for ebony spindles which made up the imposing double staircase, had also been

One Flame Hour

dispatched to Portugal to be turned there and then returned to Brazil for re-assembly in situ.

Carla may have forgotten the exact date of their visit, but what she would never forget was the heat, something so suffocating and powerful as to knock her off her feet. Quite literally, she'd sunk to her ankles on the steps of the beautiful opera house, unable to breathe.

"Four years ago," said Seb automatically. He wiped the sweat from his brow with a new, slate grey towel which had come, compliments of the water rower. "Why?"

"Just thinking about all the patients that have missed doctors' appointments because of lockdown."

"Yes, of course," said Seb puzzled. "I totally get how Manaus and 'sketchy' could lead there."

Carla shook her head. *Not what I meant* ... For a moment she had to fight an almost visceral yearning to go back in time, to experience once again the heady aroma of gardenia against a background of noise and the great whooshing sound of the falls. She would have given anything at that moment, to be sitting on the terrace, watching as the sun sank rapidly in a burst of fire engine red. She closed her eyes momentarily, imagining a later stroll in the dark though the nascent fear of wild animals - the coati in particular- would keep them hugging the hotel's shadow. '*Stay out too late,*' they'd been warned, '*and you'll be eaten alive.*'

Her eyes flew open. "I'll explain later," she said vaguely.

Seb shook back his hair with a look that said, *right*... What he said aloud though was, "do you remember when we got to the airport, the morning we left Paraguay?"

One Flame Hour

She did. Not only had they been happily sipping coffee in the wrong airport, but they were also doing it in the wrong *country*.

"That was a close-run thing," she agreed. "Luckily, we had time and realised that although we'd come to Iguazu from Brazil, we were leaving from Argentina. It's OK," she added in answer to his bemused expression. "I was just wondering."

Seb gave her another look. He knew she never 'just wondered.' "As long as everything's OK."

"Of course," she said brightly but already she was counting mentally. The two *were* connected because if Brazil was four years ago, then it must be at least that, if not longer since she'd had a proper check-up. She'd had a mammogram just before they travelled to South America on the first of their visits to the continent. And it must be at least four years since she'd had a smear test. Well, now was the time, *with* time to organise appointments so that the coming year was full of doctors' appointments. They should keep her nice and busy. She could always cancel. Yes, that's exactly what she'd do. She would spend the morning booking appointments. She began to clear a space in front of her, humming as she did so. Gosh, it was ridiculous how much more cheerful she felt at having something practical to do. To *achieve*. She could get her eyes checked out while she was at it. One of Les Girls (an ophthalmologist) had said that during the first lockdown some of her patients had gone blind due to missed or cancelled appointments. Carla shuddered. Definitely eyes. *And* teeth. She should see her dentist while she was at it - maybe pay for some teeth whitening. With all the tea and coffee, she'd consumed recently, they were looking decidedly sallow. She brightened. Between running up to London (doctors' visits were exempt from the travel ban) and running

One Flame Hour

to Southampton, she could be well occupied until lockdown 2 came to its interminable end. And beyond. If she was clever, she could stretch out visits well into the spring. She pieced together the letter from the breast screening unit. Luckily most of the relevant information was still legible. Including the usual COVID- related blurb: *'if you or any member of your household are suffering from any of the symptoms associated with COVID19, or are self-isolating…'*

"Well, whatever it is, you seem happier," said Seb relieved.

"Busy morning," said Carla airily. "Things to organise."

Seb frowned. He hated being kept in the dark no matter what the reason.

"Just need to make a few phone calls," she said briskly. "I'll fill you in later."

8

"*Not* Roger again?" said Seb. Her phone wasn't so much vibrating as screaming shrilly. Which was odd because she was sure she'd switched it off.

"Huh?"

She leant over the side of the bed, her fingers moving crab-like along the freshly polished floorboards feeling for her phone. They must have overslept. It was eight a.m. Early for phone calls but not that early. At least it wasn't two a.m.

"Dr Cave?"

Carla mumbled something to that effect. The use of her PhD title always surprised (and delighted) her. Once on a plane she'd been awoken suddenly and asked if she could assist with a medical emergency. The flight attendant hadn't missed a beat. '*Him?*' she'd gesticulated in Seb's direction, but Carla had had to shake her head helplessly. 'Sorry - academic too.' For a moment, Carla had been tempted to say '*yes - sure what can I do?*' 'Are you *insane?*' Even half asleep, Seb's reaction had been instantaneous as his hand clamped down on her wrist

"It's Sheila," said an unfamiliar voice. "From the breast screening facility - you've indicated you're not available on Monday afternoons. Is that still the case?"

"What? Oh," Carla giggled. "Hi." *Had she?* "Er…that's only because I couldn't see where to fill - no I'm quite free." She could *feel* Seb's expression beside her now. In fact, she'd left the whole form pretty much blank in the hope that someone would just call her as they were doing now. Voilà - it had worked.

"Good, so could you come up this afternoon?"

"*This* afternoon?" Carla sat bolt upright. "As in today, afternoon?"

There was silence.

"Yes."

No, no, no! Carla needed *months* to psyche herself up for this kind of procedure. Subconsciously, she'd already verbalised a response - a half joking *'yeah, didn't think the big C was going to be part of my next lockdown experience…'* But *nicely* because of course, for many that's exactly what it had been. Now, she might have to come up with something else. Besides the whole *point* was that all this planning was supposed to *take* months. Months of reading, (peppy self-help books on positive thinking: *'It's not only about becoming a whole integer person…'* kind of thing) of agonizing, of sleepless nights in preparation, of preparing herself in case she *did* have cancer, maybe write a new will - or even write a will to begin with - she was quite sure that once upon a time, she'd *intended* to write one. Months to adapt, maybe to a new hairstyle - in case her mid-back length hair had to come off. Instinctively, she touched her long locks, fear clutching at her entrails making her breathless. *Breastless. Stop it!* But the idea had never, ever been to have it all done and dusted by the *evening*. That was not what this was supposed to be about. And what happened to the much-broadcast delays in hospital treatment of any kind? News updates drummed home NHS woes, the fact that it was over stretched and understaffed, every department running at full capacity and then some.

One Flame Hour

"Ok," she said weakly. "I'll be there."

"What was that about?" said Seb reaching over and pulling her back under the covers. For a moment she enjoyed his warmth, being held the length of him. Only her chin exposed felt the draft of cold air around the bed. The rest of the house was lovely and warm but their bedroom which was over the kitchen extension, was always cold. But then they liked a colder bedroom. She shimmied away from him.

"Have to go. Have to wash my hair."

He caught her wrist pulling her back to him. "Surely you've time for that?"

Again, she moved to the edge of the bed. "Well, yes. But there's bread to be collected from Hoxton's. And it closes at three p.m. remember?"

"Carla," said Seb firmly. "It's only eight thirty A.M."

Carla's eyes widened in disbelief. "Is it really?"

Towards early afternoon, Carla set off from home, walking due North, up the narrow, cobbled street where they lived, towards the university campus. Seb had offered to walk with her, but she assured him that it wasn't necessary. If yesterday had been cold but beautiful, today was just cold and Carla was glad of her fox-collared coat as she scuttled across Southgate Street, head bowed against the icy wind. If she continued West, she would pass within a hundred yards of where Alfie might be studying. That is, if rowing on the river had been suspended. Usually, in the afternoons he would be out on the water. She wasn't very clear what the rules on outdoor sport were in this second lockdown. She knew that golf wasn't allowed. Which seemed particularly asinine given it was the one sport where social distancing was par for the course. *Oh, very good Carla!* Not 'sketchy' but still good. She applauded her witty self. She thought of all the times she'd passed by local clubs to see couples not within 200 metres of each other, let alone two.

Although it wasn't the most direct route, Carla strolled up the pretty Armoury passage that hugged the side of St. Thomas, the church converted into nine 'luxury' homes. The glow from the many stained windows washed the trees in brief splodges of colour. Outside, a few oversize cars were hooked to tiny electric charging points. Accommodation boasted private lifts and the soaring vaulted arches one would expect to find in a converted church. When Seb and Carla first moved to the city from the country, they had considered buying one of the three houses - the rest were apartments. Carla had been excited by the high ceilings - there'd be no problem fitting in the eight-foot French mirror that took up the whole of one wall in their Queen Anne manor house. Everything was light and airy and modern. Baulthaup kitchens (with incorporated Miele appliances) replaced temperamental AGAs and banished was any suggestion of unreliable heating. The idea of being *consistently* warm was irresistible when on any day in winter she'd had to put on a coat (sometimes two) just to go into the drawing room. Seb liked the idea of an integrated sound system and speakers that used CAT 5 cables.

Since they had come to the difficult decision to move, it was the first time, Carla had been remotely optimistic. Excited even. Looking around St. Thomas, persuaded her that she could live in the city after all. That maybe moving was a blessing in disguise. But every silver lining has a cloud, as Seb was fond of saying and in their case, it came in the shape of the ceiling to floor, stained glass window in the bedroom.

One Flame Hour

Besides being the *only* window, the giant biblical figure in violent purple seemed to be staring straight at them. They'd not even got a bed in the room and its eyes seemed to follow her. 'We'll have to blindfold the angels,' Carla had whispered, 'you know if...' Seb had enjoyed seeing her figurative discomfort. '*If?*'. 'You know... when...' she flicked her head upwards. 'Band Aids might do it. Small strips. But then, how odd would that look?'

Too odd as it turned out. They'd decided to rent for a while before landing on their feet (or in their case literally falling over the boundary wall) and moving into their current place which they both loved. It was the proximity to everything Carla most enjoyed about living in a city. A well-versed cliché but true all the same. When she'd lived in the country, she'd never walked anywhere. There were always fields with fledgling crops you were warned not to trample on, or irritable farmers or dangerous country roads to navigate - drivers were all Formula 1 bounders to a woman as far as she could make out. Pushing a pram was suicidal at the best of times but in the country, mud became lodged in wheels, a child would scream at the barest whiff of fresh air and there was nowhere to stop for a pee. It was the move to the city, that had really got Carla walking. She'd sold a pair of one too many Louboutins, swopping them for hiking boots and more recently a pair of re-issue Hunter wellies (not the high gloss but the new matt almond-toe) variety. Their house was a stone's throw from the cathedral, but it was also near fields and streams. Depending on how far you were prepared to walk, ancient walkways linked a veritable network of town and down throughout the whole of the South Coast.

Carla always marvelled that for centuries, those same byways and bridlepaths had been trodden by layman and pilgrim alike. Just as she was doing now. St. Thomas might provide luxury accommodation, but it had been constructed on the site of a much older church mentioned in Hardy's novels. It was these unexpected collisions with history that also excited her about living in this city. Rounding the Great Hall and nestling just inside the south door was a beautiful, secret garden. Named for Queen Eleanor of Province, the recreated medieval herbarium had turf seats inspired by manuscripts of the age, trim bay hedges and neat squares planted with herbs. Carla loved that Medieval medicine was based on the notion of the body having four humours relating to the elements and that this was reflected in the plants cultivated at the time. She ducked under an arbour tunnel picking her way carefully on, what would later, come spring, transform into a camomile lawn. Hexagonal beds were dotted with comfrey and sage. She also spied cumin and rue. Unable to resist, Carla hunkered down on all fours to touch the delicate, feathery fronds of dill. Even cumin and dill, thought Carla, which she'd always considered 'modern' were used hundreds of years ago. Peasant rents were sometimes even paid in cumin while dill (which meant 'to lull'), was used in cakes to aid digestion. And then of course, rue was used as a strong purgative for the plague. And ruefully (my girl, you're on *fire!*), even as she balked at its repugnant smell, Carla mused that Winchester was no stranger to pandemics.

All this fuss about COVID when the Black Death had decimated its population long before now, in the 13th century to be exact. She knew of lone churches standing in fields where its villages had simply melted away as had the plague four centuries later. The 'basin' surrounding St. Catherine's Hill which visitors often mistook for a disused moat, had in fact been a plague pit put into operation when the then bishop kicked up a fuss about victims being buried in the cathedral grounds. There was even a Georgian monument a stone's throw from where she was standing to commemorate all those who had died.

One Flame Hour

But an unwelcome phone alarm reminded her that there was no time to dawdle and she pressed on. She vaulted up the stone peacock tail of steps fanning away from the cordoned section of excavated Roman dungeons, to the sudden surprise of the vast Peninsula Barracks, with its neat white delineating columns stark against red brick. She remembered watching soldiers beating the retreat once long before it was converted into apartments. Her feet sank into gravel, the sound louder than usual in the absence of trains or airplanes or any of the normal bustle of life. Remembering that she was wearing brown suede Prada boots, Carla stopped, and lifting a foot twisted round to examine the heel. It was a while since she'd had to worry about heels as the only walking she did these days was through the muddy paths along the water meadows. For the first time too, in a while, she'd not simply shrugged on a warm jacket and wellies (walking gear she practically lived in these days) but taken pleasure in choosing a proper coat - 'a church coat' as her friend Natasha called any smart coat with a collar and shopping sites called 'duster'.

It was true that during the first lockdown, she'd suffered a small 'crise' that resulted in her selling or giving away many of her clothes to garner funds for the NHS or make PPE. She'd definitely slipped towards the middle of the summer, when restrictions lifted, non-essential shops re-opened, and she and Seb had travelled to Italy. She had, wrestling with her conscience, struggled with her nature and finally succumbed. To a degree. But then despite her best intentions and her breast beating (not that word again!), she had reverted. Would she ever really change? Did a leopard change its spots? More importantly, could it? And now, here they were in a second lockdown and apart from the odd new jumper (a necessity rather than frivolous purchase) and a dress (that Seb could give to her for the Christmas no one was really having) she had been pretty restrained. Perhaps she shouldn't try to change quite so drastically all at once and adapt a slower approach. So, the forest-green Max Mara Atelier bouclé coat with its specially dyed silk lining, although several years old now, still looked chic, still retained something of the catwalk and Carla, catching a glance of her 1920s silhouette, felt surprisingly upbeat.

The County Hospital, when she reached it, was virtually empty. Presumably COVID patients were kept well away. And unlike the time when she was attacked by two dogs in the summer, and she'd had to wait outside before staff took her temperature and then again inside, no one stopped or noticed as she slipped through the double rubber doors and made her way to the Florence Portal building. She reached in her pocket for her mask. It was funny how there'd been a time when she never went out without lippy and now it was a mask. It had become second nature. The ward in question was easy to locate up one flight of stairs and along a corridor. A woman behind a small window directed her to a single seat. There wasn't another nurse or patient in sight. When Carla had had a mammogram privately in London, she'd had to wait half an hour, she'd hardly been in her chair two minutes before a radiologist summoned her. And then she'd been examined, put her blouse back on, grabbed her coat and bag and she was out once more in the cold afternoon air. The whole appointment had taken less than twenty minutes.

"That was quick," said Seb when she let herself into the house. "I was expecting you much later." He looked sheepish. He was in the kitchen unloading shopping. There was crab and avocado, a bottle of white wine, nectarines and seeded bread. "In case, you needed cheering up," he said. "I thought we'd have a romantic supper. But that's just a starter. I've a leg of-"

One Flame Hour

Carla went to him, still in her coat and pressed her cold cheek against his warm one. He held her close.

"And as you're back so early…" his hands massaged her back as she remained impassive.

"Oh, yes?"

Seb tilted her face to his. "Just think, a beach…"

Still, she didn't move.

"The sweet lap of waves…"

She was so comfortable against him she closed her eyes.

"And it's balmy …"

"So not this country, then."

"You're being way too analytical. Relax. But if it's important than no, not this country. Let's see… Cocktails on the terrace, the sun sinking on the horizon. How am I doing?"

"Better…"

"More?"

"OK. Think arriving at Terminal 5…"

Carla's eyes flew open.

"Go on."

"Close your eyes," Seb's tone was stern. "One last effort. Think BA check in. Think luggage trolley -"

Carla moaned. "One with a wonky wheel even! God, Seb, *yes!*"

9

"*W*hat did you say you've done?"

Les Girls Zoomed once a week, usually on a Sunday evening and Carla looked forward to these calls. It was also the only time that she thought about what she might wear, even if only from the waist up. Sometimes, she even washed her hair in their honour. They hardly spoke to one another in between times, preferring to communicate on their WhatsApp group. But the weekly call had become sacrosanct. Carla had been on her way out, rummaging for her boots in the funny little L-shaped cupboard under the stairs. No more than three feet high at one end, it became an unfathomable abyss at the other particularly if the light had gone out (which it had), and only really worked if everyone hung up their gear (which they hadn't). Strips of anti-insect repellent plastered with dead moths had become stuck to the hem of some of the coats and the floor was a jumble of mismatched boots and shoes. Carla backing out of the cupboard to answer the phone, banged her head on the door jamb for her trouble. But then it had to be important if one of Les Girls was calling midweek.

"Are you *sure* that's a good idea? I mean we've *all* been tempted…" Carla said curtly and then chided herself for not being more empathetic. "You don't think it's a bit … well… *Trumpish?*"

"It's done!" Alice, preternaturally calm Alice, was shrieking. "I'm not taking it down. I *can't* take it down! You just don't get it! I'm now *behind* it!"

One Flame Hour

Carla registered the import of Alice's words. "Woops," she said dropping the one boot she'd managed to locate by touch alone - soft Italian leather amid rubber and latex.

"*Woops!*" hollered Alice. "Is that *all* you can say?"

Carla thought rapidly, trying to remember the layout of Alice's drawing room. "I meant woops - no - you're right. Calm down, Alice. Look, is there a window your side? That you could climb out of?"

"No."

"Can't hear you. Say again."

"NO!" wailed Alice. "I chose this exact spot precisely because I didn't want to be spied on through any window. I knew if Hugo or the children could *see* me…"

Carla switched her phone to loud speak propping it on a thin wooden ledge just inside the cupboard. If she twisted in such a way, she just might be able to locate the other boot while Alice talked.

"*Where* did you say you'd built it?"

There was another yelp, followed by muffled cries and a thud. Then a crash. Carla froze withdrawing her hand and picking up her phone.

"Alice, my friend," said Carla trying to keep the urgency out of her voice. "That wasn't a *hammer* was it?"

The sound of steel on stone was interrupted by the low, guttural sound of Alice's husband in the background, then heavy breathing and finally silence. Carla knew Hugo too well to think he would ever harm his wife. Carla wasn't so sure Alice might not harm Hugo though.

"*Alice?*"

"What's going on?" said Seb coming to the top of the stairs. "I heard that through my headphones!"

"It's Alice - you know Les Girls, Alice," mouthed Carla. "*Alice?*" she repeated into the phone, but all Carla could hear was more crashing about and then what sounded like wood splitting. After a few moments the sound of a drill made any further conversation impossible. "Bwuff," said Carla sitting back on her heels.

"What was that about? Sounded like someone was being beaten up." Seb sat down on the top step which Carla wished he wouldn't. She didn't want to chat just now. She still wanted to find her other boot and get out of the house.

"Well, I hope not but we might check later that Hugo is OK. I'm sure it's fine," said Carla speaking quickly but more to reassure herself than Seb.

"So, what was the problem? Too much lockdown?"

"Probably." Carla resumed looking for her boot. "Alice built a wall," she continued calmly. "Says it was surprisingly cheap. Only £140. There were even easy to follow instructions on YouTube. Or maybe she said the instructions were easy but it was really hard work. I wasn't paying enough attention."

"A wall in the garden? Not bad," said Seb impressed. "Good to have a little project."

One Flame Hour

Carla could tell Seb was thinking a little project might be good for Carla too.

"No, not the garden."

"D.I.Y?"

"Er... not exactly."

Seb twisted on the spot, hanging on to the rail to hoick himself up when something in her expression, caught his attention. He paused mid lift. "I'm missing something, aren't I?"

Carla muttered something about finding her boot.

Seb was insistent. "Come on Carla, I know you. *Where* exactly did Alice build the wall?"

"I'm sure she meant it as a joke," said Carla not meeting Seb's eye. "I mean you and me, I might believe-"

"Oh," said Seb. "I find that hurtful."

"OK, but you know what I mean. Ugh! I HATE this cupboard! Why can't anyone hang up their coats? And if something's on the floor- pick it up! Or on the stairs? Like clean clothes. For example. Do we just step over them? If they're folded on the stairs, wouldn't you think they were meant be on their way *up*, not down?"

"Low blood sugar, Carla?" said Seb which only incensed her even more. "Actually," he continued, "I don't know what you mean. I do my bit and Alfie's at school. Where?" She could tell Seb was miffed and wasn't going to let it go. If Seb was curious about something, he had to know. "Where did Alice build the wall?"

Carla dived in again and this time her hand alighted on a smooth fold of leather. *Da dum*! She pulled out the mate to her knee-high boots and began pulling them on. Skin-tight they were like stockings, but her wellies were in the car and she'd change into those when she got to Magda's. "You know how Alice's house is tiny?" said Carla standing up smoothing the leather over her thigh and rolling her eyes as Seb's gaze remained fixed on her leg. "She's been driven half-crazy during lockdown, what with Hugo's pigs in the house - you know one had piglets? And Lizzie's puppy. She just wanted, *wants* some peace. To be alone." *Don't we all…*

"Yes, I get all that. But you aren't answering my question. Where exactly did Alice build the wall?"

Carla grabbed her keys from the hall table.

"Oh," she said airily. "In the drawing room down the middle. Only I think there's a tiny bit of a problem as she might have bricked herself in."

Seb got up.

"Then she's just stupid."

"No, not stupid, desperate. Besides, didn't you once put polo mallets down the centre of your bed when you had to share with Dom?" Dom was Seb's twin who now lived in America. They didn't see each other much but were close as twins usually were and spoke frequently. But not close enough to warrant sharing a bed.

One Flame Hour

"That was different. We were younger then, at a polo weekend and there was only the one spare room left."

"You could have slept on the floor?"

Seb shot her a look. "Before a match?"

There was a scratchy (should she suggest sketchy?) silence.

"*This* is silly."

"I agree."

And no, he couldn't come with her as she'd promised Magda she'd drive to her place (technically illegal during this second lockdown) and walk with her from there to see Mylo. It would take them a good couple of hours each way. 'See Mylo'. Carla couldn't bring herself to add 'grave.' Put like that, it seemed suitably vague, less charged with emotion.

"Oh," said Seb his chirpiness evaporating. "You do realise it's technically illegal," he added helpfully.

"Ah, but is it? I'm just going to walk. Besides, have you seen how many people are out on St. Catherine's Hill? Do you remember when you were stopped by the police during the first lockdown?"

Seb nodded. A police car had shadowed Alfie and Seb as they left the house one morning in April. Carla had forgotten something and gone back to the house and when she'd emerged moments later, the police car was still there. Walking behind it and her family, she'd just known that the car had pinpointed Seb and Alfie, slowing when they did, picking up speed when Alfie sprinted across Kingsgate. It had then crept along beside them as they made their way to their parked car. And finally, it had stopped as Seb got into the driver's seat. The officer had asked Seb what he was doing. When Seb had said they were driving to a quieter spot to exercise, the officer having had to reverse to avoid a cyclist, mother with twins, child on a scooter, two joggers and five dogs, replied, 'fair enough.'

"What a good girl you are," Seb said kindly now. Which only had the effect of making her feel guilty.

"I'm really not."

"Oh, no?" There was a twinkle in his eye. "Want to remind me how not?"

Carla ignored him. She wasn't feeling *that* kind. "It's a walk as much as anything." She opened the front door as cold air rushed in. It was another beautiful, winter's day. *A chance as daughter Sophie was always telling her, just to be…*

Hellebores in the bed closest to the front door had begun to poke their waxy heads through the damp soil. Despite this outward sign of re-growth, the melancholy emanating from the house was palpable. The street on which Magda lived was quiet at the best of times, but in lockdown it was doubly so. There was no sign of life anywhere. Carla was pretty certain she could have stripped and run naked through the tidy front gardens without so much as a stirring of a net curtain. Carla rang the bell hearing its echo reverberated somewhere in the dark cavern of the house. She waited with thumping heart. *You can't make things any worse…* a friend had told her, and she was so right. *The worst has already happened.* What on earth had Carla to fear? It was Magda, who somehow had to find purpose and resolve to go on living without her beloved child. What on earth was Carla afraid of? What could she possibly say, or do now that would make things any worse?

Jack, Mylo's father, answered the door. He stood erect, dignified, composed. So much so that his very calm steadied Carla. And behind him a shadow of her former self, came Magda. Carla froze, unprepared for the grief on her friend's ashen face. Her beautiful eyes, normally so clear and sparkling seemed colourless. Describing eyes as being 'dead' was a cliché but now Carla knew why. The light was gone from her friend's, her suffering was tangible; crackling off her as though even her skin was radioactive. Tears sprang to Carla's eyes and despite every intention not to cry, Carla felt a sob rip through her, strangling further words, smothering her breathing. *Stop it, stop it, stop it! She told herself. You're here for Magda. This isn't your story. This isn't about you!* And yet Carla felt her friend's agony as if it were her own.

"Can I hug you?" said Carla not knowing what else to do, breaking all the COVID rules and not caring. Magda gave the slightest shrug, not managing even a nod and Carla launched towards her, over enthusiastically feeling the tiny bones of her friend's back, the rigid tension of her whole body, unable to pass on any comfort whatsoever.

"Come in," said Magda. "Why don't you come in? And then we can go on."

Carla hesitated only briefly. If it was debateable whether driving to go for a walk was permissible, going into anyone's house definitely wasn't. But Jack gave an almost imperceptible nod and Carla (peeling off the wretched skin-tight boots) stepped into the house. Everything was as pristine as ever in the tasteful furnishings, the fresh flowers, the almond scent of polished wood but if the light had gone from Magda's eyes, the pulse of light and life, the life of a life half lived, was equally absent from this house. Tears coursed down Carla's face and now she didn't even try to wipe them away. Somewhere from the depths of the house, a clock chimed another mournful reminder of what had transpired. Silently, Magda showed Carla the dining room table which was crowded with cards of sympathy, letters and drawings from the boys in Mylo's class. Carla half looked to see if Alfie's was among them, and then hid her embarrassment, muttering inconsequential words, 'Oh, they're beautiful,' which they were, and equally impotent phrases to fill the void; the silence screaming at every turn.

"Why don't you show me Mylo's Lego?" Carla asked at last, her mind scrambling to say something, anything that might bring him back even if only in their imagination.

Mylo's Lego was legendary as was the room in which it was housed. Alfie (and even Tom) had thought Mylo the luckiest boy alive to have such a place of his own. Situated on the far side of the kitchen and accessed by a wide staircase, the mezzanine's vast, vaulted airy extension encompassed an entire floor. And on that floor, Mylo had recreated, an entire town out of Lego. There was a house, garage, hospital, train station and a school. It was the school that had occupied Mylo during his illness.

With an 'Oh!' I'd forgotten how wonderful!' Carla sank to the floor peering into its tiny windows. But this was no ordinary model school. Yes, there was the furniture and the diminutive figurines every parent was familiar with (especially when you trod on one accidentally in the dark), the pinprick size accessories: utensils, plastic clothing in primary colours, a surfeit of headgear and weapons, but where Mylo was exceptional, was in creating microscopic-size books, printed, then reduced and cut and shaped to the right size that filled the tiny bookshelves. The sheet music that hung on the walls of the auditorium, were actual compositions, the G-clef on the second line of the stave just visible. The programmes from actual performances had also been scanned, reduced, and reprinted to the required dimension. Carla was speechless. The boy had been a genius. It was just a pity his immense talent hadn't been more widely acknowledged when he was alive.

Jack beamed with pride, but Magda merely nodded, her eyes mournful. It was only what she'd known about her boy all along, the creation of the city was something she'd seen him build first-hand, holding his, every step of the way. Where was the surprise in that?

When the agony of sitting there with their pain became unbearable, Carla slowly got to her feet. Sudden movements seemed inappropriate but her right leg had pins and needles and her hands were shaking. She was behaving as though she were the one who had lost a child. Get a grip! she told herself sternly and only succeeded in crying even more. Her nose was dripping unattractively. She rooted around in her pocket for a tissue but finding only a limp mask had to use that instead.

"Shall we walk?" said Carla giving her eyes a final wipe. If she hadn't had COVID before, she'd certainly given herself a head start now in wiping her mouth, nose and eyes with the grubby mask.

Magda observed her impassively, showing neither disapproval nor disgust before leading the way downstairs on silent stocking feet. Carla followed her through the immaculate kitchen, then the sitting room with its freshly plumped cushions - dusted surfaces and polished brass. Everything was perfectly arranged, new candles on the coffee table, a tray set with coffee and a plate of homemade shortbread. There was an expectancy about the place - a stage

One Flame Hour

set waiting for actors to bring it to life. But the only presence Magda yearned for was that of her boy.

Tucking the gold curtain of her hair behind an ear she stood in the hall and reached for her raincoat. Magda was probably a decade younger than Carla but now she looked like a little girl doing up the buttons of her coat. She was always immaculately turned out and today was no different. Like Carla, Magda had grown up abroad and taking care of oneself was a given for European women. But Carla understood the discipline required behind looking just so, even if internally, she was suffering. Looking good was as much a defence as a vanity. It was armour against the bows and arrows of outrageous fortune. Carla shuddered inwardly. Outrageous fortune it was. Why had it happened? Why had any of it happened? And they could begin with the pandemic. It all seemed so surreal as they stepped out of the quiet of Magda's lovely home into the weird, COVID-infested world. Most surreal of all was that Mylo was gone.

Magda's bewildered face, with its vacant eyes was real enough though as they left her neighbourhood as was the squelch of their feet on a pavement sticky with wet leaves. They crossed busy roads, cars passing within inches of them as they snaked in single file along the main road. Carla was beginning to think it was an endurance test as they waded through icy puddles, flooded cattle grids before at last coming to open countryside. Never had she been so happy to see rows of rape as her feet sank into sodden ground peppered with small stones. The wind whipped their hair, tearing at their clothes, so that soon all they could do was concentrate on walking, one behind the other, bracing themselves against the increasingly inclement weather. Even in her lined gloves, Carla's fingers felt frigid. She stuffed her hands in her pockets taking care to place her foot directly in Magda's assured track, following the steady rhythm of her friend's tread. It wasn't until they had passed the wood, that Magda began to talk.

"Do you know something?" she said as they came, to Carla's dismay, to yet another dual carriageway. They were huddled together on a narrow strip of grass as cars shot past them in both directions. Given that the rule about driving *anywhere* was supposed to be 'all but essential travel', the motorways were suspiciously busy. Or then, maybe people were driving to exercise just as she had. Carla had barely managed a, "No, tell me," before Magda had spun on her heel again and begun marching on ahead, down the ever-narrowing centre reservoir, and Carla was forced to quicken her pace to keep up. There was something terrifying about seeing Magda listing in the wind just ahead of her - an arm's-length away - close enough in normal circumstances to grab hold of but would Carla be able to reach her in time should Magda…? She never would, would she…? And then Magda had stopped suddenly, seemingly unaware of the cars flying past, splattering them both with mud. She was utterly composed, her face a pale shape against her hood, her eyes expressionless.

"Mylo was born at ten forty-seven a.m., and he died at ten forty-seven p.m."

Carla swallowed. "That's …" *What?* Incredible? Astonishing? *Extraordinary?* Carla struggled to find the appropriate word, wanting to say something along the lines of it being fate or karma but did she believe that herself? What possible comfort could there be in knowing that anyway? To try and draw meaning from a coincidence. '*There are no coincidences in nature, only consequences…*' where had she read that? Where was the consequence then? Except for the consequence of COVID. Because 'the big C' hadn't been COVID, but Cancer. Carla's meaningless reply was caught up in the screech of a

One Flame Hour

lorry's breaks as Magda took a step onto the dual carriageway. Carla's heart gave a painful lurch and she emitted a squeak that sounded like air squirting from a balloon.

"What is it?" Magda turned calmly. "Are you Ok? You should be careful!"

Carla felt fresh tears spurt as she strangled a sob. The sob became a giggle. Was *she* OK? Yes, she was. Now. Reassured in any event that Magda wasn't planning on killing herself just yet. That had to have been proof. It could have been so easy to turn quickly, launch herself into the road. And who would say that it had been deliberate? A slip in this horrid weather? So easily done. Grit in the eye? Carla who wore contact lenses knew that issue only too well. An unthinking stumble and wham. But thankfully, it was clear to Carla that self-preservation was still instinctive in her friend. Carla had felt her knees spasm and she'd leant down to adjust the buckle on her smart wellies breathing heavily. And then, as she straightened, Magda was turning again, facing Carla but not looking in her direction. Carla looked over her shoulder as a police car hugging the verge, slowed beside them.

"Everything OK, ladies?" said the officer rolling down his window.

Carla who'd had more encounters with the police during the first lockdown than in her entire life (she'd seen a naked man by the water meadows who'd later been arrested on suspicion of indecent exposure and on a separate occasion, she'd been attacked by a couple of rottweilers when out walking), was struck dumb. She was uncomfortably aware that technically, she was probably not supposed to be walking this far from home.

Their 'everything's fine, thanks' was clearly insufficient as the officer switched off his engine.

"You're sure you're OK?"

Carla played out several scenarios in her mind - none of them particularly convincing. Nor did she need the policeman to ask if she lived nearby. If they'd come far. Believing that honesty was the best policy, Carla was about to paint the portrait of the grief-stricken mother when Magda, looking at that moment anything but, explained coolly that they were simply out on a country walk. Carla lowered her gaze hiding a smirk of delight. She was full of admiration for her friend's sang froid. It was a stretch by anyone's imagination to equate crossing the A31 to a country walk.

The police officer looked them up and down. Various parts of his vest seemed to be pinging at the same time. He had two phones in his breast pocket and a voice from one of these was sending him 'South.'

"As long as you're OK," he reiterated.

Carla gave a panicked smile. "Yes, we're fine. We-"

"We're fine," repeated Magda gripping Carla's arm firmly and Carla had nodded, head bobbing inanely.

"Yes, fine," she'd echoed.

"Good," said Magda when the police car drove away.

Carla held her breath. She couldn't be sure, but she imagined a hint of a smile. Magda didn't let go of her arm and at last Carla found herself relaxing. It would be all right, she thought. One day it will be all right. But there was no more to

One Flame Hour

be said just then and they'd walked like that, arms linked until they got to the churchyard where they were absorbed under the trees, tidying Mylo's grave and remembering how he was.

10

"And you *didn't* speak?" said Seb genuinely surprised which didn't help Carla's mood. Unlike Carla, who was disgruntled with cold, her hair sticking out at odd intervals, her hands useless lumps of brick, Seb was composed, buoyant even, from a good day's work. He looked cosy in jeans and a cashmere jumper; his long locks so artfully disarrayed that she wasn't convinced he'd not spent time in front of a mirror running his hands through them. He certainly looked younger than his fifty-eight years while Carla, at that moment, felt considerably older.

"*Don't* sound so shocked. Of course, I *spoke*. What I *meant* was that I think I listened more. Unusual I grant, but you'd have been proud of me." She sank into a kitchen chair exhausted, stretching out her legs and tried unzipping her coat. She shook her hands - each finger tingled.

"Wish, I'd been there." Seb took her hands in his large warm ones massaging them. "Oh, you *are* cold," he added sympathetically.

Carla made a face and tried to summarise her walk without emphasising the fact that Magda being younger was fitter and hadn't appeared to tire at all nor need the loo. But how to recount even a fraction of what they'd talked about? Magda had described Mylo as a baby, a toddler, and finally as a boy on the brink of manhood. She lamented the fact that with every passing year as his friends grew older, as their mothers commented on how much their boys had grown, how they'd surpassed their fathers in height, Magda would never be able to join in. Every birthday would bring fresh grief for the man Mylo would never be, the children he would never father.

One Flame Hour

Magda had gone on to describe the day before he died which had been beautiful and balmy. In short, a perfect end of summer's day and so warm they'd been able to sit in the garden and eat cake. Mylo had been happy and nothing whatsoever had prepared any of them for the fact that he would die that very night. The shock was too great. Magda had believed they still had weeks. And so, did Mylo. In fact, Magda had been doing everything in her power to get Mylo accepted on a programme in Holland. But it had meant negotiating a fine balance between Mylo being ill enough to qualify and not so ill that the treatment would leave him completely incapacitated. This last bit she shared with Seb.

"Holland?" said Seb surprised. "Didn't realise they were at the forefront of research into children's cancers.

"They're not," said Carla. She made a circular motion with her ankle, a 'pretty please' gesture. Seb said something under his breath along the lines of 'the things we do for love' but nonetheless, straddling her chair, placed her foot between his knees and peeled off her boots dropping them onto the floor with a thud. She flexed her frozen toes, feeling the underfloor heating penetrate the ball of her foot. "Mylo should have had the treatment at Great Ormond Street. Actually, you know the Biotech vaccine that you were telling me about earlier? See, I *was* paying attention? Well, apparently, it's based on similar technology - mRNA genetic material to prompt the body to make antibodies. The husband- and-wife team who worked on the vaccine had already developed a cancer drug that sold for a billion pounds."

Seb whistled. "The Turkish immigrant husband and wife?"

Carla nodded. "Although not sure I'd want to refer to them as 'immigrants."

"No, you're right. Highly skilled professionals, in any case," said Seb correcting himself and taking the kettle off the range. "I didn't know of the cancer connection."

"Neither did I." Carla virtually groaned with the pleasure of being warm again. Warm enough to take off her coat which she kept draped over her shoulders. She sighed it was good to be back home in her bright, orderly kitchen with its arrangements of hyacinths and sweet-scented narcissus, knowing that all three of her children were healthy and safe. She had let temporary physical discomfort get the better of her. How quick she was to forget just how lucky she was.

"So, what happened with Great Ormond Street?"

"COVID happened," said Carla.

"Oh." He gave her foot a final pat before going over to the cupboard. He stopped his hand halfway to reaching for a mug. "You don't really want tea, do you?"

She shook her head.

"Thought so." Seb went into the adjacent dining room to fetch crystal glasses and Gin from the drinks cabinet. Back in the kitchen, he shoved a glass under the ice dispenser filling it with ice cubes. He then cut up a lime, squeezing the rest of the juice by pressing a fork into the fruit's flesh. He finished by splashing tonic into the glass. There was nothing unusual in the way he prepared their drinks, but Carla watched his movements transfixed, lulled by the mundane task. For a moment the drink fizzed and crackled, each spark further dislodging her disconnected thoughts.

And, in as much as she wanted to relay everything to Seb, there was so much she couldn't. Not in terms of capturing the

One Flame Hour

mood, of honouring Magda's discretion, of preserving her own peace of mind. She took a long sip thinking that Magda was justifiably angry and how, as they walked, her rage had been contagious. Carla wondered how she would have reacted in Magda's place. How many children had died needlessly because their cancers had gone untreated? And not only children, but adults too? Magda would never know whether an interruption in treatment had made a difference. It was something she would never have answers to. Would have to live with. Somehow. And what distressed her more than all the above combined, was the fact that Mylo had *known* he was terminally ill. They had told him he was going to die. How on earth did you prepare your child for that? How would you ever recover? Magda wasn't convinced anymore that it had been the right thing to do and yet the care team had been adamant that Mylo know. Carla wasn't sure either. She wouldn't have been brave enough to witness her boy's fear, being helpless to offer any comfort. Parents were supposed to make things better, to have answers, at least some of the time. No, Carla wouldn't share that last with Seb.

Carla sipped her drink thoughtfully. If she and Seb were feeling gloomy, Magda and Jack must be experiencing unquantifiable despair. Lockdown was challenging enough without having to deal with bereavement - isolation within an isolation. She cast Seb a sideways look. She still found him attractive after sixteen years of marriage. He made her laugh, unexpected flashes of humour and often when she was at her most grumpy. They liked to do the same things: they liked the same music, they loved opera and travel and theatre. Before the start of the pandemic, they had spent months out of every year on the move. Not even the birth of Alfie who was now thirteen, had interrupted their globe-trotting adventures. Carla loved that she could discuss almost any subject with him - from Victorian theatre practices to Valentino clutches.

But. And there was a 'but.' How would they be if they lost Alfie? Would their marriage survive? Or what if she lost one of the twins? Carla had a boy and a girl from a previous marriage while Seb had never been married before. Would she blame him? Would she be resentful that Seb didn't grieve in the same way that she did? Not display the required emotion: too little or indeed too much? Would the damage done in the first days of mourning be too great to overcome? Would they say unforgiveable, unforgettable things that would later make the way back to each other impossible? Who could tell? She shuddered, knocking back her drink.

"Come here," said Seb pulling her to her feet. "It'll be all right."

She touched his face.

"You can be so tender," she said sweetly.

"And I'd rather be in one," he said enjoying his own joke. "Heading away from our yacht and on to an island for a picnic."

"Where?" she sighed. "Where would we be? Caribbean? South China Sea? Gulf of Thailand?"

"You choose."

"Not sure I can be bothered," said Carla feeling all gloomy again.

Seb frowned. "You're not playing along kiddo. How about… Russia? Would you go there if you had half the chance?"

One Flame Hour

Carla's eyes widened in surprise, a faint pulse of excitement beginning to beat tentatively. Alfredo had been a Russian interpreter at the United Nations first in New York and then Geneva. Her brother currently resided in Moscow, and all told, she must have visited the country a dozen times. But not recently. "Russia?" she echoed. "Whatever made you think of that? I thought you liked warm places?"

"I do, but we're just having a bit of fun, remember. A bit of escapism. Besides, Russia can be extremely hot in the summer but I'm thinking about now and how you love Christmas in cold climates. So, let's pretend we could go. We could visit your brother. Things will have changed since we were last there."

"Which was almost fourteen years ago," said Carla thoughtfully. "That time we were in St. Petersburg. I was pregnant with Alfie. We were there on 1st of May, do you remember? And it snowed!"

There was a glint in her eye. She thought of all the times she'd been to Russia and just as important, what she'd worn: lots of mink and burgundy velvet and the places she'd visited: Moss film, the chocolate factory, the Georgian restaurant near the monastery, Tolstoy's Moscow home, the fabulous Pushkin Café which was just a restaurant as opposed to the Writer's Café which was a mecca for the intelligentsia.

"That's my beautiful girl," said Seb kissing her smile. "That's what's missing."

11

"You've seen this, right?"

Seb was rowing in the cellar, his laptop propped on the (£150) wooden tablet holder (the additional hardwood 'arm' had cost a further £50). Essential he'd told her for keeping up with, among other things, the daily bio blog *Catching the Sprat* he had founded. 'Or could I say 'brat?' instead?' he'd asked when he'd been playing around with titles. Why had they thought that even funny? Her only explanation was that pre COVID they'd had a strange sense of humour. Seb had studied marine biology at university where he'd first begun writing on the subject. In recent years, he'd often complained that there was never time enough for the things he really wanted to do as opposed to wasting time on things he didn't. Well, lockdown had gone some way in addressing that, providing the impetus, if not discipline, to initiate something new.

At the moment though, Seb's time seemed to be divided between issuing calls for papers on related topics (the impact of marine plastic debris on life in the sea being a popular one) and following COVID updates with just a little too much enthusiasm for Carla's liking. Seb had set up the water rower in one half of the space that Carla used as a utility room. Which suited her very well apart from the times when she went down to do the ironing. She was used to catching up on some trashy series on Netflix. Now she had to time things so that they didn't coincide.

Carla sighed. "If it's COVID-related. I'm not interested." She gathered up a basket of laundry dragging the ironing board across the floor. If he was going to chat, she was going to have to relocate upstairs.

"Of course, it's COVID-related!" said Seb. "What other news *is* there? Other than the US election shenanigans."

"At least it's keeping us amused." She shot him a look. He certainly wasn't 'sparkling' as Jessica Smith put it, the fitness guru she'd begun following when it was clear that if she continued jumping jacks with Joe Wicks, she was going to end up with a hernia.

"I'm actually grateful for the distraction," continued Carla, hefting the ironing board under one arm. "There's not much entertainment of any kind, is there? I mean other than the elections." It had certainly seen the return of humour as relayed on social media. Which had been sorely lacking recently. There was a Lego figure depicting Trump (*'Sometimes it's hard to Lego'*) and umpteen scenarios ranging from the suggestion that Melania was working for Putin, to images of Trump and Boris's faces merging into one another (*'One down, one to go'*). Carla liked the one where the Statue of Liberty was shown peeping out from behind its base best of all. That caption read, *'Is he gone yet?'*

Seb frowned. Carla wasn't showing the required interest.

"OK," she said catching his expression. "So, if not to do with the elections, then what? What's the big news? Oh, I can guess! Please tell me that lockdown's over. We're free to travel. We're going to…Moscow!"

"Now, there's a thought," said Seb. He slowed to a halt as water swished in the cylinder. It sounded as if a boat had come aground. "No."

One Flame Hour

For some reason his answer irritated her. Of *course*, she hadn't really expected anything different but the finality of the bind in which they all found themselves was depressing. Back in March, they'd believed there'd only ever be one lockdown and that it would end after three weeks. How naïve was that? Then, towards the end of the summer had come a certain freedom and they'd been allowed to travel even though in their case, it had only been as far as the Isle of Wight. And *then*, just as she'd enjoyed filling their autumn diary with musical events, a second lockdown had come into force.

Carla would never forget trying to get up to London for a last concert and being irritated because Seb had insisted on playing one last game of polo before they set off. Which had only delayed their departure. Carla had worn her new Emilia Wickstead jumpsuit and was giddy with excitement anticipating a night in London (albeit a socially distanced one). But she was soon giddy with a different feeling, a visceral urgency to get to the city while 1200 miles of traffic had the motorways gridlocked with people panicking to *leave* it ahead of a curfew announced only hours before. She'd never witnessed anything like it. 'Moscow burning doesn't hold a candle to this,' she told Seb who for once wasn't interested in her literary allusions. 'Not just *literary*,' she'd said, twisting with impatience. 'Historical *and* factual. I'm talking about Napoleon- it's also where the word bistro comes from - in case you're interested.' Carla didn't give Seb the chance to contradict her. 'See the French soldiers wanted food to be served quickly - 'bistro' means quickly in Russian…' 'You mean before everything went up in smoke,' he said pulling on the hand brake. They weren't going anywhere. 'Well, yes.' She looked at him in amazement. How could he not be interested? *Pearls* she thought to herself *pearls*. Still… when they got to the concert, when they'd glided up to the first floor with a glass of ice-cold champagne in their hand, when they'd sunk into their favourite sofa…

And now, once again, she felt she was being thwarted at every turn, that her life was being gobbled up. Precious time squandered. She was so fed up with being told what and when and how to do everything. Why, oh why hadn't she been born in Sweden? Or in a country where its people were treated like actual adults?

"Thought so," she said grumpily. "What then?"

She set down the ironing board balancing it against the cellar door. Then dropped the laundry basket beside it. Maybe, she'd do the laundry later. When she could watch a Narco-related show in peace. The gorier the better. Or maybe start a really long series like *Spiral* or *This is Us*. The last thing she'd watched was *Grand Hotel*. All sixty-seven episodes. Then again that required *a lot* of ironing.

"Well, a Harvard study is saying there's a direct connection between having had pneumonia and COVID."

She stared at him. *This* was news?

"Being a respiratory disease, I thought you *got* pneumonia when you had COVID," she said tetchily.

"You do yes, but a *history* of pneumonia is the biggest risk factor for death from COVID-19 after age."

And?

"No, that's not right," said Carla firmly. "It's things like type 2 diabetes or heart failure. Or being Afro-Caribbean."

"What? No." Seb was equally adamant. He hunched over his knees then twisted to reach for the pristine towel draped over the matching hardwood rack. Carla hadn't noticed *that* arriving. He patted his dry brow. "And of course, given my history."

"Seb," said Carla patiently. "You had pneumonia. Once."

"For which I was hospitalised."

"You were." He was, but she couldn't remember why or when exactly. He hadn't seemed so ill to her. His twin Dom was visiting from the States at the time and had panicked. Dom never thought Carla was taking good enough care of Seb. Which was probably true.

"So, I have a propensity."

"You mean predisposition." Could she go as far as saying a *sketchy* predisposition…?

"Syntax."

Maybe not. She wasn't in the mood. "You also had the pneumonia vaccine."

"Which almost killed me."

Which also happened to be true. There was a strained silence. Carla was thinking that she really ought to have gone out for her walk. It would have helped her to be patient now.

"So, what are you saying?" she said doing her best to sound empathetic.

"I'm not saying anything," said Seb but then he suddenly pounced on his phone. "Except… I'm going to call the surgery. Right away."

One Flame Hour

Carla rolled her eyes. "Well, when you've spoken to them," said Carla. "How about a walk along the water meadows?"

Seb jumped up.

"Done. Let me grab a coat."

An hour later, they'd set off down College Street, past the book shop, with its packages waiting for 'click and collect', past the college itself with the boys - Alfie included - locked up behind its walls. They lived so close to the school and yet Alfie was in quarantine, and they couldn't see him, nor could he see them. It seemed ironic that although theoretically they were no longer restricted by Alfie's school calendar, in practice they could venture no further than St. Catherine's Hill. This being Sunday there were more walkers about than usual.

Carla quickened her pace in order to keep up with Seb who was striding on ahead.

"Which way?" he said.

She shrugged. "You choose."

She tried not to think of the time last summer when they'd walked 'the loop' and had an argument and just about here, they'd split up - Seb to walk the concrete path by way of the tennis courts and she by the water meadows. If ever a decision to take the less travelled path had suffered a consequence, it was that one. She'd marched on ahead, up the northside of the hill and promptly been mauled by two Rottweilers, not on their leads. Instinctively, she rubbed her thigh where the haematoma continued to heal. It had been months now, but the bruise had become a hard lump and there were still scars on her back and waist where one of the dogs had bitten her.

"Oi!" she heard Seb call suddenly.

Lost in thought, Carla hadn't noticed that he had walked on ahead of her. She'd been following him single file along the tow path concentrating on lifting her feet through the thick bog. For months now the meadows were water-logged, the puddles ever deeper, the mud more lugubrious. Looking up she saw Seb waving his arms at a small flock of sheep that seemed to be running around in circles. A small group of people had also gathered to watch a puppy who had jumped through the barbed wire fence and was 'rounding up the sheep.' He was having a lovely time, frolicking and playing, completely oblivious of the terror his antics was creating in the sheep or the alarm in the spectators shouting from the fence. Carla thought of the pastoral tragedy that was Gabriel Oak's in *Far from the Madding Crowd* when his new sheepdog chases his flock over the side of a cliff. Carla was about to relay this - and a 'it could be a lot worse' when she realised to her horror that Seb had also vaulted one of the barbed wire fences and was shouting at the dog owner - a young girl in her twenties. He directed several months of pent-up lockdown fury in her direction, picking up a stick and throwing it to her dog in the hope of distracting it. The dog couldn't have been more delighted, dragging the stick in amongst the sheep which wasn't the idea at all.

Cringing, Carla walked on ahead as Seb gesticulated and shouted, his South African accent more pronounced the more passionate he became. She passed the shallow bathing pool sheltered by a willow tree, which was popular with young children as it was never very deep. Beyond that point though the river thinned and twisted towards the first bridge by the

One Flame Hour

Hospital of St. Cross. And that's where she saw her, a lone sheep so frightened by the dog, that she'd run on alone and jumped into the river.

Carla turned around running back down the path.

"Seb!" she called. "Seb!"

"Yah, seen her," said Seb sprinting ahead of her. Tossing Carla his Akubra (the hat he never walked without), Seb clambered over the fence and waded into the water. Carla felt herself swell with pride as people gathered to watch. Much younger men hovered, debating the best course of action. Women fretted for the sheep. Someone said they should find a rope, someone else suggested calling the RSPCA, someone else the fire department or the College itself as it owned that bank of the river. "Bollocks to that," said Seb both hands gripping the ewe's neck and meeting resistance as his hands sank into its sodden wool. But dislodging the terrified ewe from mud wasn't as easy as Seb thought it would be. The more Seb heaved, the less the sheep was inclined to move.

"It will abort its lamb," he said grimly.

"How could you tell? That it was pregnant?"

Seb ignored her. "Pull!" he shouted at a bystander who had approached the water's edge but wasn't prepared to go in. The man leaned over at ninety degrees. Any further away and he'd be falling in the water as well. With a final heave Seb shoved the ewe onto the bank. At first, she hesitated, confused as to what she was suddenly doing amidst the bull rushes after her dip in the cold water. Unsteady at first, she continued to tremble violently before running further down the field hugging the water's edge. Penned by the rock pool at one end and the bridge at the other, there was no way she could re-join the flock.

"She's fine, now," said Seb in answer to her unspoken question. "There's nothing more we can do." The spectators clapped and Carla smiled broadly. Seb emerged sopping wet from the knees down, mud and grass clinging to his jeans.

"My husband will do anything to get out of a walk," she said to no one in particular. There was an amused murmur before the crowd dispersed.

Walking back to the house arm in arm, Carla leant against him. "I was really proud of you," she said, the old attraction returning. It was as if from somewhere far away, buried deep in memory, there was a whisper of another feeling, another forgotten sensation. Recently, they'd been so caught up with just surviving, there'd been no time just to be, as her daughter Sophie was always telling her, just to relax.

"Good oh," said Seb a twinkle in his eye. "In that case, I know exactly how you might reward me."

12

"Carla perused the aisles of their local M&S casting a scornful eye on the 'dine in' option. Was that an attempt at humour or just sarcasm? She looped round one more time hoping for inspiration. From doing a routine weekly shop before lockdown, they now visited the high street branch two or three times a day if only to have some form of exercise and contact with people other than each other. They were on first name basis with Ian, Rosanna, Kate and Gem and knew the rest of the staff by sight. It always amazed Carla that those four, who had been in situ since the get-go, hadn't come down with the virus. There'd been an unpleasant incident when some bloke high on meths, had whipped off his mask and spitting in Ian's face shouted 'I've got COVID! Hope you get it too!' It was always heartening to see the familiar faces, always smiling and friendly and steady. Steadier than many of their friends were. Some continued to be terrified and so swayed by Hancock's news updates that they wouldn't or couldn't emerge from their homes. Even for a walk.

As she left the shop, Carla's phone vibrated and pulling it out of her pocket to read the text her face fell. Seb was waiting for her, leaning against a pretty painted fire hydrant. Its delicate tree of life and prancing fawn on a turquoise background seemed a taunting reminder of when the city celebrated fairs and jolly gatherings.

"What's up?" he said.

"We won't be seeing Alfie this weekend," she said gloomily slowly unhooking the mask from behind her ear. "The boys aren't being allowed home. Apparently, in order to 'protect the boys' existing social bubble', contact with anyone outside it (including parents) has to be limited." Her stomach felt hollow. The communication made her feel like a pariah. Even the *parents?* The wording felt archaic. Since when had touching become so abhorrent? Not since hearing mysterious bible readings as a child, that referred to afflictions such as leprosy and the like had Carla felt so alienated. The words blurred as a fat tear plopped onto the screen and she used her disposable mask to blow her nose. She didn't realise how much she'd been looking forward to Alfie's home coming. They'd gone from living 24/7 to nothing. He'd not even asked for tuck either. Not since the day of Mylo's 'funeral.'

"Oh," said Seb. He too sounded flat. Carla shot him an uneasy look. Seb was never ever down. If anything, sometimes she could fault him for being *too* optimistic. They began walking slowly home past the many boarded up stores along the way. Starbucks had gone, Debenhams was in receivership and rumour had it that Pret (which had only been in the city a couple of years) was also on its way out. There was a tired, abandoned feel to the city without any of the pre-Guy Fawkes or Hallowe'en bustle.

But the mothers in Alfie's year weren't taking a cancelled leave out lying down. Carla's phone pinged with a steady stream of messages expressing their upset. *This isn't what we signed up for! Poor communication! Well, my son's coming out! Let them stop me!* And the like.

"Alfie will be fine," said Seb reassuringly. "We'll miss him but it's much better that he's at school with his friends."

"I suppose," said Carla in a subdued tone. They had now reached the tree-lined pathway that led to the cathedral. Alfie wasn't coming home... *Your children are not your children...* It had begun to rain, a fine mist which always made her hair frizzy. Not that she cared too much about that either anymore. After all they weren't dressing up to go anywhere. It certainly felt as though time had stood still since March. Perhaps, like the Tom Foolery poem said, the world had needed to take stock, people were greedy, resources were being devoured by want rather than need. And, in recognition of the fact, there'd been universal wonder at the sight of empty roads and skies and seas. But now? Now, everything was just too weird, lockdown had gone on for too long. There was a weariness and a paucity of spirit and motivation. There was an ache at the back of her throat.

"Why don't we take Alfie some tuck anyway?" she said. "Text him, will you? We could drop it off now. And there's another book on Vietnam he might like."

Anticipating a 'don't be silly,' Carla was surprised when Seb readily agreed, whipping out his mask to dart into their corner store to buy confectionary. Her turn to wait outside while he went in. She stood on the curb opposite in front of the empty pub. Normally, the place was buzzing no matter the weather. Acclaimed for its cosy fires and signature bangers and mash in winter, cocktails and outdoor dining in summer, today its doors were sealed tight. She did wonder how things would be if they ever did get back to normal. Would they find the noise overwhelming? Nowadays the loudest unexpected noise came from the whirring of bicycle wheels or a scooter's bell. She could hardly remember the sound of laughter (that wasn't canned or on Zoom), of glasses clinking, of 'last orders' being called when the doors opening onto the back patio carried the sound down the street. And almost forgotten completely were summers when large screens projected films in front of the cathedral. She would never again complain about any noise that involved human interaction. Not even being woken up by an occasional brawl.

One Flame Hour

She thought back to the first lockdown with something akin to nostalgia. There'd been such a sense of solidarity and good will, a desire to get through it not just as a matter of course, but of getting through it well. Carla had invested energy and time into thinking of imaginative entertainment not just for Alfie, but for them all. It was true that the lovely warm weather had helped but there had been a general hopefulness. They'd *believed* that an end was in sight, that it *would* end. And then it had, the first lockdown had lifted and there'd been unbridled elation. She had a photo of Alfie walking with friends through a field of poppies, rolling skies above them, their arms flung wide with the joy of being together again. Of being free.

If spring had been unseasonably warm, the summer months had been even better. Endless evenings when they'd sat al fresco having six people to supper. *Six* people! What a luxury that had felt, what an indulgence. An orgy of excess. Now, after an evening's online chat, she felt exhausted, mentally wiped. When she watched a film (when she could concentrate long enough) and there were scenes involving large numbers: crowds, a ball, Carla involuntarily recoiled. They were programmed to shrink from crowds, from gatherings of more than fifteen. The psychology of fear was successfully at work, and they had their government to thank for that.

The other day she'd seen a solitary airplane. She wondered if her feeling of delight was comparable to spotting a bomber returning safely from a mission during the war. And thinking of airplanes. There was one final message but not from the mothers, it was a TikTok meme from Les Girls: it depicted a man drinking a glass of champagne and staring out of the window of an aircraft. Carla closed her eyes momentarily - oh to be on a plane! Oh, for this all to end! To have the freedom to hop on a plane and go ... anywhere! But when she'd opened her eyes again, the skit had moved on.

One Flame Hour

What the man was really doing, was crouching by a screen shot of clouds, holding a loo seat to his head while listening to a recording of a pilot welcoming his passengers on board. It made her want to weep.

She straightened quickly, her eyes blurry with self-pity.

"Everything OK?" Seb came out of the shop cradling bars of chocolate and Caramel Wafers. He dropped them into the shopping at Carla's feet. "We'll go home and then I'll run up to Alfie's house with this lot."

And she only nodded, sniffing. He pulled her to him.

"It'll be all right," he said his lips on the side of her head. "You read history, right?"

She nodded.

"Well, just remember none of what is happening now is unique. We're part of one constantly moving spiral, a cycle. It has all happened before. Once upon a time, this country was decimated, this city was reduced to half its population because of a contagion. People complained that society as they knew it had been ravaged, a new social order was in place, it was the end of religion, of manners, of culture. It's all happened before, kiddo, just remember that."

Carla pulled back.

"So, what did happen?" she sniffed. "What happened next?"

"They partied," said Seb smiling. "People hung out in taverns, they lived in the streets. People partied till they dropped."

One Flame Hour

*

Tucked in amongst coupons for Deliveroo and Pizza Hut, was an unassuming, unsealed envelope. She'd almost binned it along with the other flyers but its stiffness warranted another feel. It *looked* like an invitation, the kind they used to receive before COVID. But of course, that was ridiculous. Impossible. Obviously. No one was going to parties or allowed to have people in their homes. She felt a surge of optimism; she could almost pretend that its contents would reveal an invite to something fabulous, to something worth dressing up for, worth *looking* forward to. She was almost afraid to open it, afraid to be disappointed. She studied the curve of the 'C', running her finger over dried ink. There was something familiar in the way her name was underlined. Puzzled, she pulled out the card.

Cocktails in the Concorde Room
6.p.m

Dress formal

Underneath was a line drawing of an airplane, but Carla didn't need an explanation. She smiled. 'Dress formal' huh... yes, she could just about manage that! Faint optimism became excitement - excitement at the thought of dressing up if only to go downstairs again. She glanced at her phone. There was time for a cup of tea and a bath. She commanded Alexa to play Césaria Évora as she vaulted up the stairs. As the breezy strains of the barefoot diva followed, she felt as though she were hearing the Sirens play music from far away, something tugging at the heart strings replaying other emotions, connecting her to other memories. This is what she had missed - the impulse of being carried away with music or inspiration - anything that wasn't contrived or transmitted via Zoom. Seb was out - she wasn't sure where and it was so rare to have the house to herself that she luxuriated in its silence. She stripped off her raincoat, her socks, mud-caked jeans and jumper letting her clothes fall where she took them off, doing exactly what she was forever chiding Alfie for doing. In her bathroom, so large that it sported a fireplace the length of one wall and an armchair, she poured bath salts under running water.

Just for today, she would pretend that everything was normal, that the States hadn't gone bonkers (or that Boris hadn't), that freedom of speech hadn't bowed before wussy wokedom, that more than a million people in the world hadn't died of COVID, that Denmark hadn't killed 17 million mink and that competitive breakdancing hadn't been scheduled for the 2024 Paris Olympics. And thinking of Paris, the former President of France, with whom her mother and grandmother had been in love, Valéry Giscard d'Estaing, had died at the age of 94. His had evoked the same sense of recognition that their current leaders' names did today. Maybe it was because she was getting older that it felt as though the landmarks of her youth were slipping away or maybe it was simply that lockdown had made her more thoughtful.

Carla stepped into her bath. Her skin tingled with the heat, her thighs instantly turning pink then disappearing completely under a layer of soap suds. She peered at her naked body twisting it this way and that. From certain angles (and in subdued lighting) it didn't look too bad although in general, she felt that she had aged during lockdown. She slept badly; every day underpinned by a low-level current of anxiety. In March there had been an unprecedented degree of novelty, the world pulled together, the necessary restrictions lifesaving in the wake of such devastation. The weather had been balmy, it had been a pleasure to take meals outside, open their eyes to the beauty of the world around them, a world no one usually had the time to observe properly. It was a marvel to note the silence, the absence of planes mothballed in abandoned hangars around the world. Life was reduced to a manageable simplicity.

Carla had purged her home of unnecessary luxuries, selling clothes to garner funds for PPE and the like. She'd home schooled Alfie, they'd 'attended' lectures on all manner of subjects thanks to TED talks, they'd walked for miles along ancient routes but new to them. They'd connected with people they'd not spoken to in years. It had all been positive. And of course, she was aware of the true suffering of those who'd lost loved ones, who'd experienced the disease first-hand. And now here they were again, only this time the weather was colder, the future more uncertain, the end was not in sight at all unless you counted the latest hurdle: 15 million doses of a vaccine being delivered by February.

Carla rubbed rose exfoliator onto her shoulders although strictly speaking, she wasn't sure that she really needed it, her skin was dry enough from too many layers of clothing and spending too much time either indoors or braving harsh elements. Still, it made her feel something of her frivolous old self again. Should she paint her nails? A quick once over? Why not? It wasn't as if she was in a rush to be anywhere. Before COVID, Carla had sometimes joked that the part she liked best about going out was the getting ready. Half the time, she'd have been just as happy to have supper and watch a good film. *Be careful what you wish for...*

One Flame Hour

She lay soaking a little longer, enjoying the pretty oil painting above the fireplace. The small landscape in her favourite sea-green colours, depicted a wintery sunset, light breaking over a white capped peak. She wondered where it was exactly. Switzerland perhaps and the Chablais Alps in particular. From long, long ago a memory snuck up on her - of how her mother and she had gasped at the beauty of Lac Léman as viewed from the school Carla eventually ended up attending.

They'd moved to the country a few months earlier, her brothers slotting in effortlessly at the all-boys' English day school in Geneva but Carla's education was more problematic. There wasn't the equivalent for girls and Eugenia didn't approve of the co-ed international schools available in the city. The only other alternative would have been a local convent but Carla's French wasn't good enough. The solution? The English-styled school located half-way around the lake. The only hitch was that being an hour by train, Carla would have to board. But there were two things in its favour - one being that Montreux was minutes from the world-famous Nestlé headquarters at Vevey (Carla thought chocolate on tap) the other was the uniform. In winter, students wore sumptuous, cashmere cloaks. With hoods. Carla had always had a thing about hoods. From Eugenia's point of view, she liked that there was every chance of bumping into Charlie Chaplin, or Roger Moore or Petula Clark or Julie Andrews (she'd been mistaken for the actress when she'd had her hair cut short) or James Hunt - the list of famous tax exiles was endless.

In the end, it was none of those things that had proven conclusive but the sheer, spellbinding beauty of the place. To this day, Carla remembered being dragged reluctantly on a tour of the purpose-built school whose classrooms faced inwards and reeked of bleach. But they'd finished the visit with one dramatic finale: tea in the headmaster's study. His secretary having ushered them into a comfortable sitting room had thrown open the French doors that looked onto the garden. They'd been met with a blast of sweet, fresh, alpine air, so clean and clear, that Carla had spontaneously closed her eyes inhaling deeply. And when she exhaled, shoulders rounded, all tension expiated, and looked across an undulating verdant lawn tumbling down to the water, she had gasped. Framed by the Dents du Midi in the distance, the shimmering lake lay spread before her, a mirror of translucent loveliness.

At the furthest point, jutting out on its own bank was the island castle - the Château du Chillon, where Byron had been imprisoned. Much later, Carla would be struck dumb by the gorgeousness of the blue mountains of the Torres del Paine, appearing twice as vast when reflected in the glaciers below, by the vistas across Colombia, the isolation of Easter Island, the majestic, dramatic drama of Rio from Corcovado, the sweetness of foggy, muggy heat as a Ya Noi mass rose from Phang Nga bay, but she had not again experienced, never again felt that visceral shock when unexpectedly confronted by wonder.

And that's what she missed most now. Wonder. Surprise. Excitement. They could all do with a different view, thought Carla. It was choice that was lacking, that spontaneity of deciding to zip over to the continent for a weekend or further on a whim. And sun. Carla longed for sun. She regretted not spending more time sunbathing when they were in Cartagena last February. They'd arrived home on March 15, just as news of the pandemic broke. Or swimming. Why had she worried so much about getting her hair wet? If they ever travelled again, Carla would spend her entire time naked in the sun being burned to a crisp.

One Flame Hour

She wrapped herself in a towel and padded into her dressing room. Cocktails? The concept was as foreign as if she'd just learned a new word in Azeri. She looked at the rail of flimsy designer frocks she'd once worn as regularly as wellington boots. There was a Prada black lace dress first outed at the House of Lords, a heavily embellished Pucci mini that had seen Windsor Castle, countless velvet and sequin jumpsuits, Missoni gowns and Chanel fantasy jackets. But the Concorde Room? Would that mean they were flying off somewhere? Probably, so she'd have to be (relatively) comfortable.

Carla couldn't remember ever having dressed for comfort in her life. Except for now. When she lived in a raincoat. She pulled out a cobalt blue Temperley jumpsuit that Carla had only worn once before. It had fitted perfectly when she tried it on in the shop at the end of the summer. It fit a little too perfectly now. Just as well as the invite said 'Cocktails'. The jumpsuit wasn't designed to wear when either sitting too long or over-eating. Skimming the floor, she could even wear it without shoes. She chose large but light filigree gold earrings, brushed her hair quickly and rubbed what was left of her Chanel lip gloss using it to highlight her cheekbones as well.

The house was in darkness when she went downstairs, the underfloor heating delicious under the balls of her feet. The only light came from the dining room, and she went towards it, her heart involuntarily skipping a beat. Tea lights nestled on the velvet dining room chairs which had been placed in two rows down the centre. At one end was a large computer monitor, the sound of a low thud of an engine revving in the background. And filtering through that, was the flower duet from *Lakmé*. Carla could almost hear the overhead lockers clicking shut. She closed her eyes… *'I could be bound by a nutshell and feel myself king of infinite space…'* Now was absolutely the moment to let the imagination fly…

"Good evening, Dr Cave," said Seb handing her a glass of champagne. He wore a pilot's cap. "I am Captain Cave welcoming you aboard this Boeing 737 with destination…"

She raised an eyebrow.

"With destination," said Seb huskily, "your choice…"

13

"If I'd only known," said Seb the following morning. "How easy it could be…Tell me, honestly, was it the cap?"

"Every girl likes a man in uniform," murmured Carla stretching her leg against his. "Surely you knew that."

"Thought so," said Seb smugly.

"Actually, all you had to do was play the music."

"You mean get you to hold for BA on the phone?"

"We-ell…"

Seb leant over the side of the bed to scoop up his laptop. It was December, just, and two days before the circuit break lockdown came to an end. It was also Saturday which meant they allowed themselves a lie in. To pretend they were still on a flight bound for somewhere exotic.

"I've a better idea. I think we should go and see your brother in Moscow. Now. The minute this lockdown ends. Like in the next few days. I've been looking into it. We can pay for fast-track visas. In addition, all that's required is a COVID test seventy-two hours prior to arrival. I've looked into that too - it's expensive but it's all doable. We'll be back in 10 days."

Carla sat up in amazement.

"What fly? You mean actually *fly*?"

One Flame Hour

Seb was too busy checking out flights to notice the look of sheer astonishment on her face.

"Yes."

"B-but won't we feel guilty? I mean," said Carla. "When so many of our friends are grounded."

"We won't tell them."

"What about Alfie?"

Seb looked at her, long and hard then. "What about Alfie?"

Carla giggled, the idea of escaping even for a short time too delicious to even contemplate. "We couldn't, could we? I mean it wouldn't be right …"

"Right doesn't come into it. Alfie's at school. He can't come home. We can't visit him. You know perfectly well that he sulks if the WIFI isn't good enough. I'm not sure how much is open anyway. It won't be like the last time we were in Russia. Besides, this is about us. It's the perfect moment. Let's do it. I'm game if you are."

He shut the lid on his laptop. His eyes bored into hers, really seeing her. Carla felt a flutter at the thought of wearing a mink coat again. And which one? She had a reversible black parka which really wasn't warm enough, a short one which meant her bum froze and a longer one with a hood. It would have to be the -

"Let's go! Yup," said Carla suddenly. "Yes! Moscow in the snow! Let's do it. Let's go!"

One Flame Hour

*

"Excuse me, is it already evening?" muttered Carla into her phone, a couple of evenings later. She was tucked up on her window seat, half hidden by a curtain, a pencil and pad on her lap. "A duck is a bird. Bears drink milk. I need to boil fish and slice mushrooms." She regretted bitterly not having listened more closely all those times her father had taken her to see Russian films as a child. She remembered one in particular: a woman walking across the screen with a little white dog. Back and forth. For three hours.

Seb passing her door, jack-knifed back.

"Everything OK?"

Carla sighed. "It's Duolingo, but I really can't see when I'm going to say any of this? I'm more of 'take me to the Bolshoi, where is GUM?' kind of girl."

Seb ripped off the end of a bread roll. He had a banana in one hand and a seed roll in the other. "Just a snack," he said as her eyes followed the food as it travelled through the air to his mouth. Convinced that he had a one in fifteen chance of dying should he contract COVID, and in a bid to stay alive he was trying to eat sensibly. And not eat in between meals. Carla could see how that was working.

"Gum?"

Carla sensed Seb mentally counting the number of calories in a stick of Wrigley's Spearmint.

"As in the famous department store facing Red Square? And no, not candy. Or *konfet*. Do you realise," said Carla

One Flame Hour

thoughtfully having been reminded of something else, "that before Pushkin, Russian simply didn't have the vocabulary to express complicated thought? Actually, not even complicated thought - Russian didn't have basic vocabulary. There are lots of words simply borrowed from other languages. Like the words for candy or potatoes. 'Caran d'ache' for example means pencil."

"I'd never have guessed."

"What?"

Seb shook his head. "Nothing. And Gum."

"Nope..." said Carla putting down her phone. "Not GUM. That's just an abbreviation."

"Oh. Well, you definitely won't be going there," said Seb in relief. "Everything's closed."

"Uh uh. Not in Russia, it's not. There's a curfew in place for restaurants. But it's six o'clock."

"That's fine."

"In the *morning*."

Seb popped the rest of the banana sandwich in his mouth brushing away the crumbs that spilled down the front of his trademark gilet.

"I'm liking the sound of this more and more! *Except*," he paused for effect. "You won't like the sound of the forms we have to fill out. I've done one, you can do the other. Wait for it. You have to list every country you've been to in the past 10 years, entry *and* exit."

One Flame Hour

Carla's eyes widened. They'd be there all night! *Antigua, Argentina, Albania, Australia, Barbados, Belize, Brazil, Costa Rica, Cuba, Chile, Colombia, El Salvador (briefly), Ecuador, Galapagos, Greece, Italy, Iceland, Morocco, New Zealand Paraguay (did coffee count?), Peru, Prague, South Africa, Spain, United States (several times), Zimbabwe* - Even making a mental inventory sounded boastful. And Russia. Carla had been to St. Petersburg once with Seb, but since she was in her early twenties, she'd visited the rest of the country at least ten times.

"And you can't make a mistake. Or go back. And save each page as a separate entry. I know. It took me three hours last night. And then I lost the whole damn thing. Do we have photos somewhere?"

"We must, but even if we don't, I'm sure Marguerite will take some for us." Carla mentioned a dear friend who had a photography shop in the centre of town which had surprisingly survived a fire, a recession and more recently the restrictions imposed by the pandemic. The more they talked about their forthcoming trip, the more of a reality it promised to be and Carla allowed herself to get excited. There was also the delicious problem of what to wear. She frowned. It was just a shame her winter boots had been left in Austria at the hotel where they spent every Christmas - those would have been perfect for Russia… Her heart began hammering wildly. Then again maybe Net had some Chloe boots - they'd have to be fur-lined obviously. And she'd have to pay extra for same day delivery...

"So, I just have to book our COVID tests. And providing those are clear, we're off. The flights are booked."

Carla beamed. "How cold is it exactly?"

One Flame Hour

Seb glanced at his phone. "Well, it's snowing."

"Oh!" Carla squealed in excitement.

"And at the moment, it's -8."

"Oh!" said Carla again this time in ecstasy. "That's just so perfect."

Already her mind raced. What if she got a *khaki*-coloured mink? She'd seen one in a fancy new shop in the Fulham Road back in May when shops had re-opened. She could wear khaki leather leggings and a cashmere roll neck with it. But then the coat didn't have a hood…

"Ohhh!" cried Carla. She'd just thought of the navy cashmere Chanel jacket from the Paris-Byzance collection. Inspired by the Empress Theodora, it had a gold-tone splatter detail threaded with beige and burgundy. The Gripoix jewelled square buttons were balanced by three quarter length sleeves. Worn with either leather trousers or jeans it was glamorous, practical and warm. It was ideal for Russia. Or would have been.

"What's the matter? You seem distracted. Just for the record, I'd rather be going to the sun," said Seb. "That's the difference between us but I know how you love your cold winters. What is it?"

"Why, oh *why* did I sell that Chanel jacket?" she wailed in full regret mode. "*Why*? It would have been so perfect! You do realise the season's runway show was inspired by an *actual* 6th century empress!"

One Flame Hour

Seb frowned. He was quite used to Carla giving away an item of clothing only to bitterly regret her decision soon after. "Which one?"

"Winter/Fall. It was showcased in Shang-"

"I meant which 6th century empress?"

"The greatest."

"Oh, *that* one," said Seb dismissively with a final wipe at his front, recalling the garment not the monarch. "You *sold* it because you got £3,000 for it. On *eBay*. I don't want to think about what you paid full price."

Neither do I... thought Carla. Besides, what had happened to all her good intentions made after the first lockdown lifted? To change and be less frivolous? And that meant *thinking* in a less frivolous way too.

"You're so right," said Carla sweetly, contritely. Then again, what if she just *looked* at the khaki mink? Or better still had it delivered so that she could try it on?

14

"You have your excuse at the ready, I hope," said Seb as they hurtled up the M3. Even by her standards, Carla knew she was driving erratically.

Given that it was still supposed to be 'Essential Travel Only' with billboards every few miles reminding people to 'Stay Home, Protect the NHS and Save lives' (revived from the altered 'Stay Alert') there was a surprising number of people on the road. More than that, as they passed the exit to the M25, the traffic was heavier than Carla remembered pre pandemic. But then again, not many she supposed, were using public transport.

"I do, besides it's perfectly legal. Or at least it will be tomorrow. You're going to the Russian Visa section and I'm going to see my elderly mother."

"God help us," said Seb under his breath.

'Elderly' they both knew was not a word to describe Eugenia who couldn't have been further from the stereotype had she tried. Eugenia might have been an octogenarian, but she could easily pass for a woman twenty years younger. She could still do the splits, still skate - still even give skating lessons (or she had until COVID struck), didn't need glasses or a hearing aid (God forbid) and travelled nonstop. Somewhere along the line she'd taken the 'fly the flag' slogan to heart and was as devoted to the Commonwealth (and former member countries) as though she were personally responsible for generating trade agreements. She'd been in Dominica, in the September prior to contracting COVID, then London, had returned to Gibraltar and was now back in

One Flame Hour

London for the Christmas period. Such as it was. She was staying in the house of a friend who had since died of COVID herself.

Eugenia, charged with making funeral arrangements had been furious that large gatherings were prohibited and had postponed a memorial until later in the year. Carla had only been once to the house to see Eugenia with Tom who was the apple of Eugenia's eye. Carla had found the house creepy, full of a dead woman's possessions, photographs of people Carla had never met or knew. Yet her mother was squatting there, as giggly as a teenager on a gap year, living out of a suitcase bumming her way around Europe. Hermetically sealed, the house was stuffy with that slightly rancid smell of sour milk, several species of mildew and, when Carla glanced over to one corner of the sofa, an orthopaedic boot. 'God,' Carla had said. 'Whose is that?' Tom also sitting on the arm of a chair (both wanted as little contact as possible with the furniture) had bent 45 degrees. 'That,' he said, 'is all that remains of the friend.'

The traffic had eased by the time they left the motorway and were heading towards West Kensington. Carla was beginning to wonder if she'd not been a little too impulsive in offering to take Eugenia to have her hair done while Seb sorted out their visas. The visa and elderly mother excuse were plausible, but hairdressing definitely wasn't. The *Daily Mail* was full of examples of beauty therapists fined for breaking the law. Plus, there was another niggling worry.

"Seb?"

"Yah?"

Carla could tell he wasn't really listening trying to work out the safest place to jump out. The Russian Visa Centre was in

One Flame Hour

Clerkenwell, but Seb planned to take an Uber from where she dropped him to save time. The return of his accent belied a calm exterior.

"Do you think Eugenia is you know, *known* to the police, since her run in with them? You know when they turned up at two a.m. at brother Roger's?"

"Don't be ridiculous!" said Seb. "*Of course*, your mother's known to them! I'm just surprised she's gone this long undetected."

"Oh," said Carla deflated. They had whizzed over the Hammersmith flyover only to come to a sudden standstill on the Talgarth Road. Carla didn't mind, she'd always been fascinated by the row of houses there designed as artists' studios. She especially loved that they had been intended for bachelor artists but with a kitchen and room in the basement for a housekeeper! Imagine how creative *she* could be with a live-in servant!

"Margot Fonteyn lived in one of those," said Carla wistfully. "And Philip Burne-Jones. You've probably never heard of him."

"Carla."

"He was the son of Edward Burne-Jones, the Pre-Raphaelite." She peered up at the barrel-vaulted windows which faced north to allow in as much light as possible. "Amazing to think that parties held here, would have once had a guest list that read like the Who's Who of the 20th century. You know that Edward Burne-Jones married one of the Macdonald sisters. Extraordinary women and not just for the notable men they married. One was Rudyard Kipling, the other-"

One Flame Hour

"Carla."

"At least he had a blue plaque to his name," she said her thoughts drifting to the fact that these personages once the epicentre of cultural life in London, were almost entirely forgotten now. She remembered working on a project which involved ascertaining the holders of copyright pertaining to the estate of Gilbert and Sullivan. 'Existing client?' the girl at the law firm had asked. It was a melancholy thought.

"*Carla!*"

"What?" Carla jumped and her foot which was hovering over the accelerator jolted forward. Luckily, very luckily not into the car in front.

"Carla, what are you talking about?"

"Sorry! I was just thinking about the Pre-Raphaelites. All those famous people - just gone. Puff -"

"No, not now." Seb's hand was on the door handle. "Just here, thanks. And for god's sake concentrate! Ach," he added more gently, "you'll have a nice time with Eugenia. Meet you here in a couple of hours?" and without a further glance in her direction, he was off.

Seb was right, not driving for much of lockdown had affected her driving. She left her existentialist thoughts with St. Paul's Studios turning into the Lillie Road where a fruit and veg market spilled onto the pavement. This part of London couldn't have differed more extravagantly from their cathedral city. Here robed Arab men announced their wares in low guttural voices: the price of dates and nuts and women in full hijab huddled together knitting. Here there was life in the shouts from the market vendors, the bustle of people

One Flame Hour

going about their business, masks being the only outward sign that they were living in a pandemic.

Eugenia was waiting impatiently on the doorstep. Despite the rain, she wore a full-length black mink coat and carried her usual two handbags. Carla took a deep breath feeling the familiar tension at the prospect of any encounter with her mother. She alighted to help her into the front seat. COVID had changed the way they greeted each other but even before the virus had made elbow knocking a thing, Eugenia was the only person Carla knew who could simultaneously kiss and push you away in a single movement. Even as she bundled the voluminous fur around her mother, Carla felt herself shrink, smaller and smaller like *Alice through the Looking Glass* until by the time she was once again behind the wheel, she felt as inadequate and misplaced had she indeed been a child pretending to drive. There were no preliminaries with Eugenia who immediately launched into a description of the people she'd met picnicking (*'wasn't Partridges just heaven'*), what mass she'd attended, and which priests had been on the altar.

Along with Catholic priests, Eugenia had developed an obsession with Catholic schools. After Carla's short-lived stint in Switzerland, Carla had been sent to complete her education at a convent in England. Carla had only been at the Sacred Heart for three years, but Carla was amazed that Eugenia should continue to be as interested in it as she still was. Carla had made life-long friendships - Les Girls were very dear to her - but that's as far as her interest in her former school went. She'd deliberately decided against sending her daughter Sophie there when the time came.

Carla let her mother talk. Eugenia loved Boris, thought Trump a true gentleman (Carla gripped the wheel tightly on hearing that pronouncement) and that the Chinese were trying to rule the world. She might have a point there.

"And I've got just the man for Sophie," said Eugenia as they parked in front of Gaston the hairdresser's house.

"Sophie *has* a man," said Carla amused. "Ed, remember? They've been going out for four years." *And they live together.* Carla didn't want an argument so she wouldn't remind Eugenia on that score.

"Pooh," said her mother inelegantly. Recently her Canadian accent had become more pronounced. Maybe it was because of the experimental anti-Alzheimer pills she was popping like *konfet*. Exorbitantly priced, they were only available to private patients, but Carla wasn't sure the evidence was there to support their hefty price tag. Or that they were making much difference other than to make Eugenia more argumentative. Or so brother Roger thought. In Carla's opinion, Eugenia had always been combative.

"I'm thinking that the Earl of Scare would be perfect."

Had Carla not already parked, she'd have hit the car in front.

"You're not serious!"

Eugenia's mouth set in that oh-too-familiar line of battle, twitched. "Completely."

"You mean the man who has just admitted assaulting a female employee?"

"Misunderstood." A favourite expression of Eugenia's. Said about most men including Carla's ex-husband.

One Flame Hour

Carla was incredulous. "Never *mind* his unfortunate looks, his behaviour alone, to which he's admitted-"

"Abso -l-u-te nonsense!" Eugenia's tone rose shrilly. Shored up frustration allowed full reign. "These quiet types make *wonderful* husbands."

Carla blinked, felt a rush of blood to the head. Normally, she let her mother spout whatever rubbish she felt like, tuning out, thinking of something else. Like khaki mink. Or whether the Roland Mouret she'd worn to the opera house in Vienna was too dated for Moscow.

"Besides the fact that Sophie has never met this man, there is so much wrong with what you're suggesting, I don't even know where to start!"

"The Earl has a castle; Sophie could ride his horses to her heart's content."

Carla switched off the engine. She remembered her Spanish aunt saying that the only freedom in the world that counted was economic freedom. Carla had been a teenager at the time, but she'd listened. She turned to her mother, noting that despite looking younger than her years, there were shadows under her eyes, as there were under her own. COVID had taken its toll. She tried never to meet her mother's eye but she did so now, unflinchingly.

"Sophie rides her own horses," said Carla coldly. "She's financially independent, because of the work she does, which she's good at. She pays for, rides and owns her own horses. She *has* a boyfriend. Over my dead body would I allow her anywhere that... this... *wanker!*"

One Flame Hour

"Carla!" said Eugenia looking away and scooping up her bags. "I don't know what's happened to you. To both of you. No standards."

She was out of the car and pressing Gaston the hairdresser's doorbell before Carla had time to unclip her seat belt, gather up her own handbag and umbrella and lock the car.

It didn't make for a pleasant start. Carla had known Gaston since she was in her teens. He'd been her mother's hairdresser for as long as she could remember. Except for an eighteen-month gap when Gaston had left the salon where he worked to become a monk in Thailand, which had lasted three weeks, he'd been doing Eugenia's hair for more than thirty years. But it wasn't Gaston who came to the door but a black Labrador retriever. Carla had been attacked by two rottweilers during the first lockdown and was nervous around dogs as a result. *You could have warned me!* she glared silently at her mother's back. What kind of person omits such a thing? A thoughtless one was what.

A short, stocky youth wearing thick-rimmed glasses appeared just in time to prevent the dog licking Carla's ankles. Carla looked at him confused. She remembered Gaston as being tall and thin and bald.

"This is Hubert," said Eugenia pulling down her mask, which defeated the purpose of wearing one completely. "You have to show him your mouth. He lip reads."

"Right," said Carla behind hers.

"And the dog is a hearing dog, you know the way blind people have them."

One Flame Hour

"Got it." She still didn't remove her mask. Given she and Seb were having COVID tests that evening - she wasn't risking anything.

"Ah!" laughed Gaston coming down the stairs in Judy Garland fashion. He was wearing a boa, a baseball cap and t-shirt. He didn't appear to have aged an hour since she last saw him.

"I tell you the whole story," he continued ignoring Hubert and Eugenia and pulling Carla up the stairs he'd just glided down. "You first," he said. "Hubert will make Eugenia coffee. We have to give you a shower first."

Carla vaulted up the stairs after Gaston who proceeded to give her a whistle stop tour of his life in the past thirty years. He had a brain tumour (partly removed through a nostril), was getting a divorce from his Eskimo lover, who had Aids, amazingly they'd not had sex during the entire time they'd been married. He wasn't in love with Hubert. Hubert was just a friend. But such a sweet, kind (gay) fellow that it had made him realise what an abusive marriage he'd been in with the Eskimo. He'd had to build up his clientele after leaving to be a monk. Thailand had been amazing but there'd been too many distractions to make it viable. And here he was in his house - or rather trying to save his house from the greedy clutches of his soon to be ex.

"Ça va?" He pulled her neck back. She'd been leaning over the edge of the bath (wearing her mask) while Gaston washed her hair or rather ran his fingers through it. She'd neither smelled nor felt any detergent come anywhere near it. She felt dizzy. He vanished into the adjoining bedroom to come back with a fresh mask. "Voilà!" he said happily.

One Flame Hour

Carla sat in the conservatory space set up as a mini salon glancing nervously at the reflection of overlooking houses. It would only take one phone call for Gaston to be shopped by nosey neighbours. And with the gigantic mirror dominating the place, it couldn't have been more obvious as to what he was doing. The small courtyard was decorated Moroccan style with overhanging lanterns, mirrors and a water feature. Gaston moved her head this way and that, waving so much spray through the tresses that it felt as if she was wearing a helmet. Eugenia sat grumpily waiting in a corner of the adjacent room, her eyes closed pretending to sleep.

It was only once she'd left, that Carla remembered what a hash of her hair Gaston had made when she got married the first time. People had commented on the 'flamenco' style which couldn't have been further from her intention. She'd almost wept when she'd seen the result of his efforts. The roses he'd ordered had been so small and green and withered, one of the wedding guests had had to pop out to the neighbouring Hilton and beg some flowers from reception. Maybe it had been an omen. Not getting her hair right. Carla glanced at her reflection, a forced smile in place. His technique hadn't improved, and she only thanked her lucky stars she'd said no to a haircut. *L'état c'est moi* wasn't far off in the Louis XIV stiff curls that (unattractively) framed her face now. She gulped in slight shock. *This* is what she'd risked driving around London for? *This* is what was going to greet her brother when they arrived in Moscow? She was going to have to re-do it. She touched the ends. The hair was sticky with lacquer.

Maybe Gaston really didn't care for women... Carla remembered another occasion when he'd 'trimmed' her hair late one night at her mother's flat. She'd been in too much of a hurry to look in the mirror before leaving. Rummaging for her car keys outside, she'd paused under a streetlight.

One Flame Hour

Something odd was happening to the pavement. A triangular shape hugged the curb, sliding off the edge like one of Dali's melting clocks. The persistence of memory indeed. To this day, she shuddered when she thought of how she'd gone from shoulder length hair to a Sassoon buzz cut in a matter of minutes. It had taken years to grow out. Now, if she'd been shocked at the sight of herself, it was nothing to the shock she had when informed her of the price for a blow dry. She'd thought he'd said 'sixteen,' but it was 'seventy.' Pounds.

"What did you expect?" shrugged Eugenia in the car on the way back and patting a similar hair do.

"This is London."

That night Carla dreamed that she'd found her mother (it wasn't clear whether she'd jumped or been pushed) at the bottom of a swimming pool. They were at a party together and Eugenia acting half her age, was running around as though she'd taken speed. Carla, standing on the side of the pool had watched as her mother slipped and fell headlong into the water. Eugenia's skirts had blossomed around her like a parachute her face gradually disappearing, smothered in silk. But Carla hadn't jumped in straight away. She'd had her hair done and was loath to ruin the blow dry.

15

"I often think of Primo Levi," said Carla as the click of seat belts being fastened ricocheted delightfully down the plane. Music to her ears. She was enjoying every minute of their journey so far, from the drive to Heathrow, to the check-in process. And unlike the previous July, when it had come as a shock to discover the lounges were all closed, she was happy to be offered complimentary drinks in the designated area. She felt groomed and sleek in her Prada suede boots whose pristine soles still looked spanking new. Her brown mink was carefully stored in the cupboard at the front of the plane (she hadn't wanted it rolled or folded) and her newly acquired re-issue Celine bag (identifiable by the missing accent) was a nod towards discretion on her part. It was just a pity that discretion was accompanied by such an outrageous price tag. She felt slightly nauseous when she thought about it. Still, she reasoned with herself, it had been a more sensible purchase (relatively speaking) than buying yet another mink coat. But best of all, travelling felt like old times. Well almost: they wore masks, wouldn't have any in flight food and had an empty seat between them.

"You do?" Seb was used to the way Carla viewed the world through a literary lens and could generally second guess her, but not this time. "Angelina Jolie's more my kind of fantasy. Plus, she's alive. You have to admit, it's in her favour."

Carla thumped his arm. "I do during lockdown. Think about Levi, I mean."

"So do I."

"I'm serious."

"S-o am- sorry," said Seb smiling. He was in obvious high spirits. As was she. Just getting on the flight, hearing that delicious (not simulated) sound of twin engines revving in the background… the slight thud in her ears and of course, the flower duet. But she was also necessarily, thoughtful. Because try as they might to pretend otherwise, as lucky and privileged as they were to be taking time out from their daily lives, things weren't the same. Nor would they ever be. From COVID testing, to queues, to masks, to hand sanitation, to the empty shops in the terminal, to the fact that admitting to a holiday was tantamount to having sex in public, to-

"Let me re-phrase," he said helping himself to some of the snacks Carla had brought with her and which were spread on the table between them. He ripped open a bag of wasabi beans with his teeth. She suspected he thought it quite a cool thing to do. She didn't.

"Tell me, Carla. Why do you often think of Primo Levi? Don't tell me it's because of Alice. She's not still walled in, is she?"

"Oh my God, *Alice*!" Carla had been so pre-occupied with travel plans for Russia that she'd not given Les Girls a second thought. She really ought to have seen that Alice was safe and sound after her ordeal.

"You never said what happened in the end. She hasn't perished behind the wall, has she? The family's not going to find her corpse bricked up-"

"God, I hope not." Carla winced as Seb tore into another sachet. She helped herself daintily to a single bean. She should probably have bought the family-size pack. "Hugo took it down. Or rather demolished it. Made quite a mess by all accounts. The carpet was ruined."

"Quite a gesture," said Seb. "I mean the wall building. Not -" he motioned to her mask that was dangling from one ear."

"You like?" she said. She shook her head. It felt like a statement earring.

"Er…not so much. Well?" he added when she still didn't reply.

"She was desperate," said Carla. "To be alone. To have some space to herself."

"A bit extreme, though, wouldn't you say?"

Not remotely.

For a moment they held each other's gaze but then Carla busied herself flicking the elastic pouches on the seat in front of her.

"The mags been removed," said Seb. "Not allowed."

"You know," said Carla after a while, "how all the talk during the first lockdown was war-like, how fighting Corona was compared to combat during the second world war - how the media was all about overcoming the enemy and pulling together?"

"Y-yes."

Carla could tell this was sounding a little too esoteric for the kind of chat they should be having on their first away trip in a year but she swivelled towards him.

"But see, there's been no thought of what happens after. Of what *we* will be like after. Whether we'll remember what it's like to have to wait for things, not be instantly gratified, to *be* grateful," she finished breathlessly.

"I see," said Seb. He'd stretched out his legs under the seat in front of him and pulled out his noise cancelling headphones. Carla could tell he was tempted to cancel her out too. "And Primo Levi? Where does he come into this?"

"Well, exactly. He wrote about his terrible experiences in Auschwitz, as you know," she said earnestly, snuggling into her cashmere jumper. She unwound the matching scarf but then, catching sight of her reflection in the window, hastily it re-arranged it closer to her face. Her neck was looking decidedly crêpey these days. "What has stayed with me almost as much as what he said about that experience, was what he observed about people *after* the war, as early as on the train journey he made when he was repatriated. He said that no sooner were people warm and safe and fed, that they quickly became bored. They were irritable and started bickering. They reverted to type. In no time at all. It's depressing. They'd survived for god's sake and they were bored! I'm just afraid that when lockdown is finally lifted, once and for all, we'll go back to the way we were."

"We or you?" said Seb pointedly.

"OK," admitted Carla. "That I will." And of course, he was right. *She* was afraid that she'd go back to all her old habits. She already had in part.

"Let's just enjoy the now, yah?" said Seb quietly taking her hand. "Every minute of this. Of now."

"Do you wonder -"

One Flame Hour

"No," said Seb firmly closing his eyes. "And neither must you. Rest. It's been an early start. And your brother will expect the sparkling, scintillating sibling that you always are to him. Shut your eyes, now. There's a good girl and get some beauty sleep."

Obediently Carla closed her eyes, but they flew open as the plane ascended into pillows of turbulent air, and she felt, rather than saw, the skies suddenly darken, the light becoming brighter inside. Moscow. And in reflecting on Moscow, she necessarily thought of Alfredo and his fascination with the Russian language. Not so much with the country. *'Not in my lifetime,'* he used to mutter. *'The end of communism will come one day, but not in my lifetime.'* But it had come in his lifetime. So hard to describe to Alfie or even the twins, what it had been like growing up during the cold war - the excitement, the absolute delight when someone her father knew had defected. Now it felt the reverse, glibly speaking of course. Here they were in the cold going towards the sun. She thought of all the countless Russian films they'd been dragged to see when they were little. But watching those old-fashioned films was the only way their father could hear and practice his Russian. What he would have made of the internet resources available for study today, she could only imagine. They would have seemed miraculous to him. He could have watched any number of Chekov based dramas simply on his *phone* without resorting to sitting in dingey cinemas at odd times of the day. Even her humble Duolingo would have felt like holding the keys to the kingdom.

Carla remembered one occasion when she'd been invited (astonishingly) to the home of a Soviet girl who was in her class at school. It was when they lived in Canada before they moved to Switzerland. Alfredo, who never walked anywhere, didn't drive, didn't 'do' children or babysitting or anything remotely connected to children had volunteered to collect her. Carla wasn't sure what she remembered more vividly, the fact that he had come to fetch her or the collective hiss of fear from her friend's mother and her friends, when they heard the knock on the door. In a move that would have floored Houdini, Alfredo had slipped off his coat, kicked off his goloshes, and settled himself on their sofa lighting a cigarette as he did so. Transfixed, the women had watched his elegant head dip to meet the flame, following its trajectory as the slender plume dispersed through the air. Leaning back Alfredo had never appeared happier, more in his element, more sophisticated. And that was the problem. Sophistication yes, but from, of, in the *West, nyet.* It could not be and the huddle of Soviet mothers froze in horror at the sight of him. Of a very real Westerner sitting in their front room. All Alfredo wanted to do was practise his Russian. Carla remembered his shyness (apologies for his Russian), his delight and then the all too tangible hurt as they finally sprang into action and his coat was handed to him. The meaning clear, he was not welcome. He must take his child (which he'd almost forgotten in his eagerness to converse) and go. Immediately.

And many years later, long after Alfredo was dead, Carla had watched the *Lady with the Dog* (*Dama s sobachkoy*) again and finally understood what the film had meant to him. As a child, she'd remembered the white dog (truth to tell a yappy little creature with a fox-like face), as an adult she saw the doomed love affair. No wonder her father hadn't told Eugenia where he was taking her of a rainy afternoon! The subject matter wasn't altogether appropriate for children as it was about two married couples both unhappy with their current partners, who meet while on holiday and fall in love - a sort of *Private Lives* without the humour. It also struck Carla that one of the reasons her father had loved the film was that it contextualised the conflicted emotions he held for Russia

One Flame Hour

herself - a place that he both loved and hated, an unfulfilled desire, a constant yearning for something that could never live up to his expectation. Now, returning to Moscow, Carla felt as close to her father as she had ever done when he was alive. Touching on the remotest sensation of memory, she was transported, grasping in the dark for a lexicon ladder that might bring her home to him.

Carla glanced at Seb who was sleeping and wiped a solitary tear from her cheek. She was exhausted from the months of lockdown, the anxiety that underpinned everything. And they were the lucky ones. Of course, they knew of people who had died of COVID, but they'd not experienced what it was to have a loved one in a care home or even hospital. She knew the answer to her question about Primo Levi. She for one hoped that she'd changed. Yes, she still had her frivolous moments, indulging her love of fashion, but gone forever was a confidence in a safe future. They had only ever pretended that they could plan for one, anyway. Life had never seemed more hazardous, more unpredictable and Seb was right, it was the now that counted.

But unlike Seb, she couldn't sleep. As she tried to decipher the Russian being spoken over the Tannoy- nowhere in the garble of unintelligible words could she pick out 'duck' or 'this is delicious milk' or 'my mother likes soft music' or any of the random sentences she'd been learning- she thought back to the other times she'd visited Russia. Her very first had been to St. Petersburg at the end of her first term at university where she was already bored reading History. During the Christmas holidays, rather than return home to Switzerland, she'd signed up for a Russian language course. There were students from SOAS (School of Oriental and African Studies), Ivy league colleges in America, the daughter of a zookeeper who had a certain allure, a boy going up to Oxford who became progressively more depressed as the

One Flame Hour

month wore on, and an American boy from Harvard who was convinced the *dejornaya* (another word borrowed from the French) was stealing handfuls of his Nivea face cream.

This being 1983, a woman sat at the end of every corridor on every floor whose sole job was to monitor the guests' comings and goings. He might have had a case because when he returned to his room in the evenings, it looked as if the top layer of face cream had been scooped out with a spoon. If the British boy became increasingly dejected, Josh became more and more paranoid, convinced he was being followed. Once, when they were walking along Nevski Prospect, a total stranger had stopped him saying, '*Maybe you are a Jew?*' Josh had nearly fainted in fear, but it hadn't stopped them accepting the man's invitation to visit his apartment. Carla had been reminded then, of Alfredo's visit to her Soviet friend's. All this Russian had wanted to do was learn about the West and practice his English. Josh had been terrified and too scared to whisper anything but in monosyllables.

The students were housed at the famous Astoria Hotel. Isadora Duncan had been one of the many famous guests who'd stayed there. Carla always remembered Isadora, not so much for being the 'mother of dance' but for the fact that all three of her children had died - two had drowned when in the care of a nanny and the third shortly after his birth. Isadora also met a tragic end when the scarf she was wearing became entangled in the wheels of her car. It led Gertrude Stein to say of her death that 'affectations can be dangerous.' Carla (sometimes) heeded this when wearing vertiginous heels when flats might have been more suitable or flimsy garments when it was several degrees below zero.

But though luxurious in its heyday, in Soviet times, the hotel was little more than a hostel equivalent in the West. Carla, being young and naïve and in Russia merely out of curiosity,

One Flame Hour

didn't notice half the deprivations that her colleagues did. In the morning they had a choice of tea and coffee *with* milk but by the evening the milk had run out, there was very little fresh food and the one food item that wasn't in short supply - ice cream - was very sweet and hardly nutritious in the depths of winter. One day, a rumour circulated that a single pear had been located at a market some five miles out of the city, priced at £10. You had to have a special pass to be allowed access to hotels (such as the Astoria) that were open only to foreigners and locals would do virtually anything to get their hands on one. By the time their language course was up, Carla had given away most of her clothes, her heavy coat and her pass, passport (for Russians) to meeting foreigners.

But while the Oxford-bound student struggled with hunger (there were no coffee shops or western style restaurants) and Josh adopted a nervous tick, what impressed Carla most was the absence of neon lights. The city at night - a linear planogram of ancient buildings was gloomy, the beauty of Nevsky Prospect or St. Isaacs's Cathedral only truly visible by moonlight and in the early morning. The illumination taken for granted in the West was altogether absent and with it all associated noise and colour. Carla would never forget how green and lush everything appeared when she returned home. She'd walked from her mother's flat in Holland Park to Knightsbridge. Even though it was May, the Russia Carla had left behind was still cold and snowy. By contrast, parks in London seemed almost psychedelic, emerald-green, their brilliance all the more exaggerated after the drabness of Moscow. Everything seemed inflated in the sweetest of springs: the aroma of seringa stronger, birdsong louder. Twenty-four years later, when Carla visited the same city with Seb, the same hotel even, the place could not have been more different. The Astoria was now a five-star Rocco Forte luxury hotel boasting eye-watering opulence - a wanton, conspicuous display of consumption.

One Flame Hour

Over the years, there were other visits to Moscow to visit Christophe, who had lived in Russia during the late noughties. Those had been fun, family orientated trips with the twins Sophie and Tom in tow. Christophe was living in a former guard house which made Carla feel more than secure - not a *dejornaya* in sight. Christophe's sentry was posted 24/7 in a little box, a stone's throw from her bedroom window and she had found it comforting to see the man's shadow pace back and forth as he smoked. Inside, Christophe's house was warm, modern and comfortable - actually warmer than her own house in England and nothing like her memories of the Astoria in the '80s when they'd shivered on their way to the communal lavatory down the draughty corridor. Moscow had seen skating on the garden turned rink at the back of the house, visits to the chocolate factory, the KGB museum, the Kremlin (the Fabergé collection and crown jewels a favourite), Novodevichy convent and its adjacent Georgian restaurant boasting delicious meat and home-grown wine, walks through Red Square at night, rugged up in fur, and finally Mos film (the equivalent of Hollywood) located in Sparrow Hills, that mound on the right bank of the Moskva River. Visible from the observation platform was the stadium where the opening ceremony for the 1980 summer Olympics had taken place. And dwarfing everything, was the iconic Moscow State University, once the tallest building in Europe.

Most memorable of all, had been the time they'd visited Moscow with Alfredo. The irony being that by the time the Soviet Union was at last dissolved, and Alfredo could visit the Russia of his dreams, he wasn't really fit to enjoy her. The man Carla accompanied to Moscow was much diminished and no longer his dashing, elegant self. However, losing Alfredo in Harrods that time when she'd taken him to the barber, should have acted as a warning. There was still life in the old *cobaka* yet. But, as they soon discovered, just because

One Flame Hour

Alfredo was in a wheelchair did not mean that he wasn't capable of extreme wilfulness. The twins, Carla and her parents had travelled to Moscow to enjoy Russian Christmas with Christophe. By then, her marriage to Angus was all but over and time away was a life saver.

Carla and the twins stayed with Christophe in the guard house, while her parents lodged at a hotel close to the Arbat district. On a particularly cold afternoon in January towards the end of their stay, Christophe had suggested they while away the afternoon at his health club as he had to work. They'd already spent the morning skating around Gorky Park, but with the temperatures nudging -30 by midday, none of them were inclined to spend a second longer than was necessary out of doors. Eugenia was white with cold, and Tom looked as though he had frostbite - in fact he *had* contracted frostbite on the tips of his ears but Carla wasn't to know this until he went back to school. Her father, who of course was in no state to skate let alone walk, had sat ensconced in a coffee shop by the park's entrance. After five minutes he was bored - in fact too bored to notice Sophie strapped to a huge cartwheel ride, still in her skates, being hurled through the air. Carla felt sick when she thought about it. What might have happened if one of Sophie's skates had come loose and flown through the air? The sharp blades could have done unthinkable damage. What might have happened had *Sophie* become dislodged and gone flying through the air?

A quiet afternoon in the *banya* or swimming was just what they needed. After a quick borsch lunch (all these years later it still featured on the menu although now it was thick with vegetables and served with delicious sour cream rather than being the thin pink gruel of the '80s), Christophe had bundled them into the white ex-army vehicle in which he hurtled around Moscow. Heaving their father up and into the jeep was a mission in itself, not to mention strapping in the rumbustious twins, and a petulant Eugenia. With undisguised relief Christophe had deposited them (and the folded wheelchair) in the foyer of his club signing them in and waving a cheery *dasvadanya* - don't rush home,' as he left.

"What did he say?" said her father. He was a dead weight against her as he stopped short, stooping over the threshold, the door to the club still wide open, to grope for a cigarette and the tiny bit of chocolate he always kept in his pocket.

"Let's just get inside," said Carla as Alfredo curved away from her as mistrustful and jittery as any highly strung racehorse being coaxed into its stall. Though so thin, he was almost transparent, he was still over six foot and gangly - all elbows and flaying hands as he tried to light his tobacco. Carla motioned to the twins to unfold his chair which they managed to do in record time and then sat in it themselves, flicking up the footrest and pushing each other around the small vestibule.

"Children, children," said Eugenia in that melodramatic Victorian voice she used in public as though expecting some uniformed nanny to appear out of nowhere.

Carla was less patient. "Get out!" she said through gritted teeth. "Off!"

Sophie gave Tom a shove so that he landed on the floor and took his place. "Push me!" she commanded.

"Don't you *dare!*" countered Carla while her father giggled enjoying the distraction. "Out!" she repeated grabbing Sophie's hood. Carla was panting with the effort of holding up her father, his cigarette dangling precariously. At last, she managed to collapse him down into his chair. Despite the exertion, Carla's fingertips were still numb, the cold fusing her backbone. All she wanted to do was nestle down herself preferably into crisp linen sheets and sleep.

"What did he say?" repeated her father.

"Who?" Carla looked longingly at the wheelchair. Maybe if she sat in it one of the twins could push *her*.

"The man who dropped us here."

Carla blinked, swallowing back tears.

"He says," said Carla sadly, "to have a nice time." Poor Christophe, thought Carla, all her brother's efforts on their behalf and Alfredo didn't know who he was anymore.

Her father's thin shoulders rolled forward and he bowed his head in the bashful gesture which he'd adopted of late, when he either didn't understand something, or hadn't heard, or felt sad or was simply cast adrift as he clung to the wreckage of a disintegrating mind. Not so disintegrating as it happened. Later Carla resolved to be more circumspect in thinking she could second guess him. An expression she'd taken for shyness was in fact, one of pure cunning.

"Nice *chelovek*, anyway," said her father. "Do we know him?"

"As much as it's possible to know anyone," intoned Eugenia gloomily. She sank into a faux leather armchair, frozen to the bone, her sleek slacks and polo neck jumper while elegant for an indoor rink, were completely inadequate for an outdoor one. Only her head wrapped in a sable *ushanka* felt warm.

One Flame Hour

Bored with the wheelchair idea, the twins were creating at a nearby table, emptying sachets of sugar into glasses of water and adding bits of paper to make a paste. The adults watched them too traumatised by the cold (Carla by the cold *and* her father) to make any effort to stop them until the fierce looking woman behind the counter shouted at them in Russian. Or maybe it was English but spoken with such an exaggerated accent, it might as well have been Russian. Everyone stiffened. They'd forgotten they were not alone. The woman (Olga) if the name tag was anything to go by, had poker straight black hair that reached to her waist and alabaster skin. Carla was fascinated by its lustre. As was Sophie.

"You're pretty," said Sophie.

"You're *krasnaya*," translated Carla pleased with herself. But Olga only glowered.

"She didn't like the compliment," said Carla a little stung.

Her father's cigarette dropped ash all over his lap. "It's not that," he said with a flash of lucidity. "You've said that she looks 'red.' Of course, had she *any* imagination, she would have understood you perfectly. Red used to mean either the colour or 'beautiful' because the word for both is derived from the same root. As when Red Square was originally named. Now, it just means the colour. Did you know that the Alhambra also means 'red'?"

Carla shook her head. She'd had no idea. Alfredo would never cease to amaze her. She smiled at him delightedly. His sweet, intelligent sane self, seemed to have returned albeit briefly. She felt so much better at leaving him. They'd make it quick though, so as not to leave him on his own for long.

One Flame Hour

"Twins," she said dragging herself to her feet. "Time to swim." She felt lethargic and loath to strip off when she'd just managed to get warm again. But the sound of breaking glass and a 'Tom, that was you!' from Sophie was the impetus that was needed.

"*Nos vamos?*" said her father hopefully in Spanish. *Are we going?*

"No, Alfredo," Eugenia said firmly. "You're staying here. Right here. Don't move. We won't be long."

"Ah," said her father mournfully. "So, you're all going."

"Oh, Avi," said Sophie putting her chubby arms around his neck, using the Catalan for 'grandfather' and kissing his cheek. "We'll come straight back."

"Yes," said Tom roughing his hair. "Right back."

Which of course they hadn't. Once in the pool area, with the sauna close to hand, they'd spent a happy couple of hours sweating and over-heating and making sure they could cling to the memory of being this warm when they went back out into the frigid air. At last it was time to leave and they'd emerged into the club foyer, bright skinned, shining, with slightly chlorinated eyes, tired but relaxed. It was later than they thought and there was a different girl on reception.

Eugenia frowned. "Where's Alfredo?" she said as though missing a scarf, an item of clothing. "Where's your father, Carla?"

How should I know? Carla wanted to say but refrained, stemming a familiar panic. She'd been here before… Eugenia continued to stare at her and Carla realised with a start that for once, her mother seemed generally concerned. And surprisingly helpless. Unlike the receptionist. Carla wracked her brains for the vocabulary.

"*Gde Papou*?" she said not worrying about declensions, repeating the words when she got no response. Like the girl she'd replaced, this one also had arched eyebrows painted on like a matryoshka's and long fingernails that clacked against the keyboard. She didn't even look up.

Eugenia peered round the counter.

"Carla," said her mother in wonder. "His wheelchair's gone too."

"Then presumably he must have got bored and gone back to the hotel," said Carla in relief. "He must have taken a taxi."

"*Nyet*," said the girl. Her fingers walked across the keyboard. "*Nyet tacksi*."

"I don't understand," said Eugenia haughtily. "What is she saying Carla?"

The girl continued typing.

"No taxi," said Carla.

"But that's ridiculous," said Eugenia. "How else could he have left? There's no way he could have gone out by himself. In that cold! In a wheelchair? Not alone."

"Exactly," said Carla reassured by this logic. The twins had resumed their earlier game of tearing up sugar sachets and this time they used it to draw patterns on the table. Carla felt a tick in her cheek and a pulse at her temple began to throb.

One Flame Hour

There was a new pain by her right kidney while her stomach coiled with anxiety.

"What we can't do is call Christophe," said Eugenia firmly.

For once they were in complete agreement. They were both terrified of Christophe. Besides how to explain that they'd lost their father? Their *disabled* father. From the foyer of a health club?

"Oh, goodness." It was Carla's turn to sink into an armchair, her real leather leggings making a squelching sound against the faux leather seat. She just wanted to be home alone, to have a cup of tea and curl up with a book, shutting out the rest of the world. They had to find Alfredo first. Carla went to the entrance and put her head out the door. The cold air slammed against her face, taking her breath away. Tiny pin pricks of pain and fear made her suddenly dizzy. Her father would never survive this. One thing was to be outside in an English winter, as when he'd disappeared from Harrods, it was quite another to last long here. It was impossible. She thought with a clammy terror of the young Russian man she'd met at a party only the summer before who'd come out to Moscow with his brother. They'd been given a lift from a party and for some reason the boy had got out of the car. The next morning he'd been found frozen to death. Her father wouldn't survive two minutes in this cold, not the way he was dressed, in his ubiquitous cashmere coat, no hat or gloves or boots. Carla never thought he was ever dressed warmly enough as it was, but then he was never out of doors for very long.

The twins were singing 'I want to be a Rockstar,' at the top of their voices. Sophie was standing on the table and Tom was pretending to use a microphone.

One Flame Hour

"Get down," said Carla wearily.

"We're going to have to tell him," said Eugenia.

"I know."

Carla rummaged in her handbag for her cell phone and called Christophe, turning her back to her mother.

"Well?" said Eugenia. "What did he say?"

Carla hesitated, tucking her phone into her bag.

"He said he's finishing late - he'll organise transport."

There was a small silence.

"You didn't tell him."

Carla chewed her lip. "I thought I'd suss out if Pa was with him."

"And he wasn't."

"No."

"Oh, Good God," said Eugenia.

"God, God!" sang the twins. "Granny said God!"

"Did you know that God is 'bog' in Russian and 'bog' is God?"

For a moment the twins stopped dancing.

"How is that helpful?" said Eugenia frowning.

One Flame Hour

"It isn't. Sorry." Carla shook her head. It was the kind of linguistic tangent Alfredo might have appreciated. "Oh, Bog, Bog. What on earth do we do now?"

And then she had a thought. Maybe just maybe...

"What's your room number again?" she said dialling the Arbat hotel. "Yes, Count de Riva," she said in English. There was a click while the call was connected. To her amazement someone answered. "*Daddy?*" she said incredulously.

"*Carla?*" said her father chirpily, relaxed, suave, charming, totally at ease and at home. Because he was, home that is. "*Aqui para servirle*. What can I do for you?"

Carla often thought of that episode. And whenever people commented on the brutality that was modern Moscow, how Muscovites were inhospitable, how you never went to the police for help, not initially anyway, she described that adventure with her father. Because her father had left the health club alone, pushing his wheelchair, stumbling in the dark on the ice, on the uneven pavements, hatless, gloveless, and confused. Though not for long. A car had stopped, helped him in, wheelchair and all and even given him a Dolce Gabana cashmere cap and told him that it was a disgrace that he should have been abandoned by his family, an old man like him, left wandering alone. Alfredo couldn't have agreed more. In that moment his Russian and his memory returning like flickering tree lights. He was able to tell the nice people the name of his hotel, how he was a widower ('wishful thinking' glowered Eugenia), how his children mistreated him (well clearly, as was evident in the way the old man was dressed, or more specifically the way he wasn't, at least not for winter) and how all he wanted was to make light

One Flame Hour

conversation and practise his Russian. And they'd deposited him at the hotel. Kind unknown people whom Carla could never thank. The comfort of strangers.

And now as they sped along the Sofiiskaya embankment, Carla pondered that each subsequent visit had been more exotic and certainly more comfortable than the last. The drabness of that very first visit to St. Petersburg could not have contrasted more dramatically with all the ones that came after. So much had changed in the intervening years and not just for the country. Carla reflected on the girl she'd been at nineteen, and the woman she was now. She'd married Angus who was father of the twins, divorced Angus, married Seb, had Alfie, moved house half a dozen times and gone back to school. But this visit seemed to bring everything full circuit. Here she was, all these years later, once again on a trip to visit her brother. Time had not stood still for Christophe either though. Her brother had met his wife during his first posting to Moscow, when they were both in their twenties. They'd had four children in the intervening years and travelled the world before recently returning to Russia. Only this time Christophe was no longer billeted to the guard house. Fifteen or so years later, home was the residence itself.

16

The car turned right towards the southern bank of the Moscow River where elaborate railings encompassing the entire length of the block, seemed barely able to contain the sprawling cube-shaped mansion behind them. Across the narrow tributary, the gold cupolas of St. Basil's cathedral and the Ivan Veliky belltower sparkled against a sky puffy with snow.

"Wow!" said Seb staring at the house as the car came to a stop and the gates magically swung open. The guard popped out of his cubicle with a smart salute and Carla shivered with a frisson of déjà vue. This time though, they weren't turning left but stopping under the grand porte-cochère. "A lot going on here. What have we? Art Nouveau, pseudo-Moorish, neo-Classical?"

"It's still awe-inspiring," said Carla defensively. She actually loved the pale green tiled roof and mellow yellow plasterwork. "You'd have agreed with Lord Hailsham. When he visited in the '60s, he hated the place so much he said he wanted to blow it up and start again!"

"I was being facetious," said Seb grasping her hand suddenly and kissing it. "It's magnificent."

He sprang from the car, stretched and stood staring up at the tall pedimented windows and the white plaster medallions flanking the entrance. Snowflakes fell on his face and eyelashes. He'd always had long lashes like a camel's which Alfie had also inherited. Carla felt a wrench at the thought of how much their son would have enjoyed the snowy landscape. As Seb rapidly blinked away the snow, so too

One Flame Hour

Carla brushed aside the nostalgic pang. Meanwhile, the driver opened the boot to lift out their bags. Carla always travelled light - usually with just hand luggage making it a personal challenge to see how little she could take with her. She'd once travelled to Marbella with a week's worth of clothes rolled into her Hermès Birkin. But that was before Easy and other airlines got so finickity about the *size* of the hand luggage. And obviously now with COVID, the general hysteria about touching things meant everything had to be stored in the hold. Carla managed a shaky *'cpacebo,'* confidence in her language abilities sorely shaken after understanding so little on the plane.

"Oh, isn't it *heaven*?" said Carla snuggling into her mink and pulling up its hood. There certainly couldn't be a better view in Moscow directly opposite the Kremlin as they were - the gold onion-domes (she counted ten of the thirty) shining brightly through the snow.

"See," she said pointing. The letters CCCP that she remembered embedded between the upper arches had been replaced by double-headed eagles. "The Bolsheviks had already removed them once before."

"What a merry-go-round," said Seb.

"History is a bit." She too blinked away melting snowflakes. "Oh, but I love this! I really can't believe we're here."

"I can't believe we're staying in a house that has a West *and* an East Wing."

"Oh, darling," said Carla taking a step towards the house. "Can't you?"

One Flame Hour

"Why CD 001?" said Seb pointing to the car's license plate. The driver having deposited their bags on the bottom step, got back into the car and drove slowly past, skidding slightly on a patch of ice.

"The '1' is because Britain was the first country to recognise the Soviet Union," said Carla.

"Wouldn't 007 have been cooler?"

"Agreed, but of course Bond came so much later. Anyway, that went to France."

"Really?" Seb expressed genuine surprise. "Trust the French."

"We do, sometimes."

She smiled, hand on the brass handle shaped like a dog holding a bone. As if she'd pressed a secret panel, it opened at her touch and Christophe stepped forward to greet them.

"Welcome, welcome!" said her brother, bending his head to kiss Carla, tapping his heels in Seb's direction, bowing slightly. Carla felt a rush of affection for her sibling. For a moment they beamed at each other before he stood back to allow them to enter. The large entrance hall was exactly as she remembered it - all dark linenfold panelling, pointed doorways and Gothic décor. Huge tapestries dwarfed the red carpeted staircase which gleamed in the low lighting.

"Come on up," he said taking the broad stairs two at a time. Carla had forgotten that the reception rooms were on the first floor. Shrugging off her coat she followed, hand feeling for the heavily embellished balustrade. A carving of a dragon doubling towards its tail dominated one of the newel posts.

One Flame Hour

"The twins were convinced there was a hidden camera in one of its eyes," she told Seb breathlessly when they'd reached the top. Christophe shot her a funny look. The rest of what she was about to say, died on her lips. *Really? Even now?* It was years since she'd thought about listening devices and the like. She'd forgotten all about censorship or the fact that she'd once smuggled in magazines, Bic biros and nylon tights. But then she also remembered a later visit when even Pizza Express boasted lobsters on the menu and the amount of food available had been mind boggling. A merry-go-round indeed.

"Drink?" said Christophe crossing the Gothic landing equally resplendent with opulent wall hangings and a burnished fireplace. He pushed open the door. "This is the Red Room," he announced gravely although he needn't have as it was quite obvious. Small and cosy, a fire blazed in the tall carved fireplace. It was decorated with a porcupine and a salamander, the emblems of Louis XII and Francois I of France. Glancing upwards Carla noted that the ceiling with its squares cut out in relief, looked like a fat bar of Nestlé's milk chocolate. Carla's tummy rumbled respectively. Two sofas faced each other across a small coffee table laid out with an ice bucket and tubs of caviar. Everything, bar the caviar, was in various shades of crimson. Even the champagne had a rosy tinge.

It felt completely surreal to be ensconced in such luxury, subjected to such freedom after the restrictions they were subjected to back home. Images from the first lockdown came back to her, the second so-called circuit break and of course, Mylo's death. And it wasn't over - there were still uncertainties going into the future. Christophe leapt to his feet having settled briefly against red damask cushions. Her brother, ex-army and always energetic, could never relax for very long. He went to the window to pull back the heavy vermillion brocade curtains. "That's better," he said and as

One Flame Hour

once before, when Carla and her mother had first seen her school against the backdrop of the Dents du Midi, Carla gasped as the river and Kremlin came into view. Christophe looked pleased by her reaction. "I'm glad you like it," he said. "I never tire of it."

Carla knocked back her champagne, giddy with excitement at being in Russia, having got away at all, and of course, at being with Christophe. She stood beside him, taking his arm. He was a head taller than her, dark like her, with green eyes like hers. Only their noses were different. They'd all broken their noses at some point in childhood, much to their father's distress - he'd held great store by noses. They didn't have to be straight, but they had to be unbroken. Christophe's was the exception. While they'd all had endless skirmishes and cuts resulting in stitches, Christophe's nose remained intact. It was a nose that amused their father. He would laugh whenever he saw a photo of Christophe. 'It's because he *has* no nose' he'd say. When they were young, Carla and her brother were sometimes mistaken for twins, but Christophe was so handsome, she often thought that he was the more beautiful. Her friends certainly thought so. She didn't have a girlfriend who wouldn't have happily dated him. Handsome or not, she'd forgotten how much she adored being with her brothers. There was only Roger missing.

"It's incredible," she said. "I'm so grateful." She felt foolish tears prick her eyes.

"It's nothing. I only wish the rest of the family could be here too."

He was thinking of his wife Julia and the children who were already back in the UK ahead of their Christmas leave. With everything going on, Christophe wasn't sure that he'd be able to join them. Carla was thinking rather of Eugenia. They stood for a little while longer. The river rushed past, inky and swollen.

"Don't mind me," said Seb only half joking.

"Darling!" exclaimed Carla turning.

"Sorry," said Christophe. He moved to perch on the end of Seb's sofa in a friendly gesture, one leg crossed over the other, leaning slightly forward as he nursed his glass. Carla noticed with approval that he wore socks long enough so as not to expose any skin. Along with noses, Alfredo had been very particular about sock length. Alfredo… whose underwear had even been handmade, and his coat of arms embroidered on every item of clothing. Who cared about that kind of thing anymore? Perhaps only fictitious characters such as Count Rostov did. Carla though fondly of the count. She'd read *A Gentleman in Moscow* not once but twice recently because if there was ever a personage fictitious or otherwise who was more like her father, it was Alexander Rostov. Reading about him, brought Alfredo close again. She frowned. She was trying not to think about him, and yet here in this place, with its dark panelled recesses, medieval style paintings and Byzantine grandeur, their father was everywhere.

"So, tell me," continued Christophe addressing Seb now. "How is it back home? How has lockdown been for you?" Christophe had heard all about Carla's adventures, but he was less up to date with Seb's. "I heard about the niece," he said pleasantly. "But didn't know you had another brother apart from your twin."

"I don't," said Seb knocking back his champagne. Carla knew what was coming.

One Flame Hour

"But I thought Dom was gay," said Christophe in one of his less diplomatic efforts. Carla loved that her worldly brother could also be such an innocent.

"He was. Is."

"But the baby?" Christophe rubbed his forehead with his thumb, perplexed.

Seb was fiddling with his hair, always a bad sign and nodded when Christophe waved the bottle in front of his glass. The male servant had come in with another bottle. Small and ugly, with sticking out ears and a pointed nose he looked like a Russian leprechaun except Carla could tell by the expression in his eyes that he was probably the very sweetest of men. She too accepted a re-fill.

"Baby," said Carla interrupting so as not to prolong Seb's discomfort, "is eighteen. It was a long time ago before Dom moved to the States and came out."

"Thank you," said Seb but it was with relief not sarcasm. He always found it difficult talking about Dom.

"Interesting," said Christophe. "Have you met her?"

Seb and Carla exchanged glances. Zoe had been the subject of a hissy fit on Carla's part when she'd accused Seb of having an affair with a gorgeous blonde who he kept meeting secretly (well twice) and Alfie had unwittingly filmed with his drone. Zoe, in trying to locate Dom, had got in touch with Seb when she'd had a DNA test. It wasn't as confusing as it sounded. Zoe had been on a gap year travelling around Europe but had since returned to South Africa when it looked as though England might go into a Tier system.

One Flame Hour

Seb nodded. "Zoe's a lovely girl. I hope she'll spend some time with us when this is all over. When we can travel freely, when Dom can come to us or we can go to him or Zoe can."

Carla agreed warmly. Dom still wasn't entirely on board, but in time, when he got to know Zoe, Carla was certain he would fall for the girl's charm as they had. Youth itself was infectious. Who wouldn't love a beautiful, bright artless creature without any guile or malice whatsoever?

And then she let Seb recount their more recent news. They'd laughed about the police visiting Eugenia at two a.m. and grown sombre talking about the people they knew who had died or been affected by the virus or the so-called 'long COVID'. Which brought them to pause and remember poor little Mylo and then Seb reminded of his own precious mortality, reminded Christophe, that he had a one in fifteen chance of dying. And that Dom had done his utmost to stop Seb travelling to Russia. Which was rich thought Carla, given that Dom in the States (with 65,000 deaths to date), was in a far more COVID-infested part of the world than the Russians were. Come to think of it, the UK was probably worse off than either of those two countries anyway. Being diplomatic not only by profession, Christophe steered the conversation to more general science: the pros and cons of the Pfizer versus Astra Zeneca and the catchy 'cabs for jab's policy designed to get the elderly and less mobile vaccinated first, the fact that Boris was still trying to 'save Christmas' enticing the populace with the idea that they might soon be able 'to kiss granny'.

"As if that were going to clinch matters," muttered Seb. Carla giggled. It would take a seismic shift in relations to get Eugenia anywhere near Seb - or vice versa.

One Flame Hour

"Yes, well," said Christophe. "You must be exhausted. I certainly am. It's full on here. We're not really lockdowned at all. So, if you don't mind, I'm going to call it a night. I've put you two in the Churchill Room."

He got up, finished his drink and set the glass down on the silver tray. In the flickering flames the striped brocade wallpaper appeared as elongated tongues of fire, and the little carved man on top of one of the door frames seemed to rub his hands in glee.

"I'll show you the rest tomorrow, before we set off."

"Set off?" Carla echoed.

Christophe touched the side of his nose, the 'no nose' their father had so admired. "It's a surprise. Dress warmly. We'll be gone all day."

17

"Did you know," said Carla looking up from her phone, "that Churchill said Russia was 'a riddle, wrapped in a mystery, inside an enigma?'"

"Ah," said Seb sleepily. "I'd forgotten."

"Did you really know that?" Carla dug her heels into the mattress and raised herself up to a half sitting position. Her head pushed into the overstuffed headboard. "Did you actually?"

"No," said Seb. "But it rang a bell."

She lay down again, flipping onto her stomach and resumed her Duolingo lesson.

"Except that's what I feel about the language. I mean who says things like 'the poet does not have a mouse' or the 'cat isn't an architect but an artist?'"

"I don't know," yawned Seb. "Maybe Russian cats *are* artists. Put the phone away. You're sounding suspiciously awake."

They were lying in a vast, four poster bed lavishly draped in billowing curtains. The corona above it was heavily embossed in gilt and silver with images of cherubs feasting on peaches and bunches of grapes. It reminded Carla a little of the refurbished church they had considered buying before moving into their present home. It was foggily quiet, not a sound from pipes or neighbours or the squeak of wheels from uneven luggage being wheeled up the street or bicycles or children or any of the hundred little sounds, that even in

One Flame Hour

lockdown made up the daily background noise to their neighbourhood. Eventually, Carla felt herself relax. She felt for Seb's foot. His body temperature was always several degrees warmer than hers and she snuggled close, sliding her phone under the pillow.

"And have you seen the loo?" she said her voice muffled against his ribcage.

"Oh, was there one? I couldn't find it."

"What do you mean, couldn't find it?" She sprang away from him. "The room is vast!"

"That's the point, everything is enclosed in wooden boxes. I'd no idea which one was the latrine."

"You didn't ... did you?"

Seb made the clicking sound that always sounded like an African dialect. "Ach, of course not. What do you take me for?"

Seb was right though. If the Churchill Room was impressive, it was nothing to the spectacle of the bathroom. Carla had never seen anything like it. A Gothic style frieze ran the perimeter of the room, while full length windows were festooned in Colefax and Fowler. Carla recognised the material as she'd used it herself once for curtains in a flat in London. Sophie still called it 'Colefucks.' The castellated carvings and arches and spade-shape trimmings, could easily have been the film set for *A Knight's Tale*. Carla half expected to see a longbowman pop out from behind the fan light.

"Why are you whispering?" he added now, whispering himself.

One Flame Hour

"You know, in case?"

"In case what?"

"In. Case. They're. Listening." She cast a glance at the ceiling.

Seb poked his head from out of the fourposter, using the curtains like a kerchief. He looked like a man in drag.

"Well, I hope someone is!" he said addressing the ceiling as though there was a hidden camera in one of the vents. "Labels in the bathroom might be jolly useful. You know little Post-Its on the basin and loo. Especially the loo."

Carla pulled his arm. "Sh!" she said alarmed. "You just never know. Write it down if you want to say something."

"Something?" Seb flopped back onto the pillows taking her with him.

"Yes. You know, that you don't want anyone," again she raised her eyes to the ceiling, "to hear."

"Right."

Carla could feel the even, clean tempo of his heartbeat under her cheek. Hers often felt gridlocked, as if the tiny mechanisms strained with the effort of pumping blood through its valves. Strained and failed. Sometimes she thought with certainty, that her death would be by way of a cardiac arrest.

"Hey," said Seb. "Come back? I've lost you. What is it?"

One Flame Hour

"Nothing," lied Carla. "Just wondering if we should get up. But we don't have to just yet, do we? And where do you think we're going today?" How wonderful to have a plan and somewhere to visit.

That was what she had missed in both lockdowns - having a choice or at least the illusion of. She was so fed up with being told what she could and could not do and with whom she could do it! Christophe had told them that Moscow was pretty much business as usual with restaurants, theatres and shops all staying open. Amazingly, she had no desire to mooch around shopping malls, but it *would* be fun to have dinner sitting at a table with white tablecloths, not slurping a coffee on a park bench and shivering in the rain as they had to do back home. Les girls had tweeted, that to prevent people from gathering even out of doors benches were being removed from some city centres. It beggared belief. What on earth would come next? Carla shrugged mentally, thrusting aside that and any other depressing thought that threatened to prick her mood. Especially, the dull ache pulling at her heart strings every time she thought about Alfie and how much she missed him. But that's because he was boarding, and he'd been in isolation. Alice (before the wall in the living room debacle), had confessed that she wished her children would take up smoking because at least that way they'd be going outside. 'But they're only kids!' Les Girls had protested. '*And?*' It seemed they were all living extremes - those with too many at home wanted to be alone and those alone…

Seb rotated his shoulders, moving her hand away and coaxing her back to the present. "No idea. I wouldn't have minded seeing more of Moscow now that we're here."

"I suppose Christophe imagines you've already been to the Bolshoi and Conservatoire." Even as she said it, she realised she might have been confusing husbands. It was Angus, not Seb who knew the capital.

Seb threw back the covers. As if on cue, the alarm sounded on his phone.

"Except I haven't. I've only ever been to St. Petersburg with you," he said a touch tetchily.

Carla shot him a look as Seb shrugged on his dressing gown.

"Right," she said smoothly. "Well, I'm sure there's time to do both and at least this way, brother Dom will be happy you aren't over-exposing yourself to COVID." And then, realising she was edging towards murky waters, added brightly. "But isn't this romantic, Seb darling? *And* it's snowing!"

A couple of hours later as they headed out of the city, the pretty dawn sky with its polka dots of white flakes had turned anthracite. It was more than snowing; they were headed into a storm.

"Will it be all right?" asked Carla anxiously as ice caked the windscreen and the wipers groaned with the effort of trying to shift it. From time to time, there was only the tiniest clear patch through which to see. The air all around them was grey and heavy with swirling snow. "Do you think it's still OK?"

"Oh, this is nothing," said Christophe who was sitting alongside their driver. "Surely, you remember Montreal or Geneva?"

Seb raised an eyebrow as if waiting for Carla to expand further, but she merely nodded vaguely. Both siblings had been born in one city and lived in the other, but Carla hadn't been back to Canada since their parents left for good. She

One Flame Hour

pressed her forehead against the frosty windowpane, trying to make sense of the shapes through the snow. They slipped down Sofiiskaya Street, hugging the high wall of the Kremlin where bridges and buildings were illuminated under multicoloured lights. It was all a far cry from her earlier memories of the capital, and all the time, the further they drove, the further Carla felt from herself. Initially, she'd imagined that she was becoming closer to Alfredo, hoping to discover aspects of her father she could never know. Now, she realised it was part of herself, discarded during COVID, that she hoped to retrieve.

The overheated car, softly purring engine and the stop-start of the traffic lights were soporific. There was a four-hour time difference with London and Carla felt more jet lagged coming to Russia than had she travelled half-way around the world. But just as she felt herself slip slide into sleep, the loud honk of a horn would startle her. She forced herself to sit up and look at the scenery. She'd sleep better that night if she didn't nap now. Once again, she pressed her forehead against the cold pane dazzled by the glitzy designer stores, the profusion of restaurants buzzing with diners. She thought of their own High Street back home, where every other shop was either permanently out of business or on the brink of going under, and the few eateries that were open only offered takeaway. She was reminded of a child's geography book. Only in this case the countries had been swopped over - where one was barely coloured in, jagged scratch marks nowhere close to fitting within the desired shape, the other was exuberant - Klimt-like in opulent jewel-like colours and bold accents of gold. All of which only reminded Carla of her Chanel Byzantine jacket. It would have been the ideal garment to wear among these sleek and gleaming creatures. Hairdressing and beauty salons were also clearly open if their swishy hair was anything to go by. Carla supressed a sigh, she could be a truly good woman if she always had coiffed, blow-dried hair.

One Flame Hour

Seb too appeared captivated by what he was seeing. Carla tugged at his hand.

"I can see why you love the place," he said hardly tearing his eyes away from the skinny dark-haired beauties swaddled in fur gliding from pavement to waiting car. His eyes widened as a gold four-wheel drive cut in front of them. It wasn't just a metallic yellow colour either but looked like twenty-four carat gold.

"It's not all like this," she said tartly as they headed for the Garden Ring. *Where oh where was a good old fat babushka when you needed her?*

"No, I can see." It was Seb's turn to consult his phone. He had pulled up a map of the city. "From the air, Moscow looks like a giant dartboard with the Kremlin as its bullseye."

She leaned over his shoulder. "See the rings?"

The city was encircled by ring after ring of elaborate motorways with a central four-leaf clover formation. The ariel view was beautiful. "Actually, not sure we should get too hung up on the 'rings,'" said Christophe twisting round in his seat to talk to them. "As the first one technically isn't a ring but a half-circle. And the Boulevard ring isn't a ring at all but has boulevards."

"And the Garden ring is a ring but there aren't any gardens!" said Carla not to be outdone.

"Sounds… very Russian," said Seb smothering Carla's hand with his. He had felt her body tense as cars honked either side, flashing by at speed. Ever since their car crash a few

One Flame Hour

years back, Carla was a nervous driver and an even worse passenger. "An enigma within a mystery," he added dryly.

"Ah, but as with all things there's an explanation," said Christophe. "The Garden Ring is so named because in Tsarist times, homeowners were obliged to plant front gardens. But having been introduced during Tsarist times, the Soviets of course got rid of them. In all cities, Kremlin was always the first level of defence. You then had walls or rings surrounding it. As you do with the *Bely Gorod* or 'White Town' that you see in Moscow. As the population grew and people lived outside the walls, another wall or ring was built. Hence 'Ground Town.' The greatest threat apart from attacking armies was from fire, and the city being burned to the ground. There was little concern for whether future tourists might get lost! Sometimes, the walls simply crumbled or were redundant, but the roads remained."

As they veered from the MKAD - which in the 60's had been *the* definitive, final ring road, but was no longer, Carla's head swivelled. "We're not headed for *Tula*?" she said suspiciously.

Christophe had removed his glasses and was wiping them on the little bit of cloth that came with glass cases. Carla always lost hers within days.

"You've always wanted to visit," he said evenly but Carla could tell that his little surprise had worked, and he was pleased.

"Tula?" echoed Seb frowning. He hated to be excluded and she could tell he thought it a special word between them and nothing to do with ring roads or city planning.

"Oh my *God*!" exclaimed Carla. "I'm so excited!"

One Flame Hour

"What's so special about Tula?" he said edgily.

"Tula itself is worth visiting," said Christophe pleasantly. "It has a Kremlin of course -"

"It's not *Tula*!" interrupted Carla. "Tula's the closest city to Yasnaya Polyana."

Seb sighed. "Tula's easier to pronounce. Sorry, I'm none the wiser."

"Oh," said Carla. "Of course, you aren't. I'm so sorry. Tolstoy. It's to do with Tolstoy. Yasnaya Polyana was Tolstoy's country estate and a place that I've always wanted to visit. It's also where he wrote his greatest fiction."

"I thought you had a thing for *A Gentleman in Moscow*?"

"Yes," said Carla. "You've reminded me!" She touched Christoph's shoulder. "If Amor Towles *ever* wants to visit, will you *please* invite us again?"

It was no good, the calmer Christophe became, the steadier, the more frivolous and excitable Carla appeared. She'd adored Towles's book, but Tolstoy was in another category. A bright orange sun had risen suddenly between stripped birch trees and it had stopped snowing. "Besides we're making the trip in reverse," she mused.

"Who 'we'? A 'gentleman'?"

Seb was used to Carla's odd, disjointed literary references as he knew she often spoke aloud, completing some stream of consciousness that was obvious to her, but oblique to everyone else. Seb waited for Carla to elaborate as he knew she would eventually but Christophe raised his eyebrows impatiently. Since they'd last seen each other, Christophe seemed to have become even more measured, more patrician and statesmanlike in his present position. With his thick, elegant, (gently) greying hair and black rimmed glasses he was a mixture of urbane Brahmin professor and adroit diplomat. He was also more of the 'great minds discussed ideas' vein, while she happily sank to the 'small minds discuss people' level. But then she had always found people's stories irresistible.

"Reverse?" He sounded bored and was studying his phone, and without waiting for an answer began chatting to the driver in Russian.

Seb catching Carla's expression prompted her.

"What did you mean, darkling?" he said kindly.

"It's just," Carla shook her head trying to clarify her thoughts. "It's just that it took Tolstoy twenty years to return to Moscow from Yasnaya Polyana, where we're headed to now," she said more for Seb's benefit than her brother's. Christophe wasn't listening anyway. He'd probably visited the writer's birthplace a hundred times already. "Tolstoy's wife missed city life, ballet and music. She dreamed of Moscow."

"I've heard that line before," said Seb.

Carla smiled. "Yes, Chekov, well done. And probably for the same reason. More a state of mind than one of geography. It has famously been said that all the three sisters ever had to do was buy a train ticket. For whatever reason, they don't or can't. But that's fiction. Tolstoy's refusal or reluctance if you will, to live in the city was very real, if just as complex."

"So, he never left?" Seb slid away his hand.

"No, he did. He finally agreed to the move but as his family soon discovered, all he did was create a mini Yasnaya Polyana in the capital. In his case quite literally. He had three peasant cottages from the estate transported to Moscow and rebuilt around an open courtyard. There was a summerhouse and orchard too."

"You can take the man out of the country…" murmured Seb.

"Exactly," said Carla. "He also wanted to continue the simplicity of life that he had developed in the country, in the city. He preferred wooden utensils to Sofia's silver for example, and he took to dressing in britches and a smock. He teased his sons that while they dressed like gentlemen to live in the country, he dressed as a peasant to live in the city."

"And did he manage all that?"

Carla nodded.

"Well then, I don't think it such an unreasonable ideal," said Seb. "Sounds like an enterprising kind of chap."

Carla was silent.

"Was it a happy ever after kind of story?"

Carla rubbed a circle on the fogged-up pane.

"No," she said thoughtfully. "No, it wasn't"

Which was something of an understatement. Carla had always been intrigued by the Tolstoy marriage described in all its gory detail by his wife Sofia in her diaries. Then again, perhaps it was tit for tat. Tolstoy had shown Sofia *his* diaries on their wedding night. Carla often thought Sofia's were a lifetime's revenge for what she had read there and a way of expressing her grief. Tolstoy had carefully documented every desire, every affair and sexual conquest. He had even pointed out the fruit of these unions, the result of which could be seen running around the estate of which she was to be mistress. To his enduring surprise and disappointment, she had not been sympathetic to these revelations. At the tender age of eighteen (Tolstoy was sixteen years older), Sofia was horrified. Worse, her faith, trust and admiration in her new husband were completely shattered.

"You see," Carla explained not quite finished with her favourite subject. "The man Sofia revered, turned out very much to have feet of clay. And yet she remained loyal, bore his thirteen children (burying five of them in childhood), and put up with his lunatic schemes. More importantly, she became his scribe, painstakingly copying page after page only to have Leo change it all, when she thought they'd finished. At the same time, she oversaw the children's education and at times had to find work to supplement her ever-decreasing allowance while Tolstoy simply gave it all away. He didn't wish to be troubled by money matters believing that happiness didn't depend on it but as he lectured her, on 'what they made of themselves.' "

"I'd agree with that," said Seb with feeling. "Wouldn't you?"

"Obviously," said Carla her tone rising defensively. "But Sofia had children to clothe and feed." Phrased in that way, of course, Tolstoy sounded reasonable but Seb was missing the point. As far as she was concerned, Sofia was a saint. *He* was immortalised but she made it all possible.

"You clearly admire this woman… this Sofia," said Seb supressing a yawn.

"I do," said Carla. "Passionately. I love that she never lost her sense of humour. In spite of being very miserable a lot of the time."

"I see," said Seb puzzled and then brightened thinking of something. "Would you love me even more if I was just a little bit like Tolstoy?"

Carla snorted. "No." Hadn't he been listening? "The final straw for Sofia came when Tolstoy started preaching universal love."

"Er… isn't that a good thing?"

"It might have been had Sofia not felt that he'd stopped loving his own family but was willing to share his private life 'with anyone and everyone.'"

"But not with her."

"But not with her," she repeated.

Carla glanced at Seb. He could be uncannily astute sometimes. Did *he* love more than she did? All she knew was that jealous sparks could be detonated unexpectedly but was that ever an indication of love? Did jealousy ever denote love for the other person? Was it not rather *self*-love, insecurity, control or a fear of exclusion and nothing whatsoever to do with the beloved? Because if you really truly loved, you allowed your partner the freedom just to be, as daughter Sophie was always saying, you loved them just as they were. COVID had certainly highlighted what was important, what was irrelevant what brought real happiness. The line from their one-time poet laureate came to her. *'Let the less loving one be me ...'*

But then again, there was always an ebb and flow in any relationship. The same even applied to Christophe. Her brother was laughing at something the driver was saying. She caught a glimpse of a slice of high cheekbone, a discretely expensive clad shoulder pressed into the back of the seat. As he approached middle age, Christophe presented to the world a man who was happy in his skin, who had achieved what he had set out to achieve, could leave this world, were his life to end now, satisfied. When they were young, they'd been close, confiding in one another, allies against Eugenia's erratic behaviour. But now, would she say they were close? She wasn't so sure. And was she happy in her skin? Yes, while she felt useful, while she felt loved.

"So, what plans for Christmas?" said Christophe, half turning. His phone was back in his coat pocket which meant they had his attention. Until the next call...

"You mean if Boris saves it in time? Jury's still out as to whether or not it's going ahead. But you probably know better than any of us."

"Yeah," joined in Carla. "BoJo says it's just one day. That it shouldn't matter. That we can look forward to *next* Christmas."

"Well, that's not true," said Christophe kindly. For a moment their eyes met. *On the same page at last.* And in that moment, all the Christmases they'd ever spent together growing up came flooding back to her. Frame after frame ... "Of course, we celebrate Christmas here on the seventh of January," he was saying, his voice dipping in and out of her recollections, "because the Russian Orthodox Church uses the Julian calendar so it's different anyway. It's a while since I was in England for Christmas or with the rest of the family for that matter."

"And Christmas in Zim is hot, so different again," chipped in Seb.

"Quite."

There was a small silence as both Christophe and Carla tried to imagine what it would be like to be in a hot climate in December. Seb had occasionally suggested they go to South Africa for the holiday but neither Alfie nor Carla could quite face a beach when they were used to log fires and snow. Even – twenty-five which is what it was outside, was welcome. In fact, the colder the better. It was what Carla and her brother were used to. Hypnotically, the windscreen wipers pushed heavy snow away from the centre, but Carla felt cosy and snug and yes, happy. Or she did until Christophe, swivelling in his seat, elbow crooked asked,

"Do you remember the Japanese hitchhiker?"

Caroline blinked. "You mean with Pa?"

"*Was* there another?" Her brother seemed genuinely surprised.

No, of course there wasn't… She just wasn't sure that she wanted to think about him right now. It was still only mid-morning and Carla's tummy rumbled. A hot chocolate and a hot roll of any description wouldn't go amiss.

But Seb had picked up on this titbit from her past. "Japanese hitchhiker?" echoed Seb. "Darling, there's so much I don't know about you…"

One Flame Hour

"Yes, well..." *Cinnamon toast cut up in small triangles the way Rosa, their Guatemalan maid used to prepare it...*

"Spill, as Alfie would say."

Carla made a sort of grimace. She really was hungry, starving even but then the Japanese hitchhiker had also been hungry *and* cold that snowy Christmas Eve. To this day, she felt a pang of remorse thinking about him. But then it was just another example of the complexity of people - the contradictions that rendered them neither good nor bad, just people. And in her father's case, a man who could be charm personified, on occasion, he could also be harsh and uncompromising.

"Yes?" encouraged Seb.

"Not much of a story. Nothing really to spill..."

Avoiding Seb's searching look, the slight pursing of his lips as he steeled himself to hear something that didn't, or couldn't include him, she turned to the snowy landscape. And because it was so like the Swiss backdrop of her childhood, it took no effort at all to leapfrog over the years...

18

In that frame, Carla was ten years old again, squashed between her brothers in their mother's Pontiac while their dog rode up front. They were bickering as usual, the windscreen misting up with their collective breath. Music, in the form of one of the only two cassettes in their possession, was *The Long and Winding Road*. Needless to say, the journey was fast becoming both. Eugenia, because it was Christmas Eve, was growing more maudlin by the minute as she remembered *her* past Christmases. With every fresh sniff, she lamented the fact that her children didn't want to listen to Christmas music or (in her opinion) make sophisticated, intelligent conversation.

"But we've been listening to carols all afternoon!" protested Christophe. He was the only one of the three Eugenia listened to. She spoiled Roger, antagonised Carla, but respected and was afraid of Christophe. "And slow down!"

It was true, Eugenia who normally drove at a snail's pace with the window rolled down, her elbow propped on the frame, a lit cigarette hanging over the side, varnished fingertips tapping the door, was bombing down the freeway.

"You do know there's risk of avalanche, right, Mère?" said Christophe as they shot over the border into France. Christophe had taken to calling Eugenia 'mother' in French. Phonetically, it could also be the word for 'sea'. Carla and Roger thought this typically pretentious, until Christophe pointed out that he was making a pun on *mal de mer* which meant seasick. Or in his case, 'sick of mother'.

One Flame Hour

They lived in Ferney-Voltaire which was only six kilometres from Geneva and the UN where their father worked. Many expats chose to live in France, rather than Switzerland, as rents there were cheaper but it was still an easy commute. Diplomatic plates meant that Eugenia barely had to slow down as she flicked ash in the guard's face.

"I do," conceded Eugenia now. "Which is why I'm trying to get home as quickly as I can."

"Wouldn't it be fun to have a house in no-man's-land?" piped up Roger completely oblivious of the tension in the car. At the time he was obsessed with the small area between borders. "Could we live in a house like that? Christophe could be in one bedroom, but he'd actually be living in another country!"

"Suits me," said Christophe who was ten years older and would have happily ditched his siblings there and then, if it meant having any sort of privacy. He huddled against the window peering moodily up at the darkening sky, trying not to feel sick as the road narrowed, winding through the valley. Carla leaned against him following his gaze. At the time, everything he did was smarter, better, more imaginative. He didn't feel the same way about her though and pushed her off him as though she were a bug.

"Oh, my God, what is that?" Carla shrieked moments later. A dark yeti-type figure was flattened against a snowbank. "Stop!" she shrieked again. "Stop the car!"

"Don't do that!" said Christophe flinching. "Do you have to *squeal*? Jeez…"

"Eugenia," said Roger who was pushed against the door handle on the other side and Carla who see-sawed somewhere in the middle. "Chris said -"

One Flame Hour

"I heard him," said Eugenia. She was hunched over the steering wheel peering into the darkness.

"Why does Maple have to sit up front anyway?" grumbled Roger.

"Because it's illegal," said Eugenia vaguely.

"What is?" said Roger.

Carla elbowed him in the ribs. "For a kid to sit up front. You know that."

"But why can Maple?"

"Duh," said Christophe. "Because Maple's a dog. D-O-G."

"I know that," said Roger his voice warbling.

"Then why did you ask?"

"Stop fighting!"

"We're not!" said Christophe in amazement. This was just normal banter as far as he was concerned.

Eugenia fumbled for a cigarette. "Light one will you, honey?" she said to Christophe who responded immediately by pushing Carla out of the way and leaning into the front seat. He made an exaggerated show of rooting around in their mother's handbag before fishing out a packet of Rothmans. Leaning back, he lit one and inhaled.

"Christophe's smoking!" said Roger eyes wide as saucers. "Eugeniaaaa!"

One Flame Hour

"I heard you."

Carla, who wasn't wearing a seatbelt, in fact none of them were, twisted round sitting on her haunches, to look out of the back window. "He's there!" she shrieked again. "Go back! What if he really is a yeti! Do you have a gun Eugenia?"

Out of the shadows, dirty, dishevelled, long-haired and completely bewildered wasn't of course a yeti, but a hitchhiker. Or at least that's what they thought he was. What else would a person be doing out of doors in this weather, on Christmas Eve and in the middle of nowhere? He was also Japanese or Oriental and, as they soon discovered, didn't speak a word of English. Eugenia, reversed unsteadily down the snow-banked road, tyres spinning, her breath unfurling in the darkening air. She rolled down the window as the man lumbered towards her. His shoulder-length hair was thick with snow, his nose red and dripping. He clutched a road map that he was trying to decipher upside down.

"We have to look after him, Eugenia!" said Carla excitedly.

This was promising to be the biggest adventure ever. She gave the man her most winsome smile. She had a nurse's outfit that the Three Kings had given her *last* Christmas which she was hoping might still fit. Being half Spanish, Carla and her brothers were truly spoiled because not only did they receive presents on Christmas day, but they also had gifts on the sixth of January - the Epiphany - which was celebrated in Spain. It was the Three Kings rather than Santa Claus who left presents and traditionally, these consisted of sweets and costumes for dressing up. Carla thought she looked terrific in hers. At first, she'd been suspicious. It didn't look shop bought like her brothers' cowboy outfits. Exquisitely tailored, it was an exact copy of a Spanish nurse's.

One Flame Hour

The dress was Egyptian cotton and the apron was made of voile. But the best part of it - the pièce de résistance - was the beautiful cashmere cloak. Carla thought her hood fetish must have begun then. *'Makes me almost want to become a nurse too'* - Eugenia had breathed when she first saw it. The complicated tie system - straps that crossed in the front and buttoned at the back - prevented it flapping away or falling off the shoulders.

Perhaps, thinking of Alfredo, Eugenia hesitated briefly. It was understood in the family, that their father, generous in so many ways, was patholocially allergic to house guests of any description. But then this Japanese man was in a category all of his own.

"You're right," said Eugenia. Carla felt a glow that their mother should have singled her out for approval.

"If you do it to the least of these, you do it to me…" she quoted under her breath.

"Yes, OK," said Eugenia. Christophe rolled his eyes.

"Let him in kids."

Christophe didn't budge. "Let him in where?" he said reasonably. "Unless the infants want to walk."

"Ha, ha," said Carla.

"Come *on*!' said Eugenia. "It's cold and late and your father will be waiting for us. But we won't tell him. Don't tell Alfredo." *Alfredo… Don't tell Alfred.* Nancy Mitford had nothing on *their* father.

One Flame Hour

"So, maybe this will work if-" Christophe opened the car door and Maple leapt out, rolling in the snow and chasing imaginary rabbits.

"Now look what you've done!" said Roger.

"I'll get him," said Eugenia unexpectedly. She tossed her cigarette out of the window and they watched it, momentarily transfixed, a glow worm flying through the air. Seconds later it lay fizzing on the snow.

"*Out out brief candle,*" said Carla.

"In, in!" commanded Christophe motioning to the hitchhiker. The man didn't need any encouragement. Skirting the front of the car, he collapsed gratefully on to the front seat. Shaking with cold, he tucked his rucksack under his feet and closed his eyes.

"Do you think he's dead?" whispered Roger.

"Of course, he's not *dead* dummy!" said Christophe. "The mirror's misting up."

They observed Eugenia, mink coat trailing as she chased after Maple who was looping through the snow in wide figures of eight. Eventually, she cornered him removing her coat to use it as a matador's cape. Breathless, she virtually threw him into the back where he lay prone, a dead weight of matted wet fur.

"Eeow!" said Carla wrinkling her nose. "He stinks."

The Japanese hitchhiker opened his eyes briefly, grunted and pointed to Maple.

One Flame Hour

"Dog," said Eugenia helpfully.

"Do the Japs eat dogs?" said Roger alarmed.

"No," said Christophe authoritatively, "that's the Vietnamese."

A cross between a mutt and a Great Dane, Maple was the most ill-disciplined, bad tempered animal Carla had yet to meet. Roger had named him after the syrup but that was wishful thinking - sweetness was not in his nature. Within hours of his arrival, he'd vanished into their wood not to be seen for three days. *'Wish I could have done the same,'* Christophe had muttered when Maple eventually pitched up, depositing several dead rabbits on the kitchen floor. And Maple was always hungry. With the outbreak of the Falklands war, a different battle began in their own household. Alfredo, being Spanish, sided with the Argentines and *Las Malvinas;* Eugenia, naturally sided with the Brits. In protest, she moved out of the matrimonial bedroom, refused to eat the Argentine beef that was delivered to the house on a monthly basis and had knickers printed with the Union Jack. Maple was soon being fed the very best fillet.

They'd been quiet on the remainder of the journey, the hitchhiker and Maple both snoring contentedly. Carla held her nose not sure who smelled more. It was a great relief, when they finally reached home, and they could all stretch their legs - Maple included. With the Japanese in tow, they piled into the house - a house that had once been three separate apartments on three different floors accessed by an external staircase. Their parents had spent the better part of sixteen years arguing as to how best to convert the house into

One Flame Hour

a single dwelling again but neither had ever come up with a satisfactory solution. Besides, it rather suited Eugenia who could frequently have people to stay without Alfredo even noticing they were there. Guests would waft down to breakfast and their unassuming father (*Don't tell Alfred*) would welcome them graciously, assuming they'd come in for a coffee. Mustering his old-world charm, he would get to his feet, tap his heels, whisk a lady's hand inches from his lips *but never ever touch* - and murmur pleasantries. '*How lovely to see you- how clever of you to find us. See you again the next time you're visiting...*' much to the bewilderment of the guest who very much hoped to see Alfredo later that very day.

The objective, when they got home this time, was to smuggle the Japanese man into the house and up to the third floor without Alfredo being aware of him. It had been a long day, Eugenia was tired and this being Christmas Eve, she still had a host of last-minute preparations to attend to. With the man safely in his room and presumably tucked up asleep, Eugenia wouldn't trouble herself about him until the morning. By then, she would have come up with some story to explain the presence of this random guest, who had appeared at breakfast, on Christmas day. Eugenia just might have got away with it too, if Papa hadn't in fact already taken to his bed with the beginnings of his seasonal 'beeruus' leaving the door open to his apartment. Excited at the prospect of having an unsolicited guest to stay, the ever-affable Roger had skipped noisily up the stairs. But their little brother had reached the top step at precisely the moment Alfredo had emerged on the landing in his pyjamas. Roger had frozen, mid hop, as had the Japanese hitchhiker while a thunderous cloud had been swift to descend on their father's usually passive features.

"So, what happened next?" said Seb. "Did you have the best Christmas ever?"

One Flame Hour

"Er… no, not exactly," said Carla. "We've definitely had worse. But that was the one to brand the soul, the one we all seem to remember."

"Christmas Japanese fashion? They're Shinto and Buddhist, right?"

"Right," agreed Carla weakly.

"In case, you really want to know," said Christophe filling the ensuing silence. "The Japanese hitchhiker went back out into the snow, never to be seen again. Roger still reminds us that it could have been Jesus himself, and that we definitely failed the test."

19

The sound of Christophe unclipping his seat belt together with a rush of cold air jolted Carla awake and she realised that she must have nodded off after all. For a moment she was confused, memories of her childhood swirling in her head. But she wasn't still in Geneva her stomach in knots with the tension (and realisation) of what they had done or not done, guiltily sitting down to a lavish tea. Her stomach rumbling with hunger was real enough as was Seb, who was already outside stretching his legs. With his borrowed ushanka and broad frame he could have passed for a local, whereas Christophe was elegantly effete - more French or Italian and light years away from the long-haired would-be-hippy of their youth.

They'd parked across the road from the entrance to the Kremlin complex, with the gold onion domes of the appropriately named Epiphany Cathedral shining even more brightly against the crisp densely packed snow. The sun was still orange in a marshmallow pink sky. The green painted roof and blue painted walls of the Assumption church beside it, was a cross between a wedding cake and a gingerbread house. Her tummy responded immediately with a Pavlovian growl.

"Interesting," said Christophe when she'd voiced her observation as they entered the walled city. He turned owl-like. "You must have known that Tula was renowned for its *pryanik* or gingerbread."

Not really, she thought. It's just that I'm so hungry!

One Flame Hour

"In fact, look." He orientated her shoulders in the direction of a giant round stone coin perched on a plinth. It had scalloped edges and curly swirls. It looked more like an Oreo cookie than the gingerbread with which Carla was familiar.

"That one measures eight feet," said Christophe clapping his hands together for warmth. His breath came out in quick bursts. Carla could feel the cold through her teeth. "Catherine the Great was given a cake that weighed more than sixty-five pounds!"

"She obviously had a big appetite," said Seb.

An ounce at this point would do just fine…

"Can we try some?" she said faintly.

"Of course!" said Christophe. "That's why we're here. You'll see there's a whole culture around the *pryanik*. It wasn't just eaten to relieve hunger. It could be used to teach children the alphabet. The little cakes often had names on them, and children had to learn their letters before being allowed to eat them."

God help me if I must do the same, thought Carla. She found it hard to remember even the simplest words. But that was learning a language when you were older, she thought dispiritedly. What was the Russian for 'eat' anyway? Why was it that she could remember odd phrases but nothing useful?

Christophe fished out his mask. "Come, we'll learn more here."

They followed Christophe into a little kiosk already so over heated, she could feel the sweat pooling at the back of her neck. She removed her mink hood bitterly regretting having donned thermal leggings under her leather trousers. Unlike in England, the Russians hadn't imposed a second lockdown or 'circuit break' and schools had remained open for the duration of the autumn. Carla watched the students sitting quietly on low benches with a pang of envy. Alfie had missed out on so much in the past year - excursions such as these, and just the chance to be with other children his own age. But unlike his classmates who would certainly have shown signs of boredom by now, fidgeting in their places, groping for their phones, these boys and girls appeared genuinely captivated as a baker told them about the various tools used in the making of gingerbread. Various kinds of cookie were displayed on the shelves above them. Dark brown with white icing, they looked like a variation of the German *lebkuchen* and came in all shapes and sizes. Some were square or round or depicted a house. There wasn't a single gingerbread person among them. Carla wondered if anyone would notice if she pinched one.

"Those are just for show," said Christophe reading her mind. They moved to stand in a corner of the room. "The recipe was a closely guarded secret," he translated when the guide resumed talking. "Passed on from family to family. There was never one formula or way of measuring. Bakers used small stones or bits of metal which were then kept under lock and key."

"And the shapes?" said Seb. "Who decided that?"

Christophe nodded, watching the baker. "She's getting to that. The mould was made from either a birch or pear tree, aged for anywhere between five and twenty years, then smeared with wax."

One Flame Hour

"Yum." Carla felt positively faint behind her mask. Her disposable, surgical mask - Seb bought them in bulk from a man in the market - had begun to shred bits of fibre and thread stuck to her lipstick.

"Are you OK?" said Christophe worriedly.

"What's she saying now?"

The baker had shot her a dark look. Christophe put a finger to his lips and motioned for them to follow him out of the room. "Cakes were also used for games. They were thrown like discs."

"They were *that* hard?"

"Maybe just the overcooked ones."

Seb pulled her to him, leaning into her while he removed his mask. He held out a heart-shaped cookie which didn't look hard at all. She caught a whiff of cinnamon and honey. Her eyes, never mind her mouth began to water and she lurched forwards. "Uh, uh," he said continuing to dangle it in front of her. "Did you know that if a guy wasn't sure his girl would accept his proposal, he sent her gingerbread?"

"Yes," said Carla without hesitating. "Yes, yes, yes."

During the twenty- minute drive from Tula to Yasnaya Polyana, Carla was still eating gingerbread.

"I'm not sure you're supposed to eat the entire box," said Seb amused. And then he frowned as a disturbing thought occurred to him. "Please tell me you're not…?"

One Flame Hour

"Pregnant?" Carla rolled her eyes. "Don't be silly."

"I'm not. That's what you said before Alfie."

"That was different."

"How?"

Carla brushed crumbs from her lap and ignored him. "I didn't realise we were skipping lunch," she hissed.

"It's because of the weather," said Seb. "Your brother wants to get back to Moscow in good time. Hang in there. You can make up for it at supper."

"Ohhhh!" breathed Carla almost choking on the last corner of cake. They'd turned off Polskaya Doroga Avenue coming to a stop in front of twin gate posts. Their spotted tops gave them the appearance of giant toadstools. And in front of these, was a troika. Bedecked in bells, three horses in special sledge harnesses, stomped the frozen ground. A Cossack in an ankle-length red coat with gold frogging, looking for all the world like a Byzantine Father Christmas, stood sentinel beside them. The horses began stomping the ground, emitting loud snorts their breath hanging in the air. Remove all colour, the vibrance of the man's scarlet coat, the glint of brass as the winter's morning sun caught the horses' harnesses, and the picture could have leapt from one of Tolstoy's own sepia photo albums.

"No," said Carla almost speechless. But not for long. "You haven't!"

"It's nothing. And very touristy," protested Christophe but he looked pleased all the same. "But *ojo*. Mind, I wouldn't do this for just anyone. And luckily there's no one to see me succumb to this… this *cursiness*."

"'Cursiness'?" repeated Seb.

Carla smiled. "Christophe's created a new word. 'Cursi' is … I don't know - I guess 'corny' would be the closest translation. But there's no other word in English that really does it justice."

Seb looked around him sceptically. "And there's no one else here? Queueing to go in, I mean. You don't think it might be closed?" he added hopefully.

Christophe shook his head alighting but leaving the car door open. "Nope. Summer's the busy time. You can book private visits at this time of the year, no problem."

"I can see why," muttered Seb still reluctant to emerge from the car.

"The Rolls would be warmer, I agree," said Christophe. "Perhaps you -"

Carla's eyes were shining as ignoring Seb, she jumped from the car to embrace her brother. "Oh, this is just too wonderful! Thank you, Christophe. Truly!"

Seb winced and a tick had begun in his cheek. As a polo player, he had a utilitarian approach to horses. To him they were '*maquinas*' - machines - tools for the game and there was nothing whatsoever sentimental in his relationship with them. Off the field, he barely tolerated them, and this kind of contrived entertainment was not his idea of fun.

One Flame Hour

"Hop in," said Christophe motioning to the sled. "It's a short ride," he added reassuringly to Seb. "And then you'll be inside again."

Seb looked doubly doubtful. The curved sides of the sledge were so low they almost touched the ground. By contrast, the seats were high, tilted precariously forward. One lurch and a passenger could easily be thrown clear.

The Cossack climbed up to his own little perch. With his back to the passengers, he wrapped himself in a blanket.

"I like those low sledges pulled by huskies myself," muttered Seb.

"Oh, darling but they don't have bells!" said Carla.

"Actually, the bells have, well *had* a practical purpose," said Christophe hopping into the sledge as if to prove a point.

"Oh?" Seb looked unimpressed on both counts.

"Yes," said Christophe. "When troikas were used in the postal service the bells acted as a warning that horses were fast approaching and to ready fresh ones. Now, of course, they're only decorative. But at the time, there might have been up to a hundred bells attached to the bridle and saddle and the special harness that dictates how each horse will perform."

Seb pulled a face. "In my game the rider dictates how a horse performs," he said tartly.

"Come on!" said Carla smoothly, recognising the tell-tale signs of a sulk and stepping equally nimbly into the troika.

One Flame Hour

"You're going to have to sit in the middle," said Christophe. He held out a thick fur rug invitingly. "For balance."

"Just great," muttered Seb. He made a sideways, crab-like movement intending to fold himself neatly onto the edge of the seat but miscalculating the angle, ended up half lying, half sitting, with his head on level with Carla's bosom. Because of an old polo injury to his knee, Seb always found it awkward bending low. The troika listed to one side.

"Won't matter," said Christophe easily. "Once we get going. See, the central horse will trot, while the outer two gallop. They can easily reach a speed of fifty kilometres. Besides, it makes for a safer ride."

Than what? Carla's stomach lurched with the troika as the Cossack cracked his whip and the horses set off, bells ringing, sledge runners shrieking as metal sliced through snow and ice. Despite being warm enough, wedged in as she was between her brother and husband, the parts of her face that were exposed, stung with cold; it felt as though there was even ice up her nostrils. She tried to wiggle away the uncomfortable sensation, but the tip of her nose was numb. She tried to move her jaw but speech was aborted in her frozen breath. Now she was very glad of her hood, her fur-lined gloves and thermals.

As the horses gathered momentum, and their gait evened, both Cossack and Seb arched backwards. High above her, the driver's long whip lassoed the air with a gun-shot crack, followed by the sound of ice snapping under the horses' hooves. Their manes flowing behind them, the horses thundered steadily down the *presphekt*. Through birch trees whose branches drooped with the weight of the snow, Christophe pointed out the English Park and the lake and ponds caked in grey ice. Carla's eyes watered with cold.

One Flame Hour

"Look," said Seb. His right hand gripped the side of the sledge, the other was firmly around Carla, more to gain purchase than out of affection. Two trees, a birch and a lime, had grown together, twisting around each other as if in an embrace. "Tolstoy and his wife?" he suggested.

Carla shook her head. "The romantic in me would love to think so but the realist knows better. Tolstoy and his art, perhaps? Tolstoy and his place in the universe once he'd renounced all worldly pleasures. Or the man and his spirituality? At peace with one another. At last."

"All a bit profound?" said Seb. His leg was solid against hers. She for one felt perfectly secure in the sledge. "This is the man who wrote *War and Peace,* right?"

"Have you ever *read War and Peace*?"

Seb made an ambivalent sound.

"I'll take that as a no," said Carla.

"Maybe. But I know about it."

"Of course, you do," she said smoothly. "But see, Tolstoy's was realist fiction at its best. He was somehow able to describe 'conscious mental life.' Even Anna Karenina, as she's about to throw herself in front of the train has a moment's doubt, a moment's hesitation. You rarely get that in novels. Mostly you get a character's action aftermath, but not what was actually going through her head."

"Well, I know what's going through mine," said Seb. "I can't feel my feet." His face was so close to hers, his mouth moving against the scarf he was using as a balaclava.

One Flame Hour

"All this, and he still wasn't happy."

"Maybe because of all this," said Christophe. He motioned with a gloved hand as the troika flew down the avenue dissecting what appeared to be the rolling plains of endless parkland. Carla recognised maple and ash and felt a pang of recognition, a nostalgic yearning for other wintery landscapes. "I think it's safe to say that he was a tortured writer - a man at odds with everything around him except nature and the peasants of course, that he loved so much."

"Love being the operative word," muttered Carla.

"There's a school on the estate that he established for his serfs," continued her brother. "You'll see it later. We pass it when we leave."

"Are those *all* apple trees?" asked Seb turning his head. The sweeping empty expanses had given way in the distance, to hectares and hectares of orchard.

Christophe nodded. "All thirty-three varieties. Some are saplings from the very trees Tolstoy planted. In fact, one of his descendants who grew up here - a young guy in his thirties who calls himself plain Mr Ilya - has taken to producing apple juice. He's growing a successful business and his logo is taken from -" Christophe stopped. "You know what, I'll show you when we get to the house. And on all the labelling he uses the same font that Tolstoy used on his Remington typewriter."

"Funny to think of Tolstoy using a typewriter," said Seb.

"Especially as he was born fifty years before it was invented!"

One Flame Hour

They grew silent with their own thoughts. Carla's were still with Tolstoy. She wondered what it was to live with such a person, deciding to support his genius while half the time probably wanting to kill the man.

But nonetheless, with every furlong covered, Carla felt mounting excitement, until, as though theatre curtains had opened onto a giant stage, they galloped through one last canopy of trees and the Volkonsky house came into view. The long building sprawled across a horizon of white tipped trees, white against white snow, and only its green roof delineated sky from land. It was perfect and just as she'd imagined it. At that moment, she felt as far removed from COVID England as it was possible to be. Tucked up in fur, flying through the snow in a troika was as surreal as was living with a pandemic.

"I count twenty windows," said Seb. "And that's only at the front!"

But they didn't stop at the front. Lanterns lighting a path skirted the house, twinkling and dancing among the snowflakes. Carla half expected the sugar plum fairy to pop out from behind a lollipop tree. The horses slowed to a walk before dragging the sledge to a small, covered veranda at the side of the house.

"This is known as the 'summer entrance,'" said Christophe sliding from the troika and standing beside one of the horses to pat its nose, "but I like coming into the house this way. It's completely unassuming as you can see. Nothing grand at all. Besides, I wanted you to see this." He motioned to the pretty balustrade which ran the length of the terrace. Carved into the wood were equestrian and female figures. "You remember I was telling you about plain Mr Ilya? Well, he uses this design as a logo for his apple products. He sells them not only in Tula province but in Moscow too."

"So… apples were the one crop that *didn't* fail?"

"That's right, Tolstoy tried his hand at virtually everything else which did."

"But he didn't really have to worry about money, did he? He was a Count, right? A landowner?" said Seb, "he could play at being a peasant."

"Yes, and no," said Carla also alighting. She touched the balustrade tracing the shape of a head, a carved skirt. The charming, naïve-style figures belied the drama of what had really taken place in the Tolstoy household. "Trying to live simply became the became the crisis of his life, the conundrum of what he'd been born to and what he believed and how he wanted to live. A cult even. People started following him, seeing him as a Christ figure. His family didn't understand it. Sofia didn't understand it. And in the end, they were all in turmoil, in conflict with one another and themselves."

"I see," said Seb hoisting himself out of the troika and flexing his knee.

"But if you think about it," said Carla thoughtfully. "All Tolstoy's characters run away in the end, from someone or something. Maybe it was something he was doing unconsciously himself from the beginning."

"I think you know his work much better than I do," said Seb not a little mystified. "You're not a teeny bit obsessed?"

One Flame Hour

"Not a teeny bit," smiled Carla. "A lot. I've always been fascinated by the pull between art and domesticity - between good intentions and what one is able to achieve. I would have said it was so much easier for a man to fulfil both but that certainly wasn't true of Tolstoy. He was tormented by the contradiction of his life and his principles. Lucky for us, they both left so many diaries. Sofia, in hers, would complain that she was little more than a nanny; he would say that she was spoilt, that he couldn't sleep or work. Neither understood the other and in the end, he left."

"Don't get any ideas," said Christophe dryly. "Leo man didn't get very far. He caught pneumonia three weeks later and died in a little railway station not far from here."

Seb looked affronted. "Dang, as Alfie would say." He kicked snow off the heel of his boot and pulled up the collar on his coat. "Shall we go in? The other thing you siblings seem to have in common is a complete disregard for cold."

20

"And the name of this place?" asked Seb as they stepped into a small lobby, into a pool of electric light and warmth. Straight ahead of them was an unprepossing staircase and then inexplicably, half-way up, double doors, that could seal off access to the next floor. The walls up to these were lined with English clocks. "Where does it originate?"

"Well, there's the Yasenko stream that runs close to the estate," volunteered Christophe shaking snow from his hat.

"I think 'Yasnaya Polyana' might mean 'Bright Glade'?" said Carla peeling off her fur coat. She unwrapped her scarf, kicked off her boots and shoved her feet into the cloth slippers visitors to museums in Russia were requested to wear - a leftover practice from Soviet days. Finally, she hooked a clean mask behind her ears. By which time, she was sweating again. "Which is slightly ironic when everything later became so dark."

"We all know that appearances can be deceptive," said Seb reluctant to remove any bit of his own clothing. His hands were thrust deep in his pockets and the collar of his coat covered his ears.

"Not in their case," said Christophe. "I don't think they made any attempt to hide exactly what they felt for one another."

They shuffled from one simply furnished room to the other, taking in the brightly coloured rugs, the family oil paintings, the two grand pianos. There was nothing remotely ostentatious about the house and although there were some thirty-two rooms, there was a convivial feel reflected in the small groupings of tables and chairs in corners and alcoves. Carla could easily imagine Sofia and her children gathered around an oil lamp, talking, or playing cards. The feeling was not so much of a reconstructed life, but of a life interrupted. As though the writer had simply popped out for a stroll. Except that his last had been in the dead of winter fleeing from a life that was no longer compatible with the ideal he had set for himself.

Having quickly visited the first floor they returned to spend the longest time in Tolstoy's study. After all, Carla reminded Seb, it was where the great writer had written *Anna Karenina* and *War and Peace*. The feeling that Tolstoy had nipped out briefly was never stronger than in this small room. His papers and candles were neatly laid out on the walnut desk together with a divider stacked with correspondence (Carla tried to see if there were any letters from Ghandi with whom Tolstoy had enjoyed a year's intense communication) and more family photographs.

Against one wall was the famous leather chesterfield on which Tolstoy and all his children had been born and which he took with him everywhere he went. An easy chair was pushed into one corner and Carla imagined the writer moving to sit there to read when he'd grown tired of writing. Above it, a single shelf bowed with the weight of leather-bound copies of his books. All told, there were apparently some twenty-two thousand books in the house. Carla could well believe it. She also knew that only half were in Russian. There was some Chekov (although no *Lady with the Dog*) which made Carla smile, because, as she told Seb, Tolstoy had considered him to be as bad a playwright as Shakespeare.

Seb picked up a slim, leather-bound edition, turning it over in his hands. "*The Kreutzer Sonata*? Oh, it's in English." He sounded relieved.

One Flame Hour

"Do you know it?" Christophe asked.

"I know Beethoven's."

"Who, incidentally, Tolstoy couldn't bear," said Carla. "In fact, when he met Tchaikovsky, they argued about Beethoven."

"How fascinating," said Christophe, looking over Seb's shoulder, "to think of the great writer meeting the great musician. But this little novella in case you're interested," he continued, "is about a man who murders his wife. There's a bit about prostitutes (which had the censors agitated) but ultimately it advocates sexual abstinence and is an analysis of jealous rage."

Seb raised an eyebrow, before putting the book carefully back where he'd found it. "Not my go-to combination."

"Nor mine," grinned Christophe. Carla cast a glance in their direction happy that they agreed on something. She never really knew what Christophe thought about Seb but had always hoped they would find common ground. But then with Christophe living abroad for so much of his career, there'd not always been the opportunity for them to spend time together. And with COVID, the last year had been pretty much lost. She thrust thoughts of the pandemic firmly away - she didn't need reminding of any of it when she was here to forget.

"But surely they were happy in the beginning? I mean Tolstoy and his wife." Seb had already cased the small space and Carla could sense he was restless to get moving although not necessarily outside. He still hadn't taken off his coat. He swooped low onto the bits of information in English on plaques and under display cabinets.

"Everyone's happy in the beginning," said Christophe wistfully.

"Sofia was only eighteen when she married," said Carla, moving to look out of the window at the endless blanket of snow, dissected only by the long avenue of birch trees. "But Tolstoy was thirty-four and quite experienced, if you know what I mean. Promiscuous even."

"Ah," said Christophe. "But that was the demon that Tolstoy was fighting so hard to overcome."

"Yes, and that decision destroyed their relationship," said Carla. "When ... when he withdrew."

"So, to speak," smirked Seb. "I hope you aren't getting ideas," he added whispering out of earshot. "I hope you weren't thinking about us?"

He traced the line of her cheekbone. Christophe cast them both an amused look and moved discretely ahead, into another room. They heard him say something to the guide in Russian, their joint laughter and finally, retreating footsteps.

"Of course, not." She pulled away. "I was actually, thinking of Tolstoy's death."

"OK, so nice cheerful thoughts."

"Yes... *no!*"

"You mean in the railway station?" Seb leant over to read the blurb in one of those laminated brochures that museums have, the kind attached by metal beads that can't be removed. He flicked a page. "He was a pacifist, having fought in the Crimean war - my God - how old was he? A vegetarian having been a bon vivant." He made a face straightening up. "Maybe, he just needed a good steak."

Carla rolled her eyes. Seb's answer to most things being South African - Zimbabwean to be exact - was to eat a good chunk of meat.

"Some truth in that," agreed Carla. "But there's no denying how conflicted he was. How he spent his entire life trying to find meaning and purpose to it."

"Don't we all?"

"Of course. But then there's no underestimating the consequence of an unhappy childhood." Which was *her* beef, so to speak. "The man had suffered immeasurable loss in his lifetime, no wonder he tried to find meaning. But no, I was thinking more specifically about the spot where he is buried."

"Glad you're feeling so Christmassy," said Seb.

Again, Carla rolled her eyes. And then as they were about to leave the room, he motioned to a marble bust positioned in a semi-circular niche on the wall. "Who's the guy?"

"Actually, that's who I was thinking about," said Carla. "That's Nicolai, Tolstoy's favourite brother. He died of consumption when he was only thirty-seven. See, the brothers had already lost their parents when they were young - really young. Leo was only two when his mother died, followed shortly by their father and then the grandparents who had stepped in to take care of the children, also died."

One Flame Hour

Carla touched the smooth marble features. "When Nicolai died, Tolstoy wrote that he had lost his best friend."

Seb nodded. Carla could tell he was thinking of his twin, Dom, with whom Seb was close.

"When his brother was twelve," continued Carla as arm in arm, they strolled through the rest of the house. "Nicolai told the family that he had a secret, that if it was revealed, there would be no more wars and no more suffering. What was more, Nicolai told the young Leo, that he had written the secret on a little green stick and buried it near a ravine on the edge of the estate. All his life, Leo would remember this story, writing that he wished to be buried on the spot where he believed the green stick to be."

"And was he?" asked Seb.

Carla nodded. "There was no religious ceremony, mourners simply knelt around the grave."

"I think I'll start reading this fellow after all," said Seb.

But she hadn't only been thinking about Nicolai and the little green stick and Tolstoy's final resting place. Yasnaya Polyana itself, seemed a small stage where artists she'd only ever read about, live personages with their quirky ways, danced through the ether and into her imagination. It was Chekov though, who stood out for being the only real man of the earth - the only Russian of the twentieth century not to have been born an aristocrat but rather the very peasant Tolstoy was so desperate to emulate. And yet while Chekov, who had trained as a medical doctor, before becoming a writer advocated self-advancement through education, Tolstoy eschewed elitist education and even medicine, wishing to turn the clock back to a simpler time. But that too was a fantasy - the yearning to live a different kind of life. And in the end, Carla pondered, when the spirit has finally achieved its maturity and is no longer compatible with its physical form, the final journey has always to be taken alone.

"What was the sigh for?" said Seb coming to stand beside her, his hands resting on her shoulders. "You don't think it's time to leave these characters behind?"

She took a deep breath about to retort something inane but thought better of it. He was right. It *was* time but then it had been a great deal more diverting to worry about the past than it was to face the uncertainty of all that awaited them when they got home. Sensing her disquiet, Seb folded her in his arms.

"What's happening really is just a blip, you know. In the scheme of things. You talk about history. Well, look around you," he said motioning to the pictures and manuscripts and references to Tolstoy's wartime experiences. "Every age has its challenges."

"I know," said Carla mournfully. "But it's not just COVID."

"What then?"

"My nature," said Carla. "Being one of them. The fact that I seem unable to change. That I'm still obsessive in my own way. And not able to shake off my worldly trappings just as Tolstoy did. I mean not that I could compare myself to such a great man. Obviously."

"You're being hard on yourself," said Seb kindly. "Anyway, not sure how successful your writer was. At changing." He looked at her meaningfully. "Besides, just maybe, you haven't tried, *really* tried. I mean, if you had really wanted to, I'm sure you would … alter," he paused to drop a kiss on her forehead, "whatever slight imperfection there might be."

"Clothes," said Carla gloomily. "I'm shackled by clothes."

"Ah," said Seb. "We're back to that."

"I can see how Tolstoy had simply to eliminate what was destroying him. There was no half-way house. Do you know that he even made his own shoes?"

"OK, now you have me worried," said Seb frowning. "You're not suggesting…"

Carla shook her head vigorously. "Of course not. I just don't want to be dictated by fashion. Any longer."

"I salute you, Carla Cave," said Seb raising his hand to his temple. "So, you mean if I were to produce that Chanel jacket, you'd sold you -"

Carla's eyes were wide. "What? Have you seen it? Have you really? Where? Have you?"

"No," said Seb.

"Oh," said Carla deflated. "That was mean."

"No, it wasn't," said Seb. "Just testing. Look there are things you enjoy, so what? Enjoy them. In moderation. Frustration comes when you can't, I guess. Or when the guilt about enjoyment overrides the pleasure."

"That's just it," muttered Carla. "There's always guilt."

One Flame Hour

"Why?" He stood beside a window facing the park, half resting a leg on its window seat. An expanse of white snow stretched endlessly before them. He reached out an arm pulling her close, his hand resting on the nape of her neck. "Look, we're coming out of a pandemic, don't be so hard on yourself. You've done whatever you had to, to survive, to come out of it."

"Or go back in," said Christophe.

Carla pulled away from Seb. She hadn't heard her brother approach. "What do you mean, 'go back in'? Is it time to leave?"

Christophe consulting his phone, looked up. "As a matter of speaking. The UK's going back into lockdown. You're having a 'circuit break,'" he said abruptly.

"What?" Carla felt a hand stay her heart. She was used to lockdown, to a different way of shopping, socialising, and working but that's because they'd believed there'd be an end to it all. Nine months ago, they'd been told it would be three weeks. And then the numbers/cases/deaths weren't where they should be so they'd had to continue wearing masks, keep two metres apart, stay home, minimise travel, protect the NHS. But it was Christmas in a couple of weeks' time. Surely, lockdown had to come to an end then, not start all over again? She felt sick. She could see why mental health issues were at a premium. She felt herself hurtle, inexplicably, towards a black abyss.

"It's true," said Seb scrolling through his phone as messages pinged nonstop. "Matt Hancock has come up with a tier system.

One Flame Hour

Carla relented and looked at hers. There were messages from Les Girls. One of them had just had a COVID test - *Like waiting for a pregnancy test* - she'd messaged. *The thin blue line...*

"London's hovering on Tier 3," she reported gloomily.

"We should go," said Christophe. "In fact, you should probably think about changing your flights. If you can."

"Right." said Seb.

"But what about the Bolshoi?" protested Carla, the reality of what was being suggested finally dawning. "What about *Nutcracker*? What-"

"There'll be another time," said Christophe kindly. "You can come back at Easter. Johnson is saying Easter will be the new Christmas."

"But that's *months* away!" wailed Carla. "Easter's not the same! I've never liked Easter. It's not the same-"

"At least we got away now," said Seb firmly trying to put a positive spin on things.

"Got away?" said Carla feeling childish tears prick her eyes. "What? For all of forty-eight hours? Why can't we just stay?"

"You can't," said Christophe firmly. "Your visas will run out and besides 'hovering on going into Tier 3' means London will certainly be Tier 3 in a few days, if not hours. Plus, there's a new strain. Apparently South African."

"Really?" Seb looked alarmed. His niece Zoe had only recently returned home.

One Flame Hour

Carla ran her finger down the chain of messages that appeared to be addressing these very questions. "Well, a new variant should still be responsive to the vaccine," she sniffed. "And who *says* it's more virulent? Oh, this is so *so* boring!"

"Oxfordshire is Tier 3," announced Christophe. "And there's been an outbreak in a vaccination centre."

"Not surprising really." Seb held up his phone to show them images of tube and train stations across the UK crammed with commuters."

"But that's not the real issue. Apparently, in addition, there's another, deadlier variant in the UK."

"Says who?" said Carla, belligerently enough for Seb to lay a restraining hand on Carla's arm and shoot her a warning look.

"Says the UK." Christophe spoke Russian into his phone adding, "Sergei will meet us around the front, with the car," he said. "We won't be taking the troika."

Seb mouthed 'well that's a relief' but Carla hung back drinking in the last details, committing an image of the room to memory, trying to bottle the feel of the place, the silence, the inky horizon, the silver birch trees swaying slightly as snow drifted from the highest branches to the shadowed spaces below.

"But what's the rush? We could still stay?" insisted Carla. Then we could go to the Bolshoi… even the Marinskii in St. Petersburg." And of course, there was Russian Christmas itself…

One Flame Hour

There was a small silence.

"Haven't you forgotten something? Or should I say someone?" said Christophe, tucking his phone into his back pocket.

Carla's brow wrinkled. *Like?* Their mother lived in Gibraltar. Their father was dead. That left Roger.

Christophe's shot his sister an amused look. "Doesn't your son Alfie spring to mind?"

"Oh, him."

"Yes, him."

"You might want to…" Seb made a jive movement. "Steer into the skid, kid."

At the entrance through which they were to exit, Carla removed the plastic shoe covers and pulled on her boots. 'Steer into the skid, kid,' indeed. What kind of language was that? She still didn't see what the issue was. There were several families she could ask to have Alfie to stay - not least brother Roger. Besides, it wasn't as if they'd not seen each other recently. They could *all* do with time apart. Resentful and cross, she exerted herself unnecessarily so that by the time she was dressed for the outdoors again, she was 'sparkling' as JessicaSmithTV called perspiration and Seb was staring at her. She looked away, uncomfortably aware that he could usually read her every thought.

"It's OK," said Seb. "Shh, it's OK."

One Flame Hour

But Carla merely glowered.

It was absolutely *not* OK. Nothing about any of this was OK and Carla was fed up with it. Fed up with being strong (or trying to be), fed up with Zoom and crafts and being creative and fed up with trying to keep positive. No, it was not OK. This time she would wallow in things not being anywhere close to OK. *Ugh!* Carla clenched her fists. Why did the Brits have to be so damned *honest? Of course,* there were variants. There always were. The virus was behaving true to form and doing exactly what viruses always did! That is mutate. Even the flu jab didn't cover every *type* of flu that popped up seasonally. What was the matter with people? Were they always going to be a nation of knee jerk reactionists? What had happened to a country that used to prize liberty above all else? How willingly they'd all been subjugated! So, the UK was planning on going into another national lockdown even though Boris had said that wouldn't happen while the rest of the world, including Russia continued as normal. Why even from July this year, nightclubs, restaurants and bars had stayed open. And, Russia had resisted lockdowns because, guess what? She addressed Seb silently, deaths had risen but they had not overwhelmed the health system!

"So, all this panic," said Carla through gritted teeth, "is to get us back to England but not because anyone's too worried about death rates here?"

Christophe had the grace to look uncomfortable.

"Carla," said Seb in that 'you might want to tread carefully' tone.

"I think they're handling things really well here," said Christophe. "Actually, it hasn't been *quite* as free as you might think. Yes, the young have been allowed to do pretty much what they want but the elderly have been forced to isolate. But then local councils - at least well-funded ones - have been really well organised and roped in workers to do the shopping for the elderly. Plus, and this is a kind of novel idea - people with symptoms were told to stay at home and call an ambulance."

"A bit overkill, no?" ventured Seb.

Christophe pulling off his own protective shoes, paused. "Not really. An ambulance arrives with a doctor who administers a test. If positive, the patient is given a smartphone. They're required to photograph themselves at home together with a thermometer reading. Seems sensible to me."

Carla made a face. "Yeah, and then there's the Sputnik V, isn't there?"

"Yes," agreed Christophe. "The Lancet has confirmed that it's 91.6 per cent effective."

"Which seems even better than the Astra Zeneca."

"It does," agreed Seb relieved to note the absence of edginess in Carla's tone but failing to see that her eyes shone triumphantly.

"Actually, you could even have it," said Christophe. "It's available to everyone. Even foreigners. And you don't have to queue or book it."

"See?" said Carla.

"See what?" Seb's eyebrows had shot together bushier than usual. Carla wondered vaguely if there were any nail scissors in their bathroom, she could use to trim them.

One Flame Hour

"There's no need for alarm. No need to rush back."

"Oh, but there is," said Christophe. "As of midnight tomorrow, Russia is planning on suspending all flights to and from the UK. If you don't leave soon, there's no telling when you might get home."

Carla looked at her brother. There were worse things… They could learn Russian, go to the opera, take long walks in the snow, skate through Gorky Park…

"Guess, not," she conceded cheerfully.

Seb stared at her. "You aren't really thinking of staying?"

"Of course not," she lied. "We couldn't stay away from Alfie…"

A few hours later however, it looked as though Carla might get her wish to stay after all. The storm that had chased them ever since they left Moscow had caught up with them in Tula. And a sky that had begun as a dark-blue definition against an undulating sea of white, was turning progressively darker. By the time they reached the end of the drive, branches were strewn across the path, and fat snowflakes flew at the windscreen like confetti as though the heavens were a piñata sliced open at a children's party. The car's engine chugged sluggishly and at one point its wheels spun without gaining purchase. The heater blasted hot air but still Carla shivered; the dark outside more menacing than ever.

Christophe, in the front seat, half turned.

One Flame Hour

"Don't think we'll make it back for dinner," he said calmly. "So, I suggest we stop and have something to eat in town."

Carla's stomach growled in appreciation. "Great idea," she agreed. The gingerbread of the morning seemed a long time ago. The car seemed to agree too, sliding and skidding on ice before coming to an undignified stop in front of Prishpekt a small café on the outskirts of the estate and known for its hot pies and borsch. Soon they were tucked up, still in their outer garments, the windows fuzzing up with condensation. There was a heaviness in the air which confused Carla until she realised it was simply the act of being huddled together in an indoor space, something they'd not done in many months. She felt lulled by the warmth, the uncertainty of what lay ahead of them.

Already in her mind, Carla had left Tolstoy and *his* troubles far behind, fictitious, or otherwise: Natasha at her first ball, the battlefield at Austerlitz, Vronsky's boredom in Switzerland and the later misunderstanding which led to Anna's impetuous, regrettable action… had all receded into the walls of the house, back to being the mere ghosts and figments of her imagination that they really were. She smiled absent-mindedly as the waitress, the very caricature of a Russian temptress with waist long black hair and dark heavily made-up eyes, whisked their plates away the second they laid down their cutlery. Her long Schiaparelli pink talons tapped the china.

Satisfied on thick hot chocolate, Seb sat back comfortably in his chair. Carla felt cosy and snug in hers. Her thoughts zig-zagged from the gold lurex figure-hugging Missoni she'd intended to wear that night to the gorgeous backless velvet pantsuit reserved for embassy drinks. And she could have groaned aloud when she realised that she wouldn't now wear the beautiful Prada number - gossamer black lace fastened on one shoulder with a silk bow which had already seen dinner at the palace. Long-sleeved, V-necked, cinched at the waist with a tortoise shell belt, was another gown in which Carla had fancied herself poised on the top step of a wide staircase, perfectly framed against polished mahogany and a blood-red carpet. Carla frowned. The word for blood in Russian was 'krof.'

"Was he the bon viveur I imagine him to be?" Seb was asking. It was a few moments before Carla realised, they were not talking about Tolstoy but Alfredo.

"Er… not exactly," answered Christophe. "As with most of us, there's more than one side. Our father (who art in heaven) could be terrific company. He could also be irritable and difficult. Especially at Christmas…"

"So, I gather. You mean like the one involving the Japanese hitchhiker?"

"Yes," Christophe said catching Carla's eye. "But there were others too…"

"Really?" Seb's eyebrows had shot up. "What, better than that one?"

Carla and Christophe exchanged looks.

Much, much better… Depending how you looked at it…

She saw, rather than heard Seb and her brother continue with their conversation as her thoughts continued their own trajectory, swerving from the present, shying from the future before careering once again into the men's talk, of Christmas. Of course, that last Christmas had been different again, with not a few 'lasts' about it: the last Christmas at the manor, the

One Flame Hour

last Christmas being married to her ex, the last Christmas Christophe had been with his. The last with her father. But there'd also been a first.

As they so often say, with a death, new life often follows.

21

Carla remembered that she'd been juggling wrapping presents with writing last minute Christmas cards, when the phone rang. She could hear it vibrating underneath the debris of recycled paper and tatty ribbon. She was already running late to collect the twins from school, but she wanted to finish wrapping this last gift although the corners didn't quite reach. Unless she cut out a separate piece and stuck it together. Despite her best attempts, the result was still amateurish, as though wrapped by one of the twins. Her heart sank further on hearing Eugenia's voice.

"Darling," said her mother uncharacteristically calm. Usually, she blazed through conversations at 100 megawatts, always breathless from delivering whatever it was she wanted to say in staccato sentences. "We've decided."

"Oh?" Carla wasn't sure whether to feel relieved that her parents wouldn't be coming to spend Christmas in Carla's new home or disappointed. "That's OK," said Carla the roll of Sellotape stubbornly refusing to adhere to the paper but firmly gluing her fingers together instead.

"No, we're coming," said Eugenia. "But I just wanted to make sure that you've asked Roger."

Carla paused unpicking tape from her thumb and losing the end of the roll in the process. "Of course, I've asked him," she said trying to keep the tetchiness out of her voice. "And I'm glad you're coming. That's wonderful." She located the end of the roll and stuck it to the side of the table where it swung, ready to fall at any moment. "The more the merrier," she added weakly. Carla made a rapid assessment. If her parents and younger brother all came, it would mean putting Roger in the attic. It wasn't the best of spare rooms but had pretty views of the forest at the back of the house. On the plus side, he'd be able to smoke out of the little dormer window. Getting the room ready, she'd found an overflowing ashtray balanced on the guttering. Presumably a leftover from the previous owners, so clearly a room favoured by smokers.

"Oh, and darling," said Eugenia. "As Lady Hermione and Mungo are coming, I think we should have separate rooms as well. Your father -"

"Separate rooms?" echoed Carla. *Since when had her parents ever had separate rooms?* Was her mother serious? The house was large but not *that* large… all Carla could think of was the extra work. The sheets…

"Well," said Eugenia. "You know-"

Carla took a deep breath. "I don't actually,"

There was a prickly silence. To other people, mother and daughter complained furiously about the other, causing untold moments of grief, but neither were ever capable of expressing dissatisfaction in a calm, unemotional way. This was the closest they'd ever got to anything remotely like an honest conversation. If you could even call it a conversation Or honest.

"Carla, what would you know? Anyway, the point is that I can't share a room with Alfredo. I don't sleep and if I don't sleep, I don't enjoy myself. And if -"

And if you aren't the centre of attention… Carla finished the thought process in her head.

One Flame Hour

"Yes, got it," said Carla crisply.

And she did. Clearly, Eugenia still hadn't got over the fact that Lady Hermione was the daughter of a Duke. Similarly, Eugenia must also have discovered that Lady H never shared a bedroom with her husband Mungo and therefore, desperate to appear as grand as Hermione, wanted separate bedrooms too. The earful that followed, persuaded Carla that it would be useless arguing. Either Eugenia and Alfredo were given different rooms, or they wouldn't come. *Which wouldn't be such a bad thing…* thought Carla except that Carla did want to see her father and the children their grandparents. What Carla couldn't deny was that Eugenia, an indifferent mother was a wonderful grandmother. Which brought Carla back to the problem of bedrooms. If the twins doubled up for one or two nights, Carla might just be able to accommodate everyone's wishes.

But then there was Christophe. He was pretty relaxed although he liked his creature comforts. He was easy going, easily pleased and she knew that he'd be willing to sleep on the floor if need be. Which shouldn't be necessary. Lady H could have the pretty white and green room - it had a four-poster bed upholstered in Chelsea Textiles and an en suite. The loo was a little temperamental, but if the twins checked it occasionally, there shouldn't be any plumbing issues. Alfredo could go into the snug (that way he wouldn't have to climb stairs) and her mother could have one of the twin's rooms. Her heart did a tiny lurch at the thought of explaining to her children that they'd have to go up to the attic (deep breath) and share. That would just leave her father-in-law Mungo… Carla massaged the bridge of her nose. She'd think about where to put *him* later.

One Flame Hour

Carla agreed to it all and rang off. *Just finish the task in hand*, she told herself. *Except I'll just unload the dishwasher first and then try and find the Christmas tree lights and the stockings… and the stand…and while it's still light go into the wood for kindling and ivy which would involve taking a stool with her as the last time she'd looked there was only ivy on the most uppermost part of the trunk of the tree on the slope going down to the walled garden, which in short she couldn't reach…But then if she did all that today, she would have the next few days free to think about food. Which was no mean feat. Lady H was a vegetarian, her father hated turkey, the twins likewise, Mungo preferred beef or ham, Eugenia didn't care too much as long as there was Christmas pudding with all the trimmings (which Alfredo detested) and Angus - she'd forgotten about her husband. Well, if the meal was liquid there wouldn't be a problem. And the twins! She let go of the wrapping paper and cello tape and scissors. Never mind Angus, she'd forgotten all about collecting the twins!*

By Christmas Eve, Carla was a bundle of nervous energy pacing through the house, making sure all was in order. Angus was working - he always worked right up to the very last minute on Christmas Eve and Carla luxuriated in the quiet of the house. It was most definitely the lull before the storm, when everything was still in place: the cushions plumped, the coffee table straight, the wood neatly arranged not spitting ash, the kitchen sink pristine and the hall entrance mud-free. Feeling increasingly cheerful, Carla switched on to Classic FM to hear Aled Jones dutifully belting out carols. She did a final inventory, mentally checking off completed tasks. Candles and fresh flower arrangements adorned all the rooms. Carla had picked blooms for their scent and association with Christmas: delicate hellebores and eucalyptus. There was a selection of Jo Malone bath oils in the bathrooms and shortbread, whisky, and tea for those still feeling peckish or needing a night cap.

One Flame Hour

There was not one, but three Christmas trees and fires roared in all the reception rooms. The mantlepieces were draped in evergreen garlands slotted with fur cones, dried orange slices and cinnamon sticks. Oversized velvet bows drew attention to the bunches of mistletoe dangling from various nooks and crannies. The very definition of optimism thought Carla wryly. Still, Sophie was particularly good at tying bows and this activity had kept her preoccupied for hours. Both children had helped to make biscuits: star shaped shortbread decorated with edible silver balls and dusted with icing sugar. Glossy oak floorboards threw off a subtle lemon and verbena aroma. Silver and crystal sparkled casting random starbursts of pattern on the walls. The enormous Christmas tree in the drawing room was reflected in the vast ceiling to floor mirror that took up the whole of one wall. The manor house, caked in snow was greeting card perfect only requiring guests to kiss it to life. And although Carla was exhausted, she was pleased with her efforts, as she chased shadows down corridors where a wintery sky bathed everything in an apricot, pine-scented light.

Tea was ready in the great hall after which they could move on to cocktails. A light supper was laid out in the library for those who wished to attend Midnight Mass. Carla marked the rooms and corresponding meals in her head. It was rather like playing a culinary Cluedo. She was hoping that most of the guests *would* go to mass so that she could play Father Christmas. Once the children were in bed, she could then safely retire having filled the stockings and, as was tradition in their family, deposit them at the children's door so that they were the first thing they would see when they woke up in the morning. It might also ensure that the adults had a little extra sleep while the children examined the content of their stockings.

One Flame Hour

Father Christmas had done the same in her home when she was a child although there had been the one time when she'd woken (or maybe she'd never gone to sleep in the first place as she was so excited) to see a shape carefully propping up her stocking against the door jamb. Her belief in Santa Claus (which had been rock solid up until that point) was briefly displaced when his face was illuminated by the burning red tip of a cigarette hanging from his mouth. She might even get a decent night's sleep. The thought cheered her no end. Her eye had begun to twitch with fatigue, never a good sign. Still, she'd had time to don a pair of velvet trousers and embroidered Emma Hope slippers, touch up her make-up to await the arrival of her guests. She'd sent the twins out into the wood to collect kindling but really it was just an excuse to keep them out of the house a while longer; and from time to time, she could hear their voices floating across the valley.

Carla paused at an upper floor window trying to make out Sophie's wine-coloured coat and Tom's green one, through the trees. Most of the land that belonged to the manor was at the front of the house. There the lawn was smooth and flat punctuated at one end by an eratically stocked herbaceous border. There was also a paddock and orchard and beyond those, standing in splendid isolation, was a lone weeping willow. Even though the tree was some distance from the house, sitting under its sprawling, drooping branches was really the only agreeable place to have meals out of doors. The back of the house, despite a wood and walled garden was problematic. The walled garden was at such a distance from the house that Carla was convinced it had never belonged to the manor at all, but to some other house in the village. And the kitchen opened on to a narrow runway of a terrace with high laurels designed to disguise the sheer drop behind them.

Carla had learned this to her detriment when she'd had her gardener rip out the hedges. She wasn't sure why she'd ever

One Flame Hour

imagined there would be the same flat lawn configuration at the back of the house as there was at the front. Frustrated by the feeling of being hemmed in, she'd often stood on the teak picnic table, peering over the hedge. At that height she could catch enticing glimpses of emerald green, spools of colour unravelling through the trees. She imagined a 360 view of rolling hills, a kaleidoscope of sky streaked by ribbon thin sunsets. More importantly, eating al fresco would be a doddle without having to schlep everything miles to the willow tree. She could entertain more easily and of an afternoon even lie out on her new wide, flagstone terrace on one of those incredibly smart loungers, book in hand, while the children frolicked on the nearby lawn. Enthused with plans, she thought she might even grow vegetables and fruit again in the walled garden, even if she might have to bicycle to get there. In high spirits, Carla remembered leaving the house having instructed her Dutch gardener to tear the hedge down. '*All of it?*' he'd asked puzzled. '*All of it!*' she'd said gaily tossing the instruction over her shoulder and thinking no more about it as she'd sped off to London.

Angus, glass in hand, stood waiting for her in front of the house when Carla got home that evening and one look at his face told her something was seriously awry. His jowls were virtually shaking with barely controlled anger. There were food stains down the front of his white shirt which ordinarily might have bothered her, but her gut told her that these would be the least of her worries. He was running his tongue over his lips in the way he did when he was either very drunk or very cross. Or both. Carla rolled down the window, her cheerful greeting dying on her lips. The front door was wide open, and even from the car, she could see down the long corridor through the kitchen and beyond. Well beyond. Taking a deep breath, she alighted. And did a double take. Quietly, silently, before Angus could protest, took the glass from out of his hand knocking back what remained of his

One Flame Hour

whisky. She had expected to look out on to a green and pleasant land with the tallest oaks swaying ever so slightly in a gentle breeze. Closer to the house, she'd hoped the clutch of seringa trees that hadn't been chopped down, would scatter chalky petals with their intoxicating scent.

"Explain this!" He'd stormed through the house to the terrace after a quaking Carla, her shopping bag limp by her side and her smile sliding with it.

He'd stood like a prize boxer, legs firmly planted to take a punch (and give one), shoulders hunched, head thrown back. His back was to… Carla's stomach heaved… what was nothing short of a void, an abyss. Her head spun as she stood on the edge of a vertiginous cliff. The laurel hedge that was, had given the narrow terrace the illusion of depth, and although she'd not realised it at the time, also shelter. Without it, the terrace was an even tinier strip, narrow and inadequate. What was worse, at least ten feet below lay a graveyard of chopped branches, ugly tree trunks, rotting plants (the ones she'd tossed over the hedge in the hope that they'd simply disappear) ditto broken wine bottles (Angus's) and long forgotten gardening tools lost in the process of trimming. What there was not, was a flat green lawn with expanding views. Furthermore, the trees she'd imagined gently swaying in the distance, seemed to be marching ever closer towards the house in *Day of the Triffids* mode.

"What the *hell* were you thinking?" shouted Angus.

Carla's toes curled. What *had* she been thinking? "I'm so sorry," was all she could stutter followed by a poor, "I'm sure it will grow."

"Yes," Angus had snarled. "Sure, in *time…*"

One Flame Hour

Well time was here, and the hedge had grown but not enough to muffle the shouts that were now coming from the direction of the walled garden. Carla hurried downstairs to the kitchen to open the back door, but the twins had come in through the front bringing with them not a neat basket of twigs and cones but mud, a bird's nest and the bottom half of some poor creature's leg.

"Are those *maggots?*" Every intention Carla had had of keeping calm no matter what transpired that afternoon, flew out the door just as surely as the squirming white things fell through it and onto her polished floor. The fresh scent of beeswax was quickly wiped by the stench of rotting flesh.

"Oh, but Mummy," said Sophie clutching the disgusting limb to her chest. Was that *blood* on her jacket? "Just look at the poor thing!"

"And my kindling?"

"Fell out," said Tom helpfully dropping his coat on the floor.

"From what?" An unwanted edge had crept into her voice. She stared at the coat. "Hang it up! And bring me the dustpan and brush."

"Can't," said Sophie rushing past her. "I have to look after him."

"He's dead, stupid," said Tom. "Besides, there isn't a 'him.' There's nothing left to it! It's just a bit of manky old rabbit!"

"It's not!" screamed Sophie throwing herself at her twin.

One Flame Hour

"Oh my, is this how we should be on Christmas Eve? Don't you think Father Christmas can hear *every* word?" said Carla her own voice rising as she peeled Sophie off her brother.

"You mean if you still believe," said Tom.

"Well, you know how it is in this family," said Carla trying a different approach. "If you don't believe, he doesn't come. Simple."

"So," said Tom rudely.

"So? Continue in that vein and there'll be no Father Christmas whether you believe in him or not."

Carla shook a maggot from her toe and was just going to fetch the dustpan and brush herself when she heard a car's engine. "Maybe that's him now," she said grimly.

"That's *not* Father Christmas!" said Sophie promptly dropping the rabbit's leg, gore and more maggots splashing against Carla's velvet clad trouser leg.

"*Avi!*" squealed Tom using the Catalan for grandfather which is how they addressed Alfredo. He too tore out of the house, slamming the door so hard that it reverberated off the woodwork.

Carla went into the kitchen to fetch her marigolds and emerged just as her mother stepped into the house.

"Oh," said Eugenia stepping over the bloody mess in the hall. "Darling, aren't you ready for us?" Her voice was tight with disapproval.

Carla felt tears prick her eyes. She *was*, she had been.

256

One Flame Hour

Eugenia peeled off her gloves but snuggled into her mink. "I'd forgotten how cold the country always is," she said ignoring the roaring fire that was belting out so much heat the mantlepiece was hot to the touch. In fact, only that mourning Carla imagined a crack in the marble surround. "Has Lady Hermione arrived?"

"Not yet."

"Oh." Eugenia was disappointed. "You might want to help your father," she added as an afterthought. She had turned to the huge sash windows through which they could see the twins deploying a huge amount of energy (with little effect) in trying to prize Alfredo from the car. He was poised in a sitting position, half-way out of the front seat, holding on to the roof of the car. But gravity was pulling him backwards and the more the twins heaved, the more he resisted. They were all giggling. Alfredo most of all. He was also trying to light a cigarette, his '*baston*' wedged between his legs.

"Avi, Avi," she could hear Tom say. "We'll help you light it."

"No," said Sophie swiping away her brother's hand. "I will."

"*Oy yoy yo*," muttered Alfredo. "Where are we?"

"The Manor," said Tom. "Home."

"Whose home?" said Alfredo.

"Avi…" said Sophie giggling and Alfredo spluttered as though the two were complicit in some illegal activity.

Carla ventured out into the cold. "Are you coming in Daddy?" she said.

One Flame Hour

Alfredo ignored her. "Where's...?" he looked around him for some sign, some object from a memory box that might help him remember. Carla followed his gaze.

"Angus?" she prompted.

Alfredo looked delighted. "Angus," he said firmly.

"At work," she said.

There was a sunbeam, a flickering of lights. "*Still?*" said Alfredo in disgust. "But it's Christmas!" He pronounced it 'Chreeeestmuss'."

"Ah, Alfredo," said Angus as if on cue, emerging from behind the magnolia tree on the front lawn which, as Carla knew only too well was directly in line with the hawthorn hedge, which was beside a gate that led to the lane, that led to the main road that led to the pub. His shirt was hanging out of his trousers. The belt that should have kept them in place was missing. Carefully, he placed one foot in front of the other as he snaked towards her. But Alfredo saw only the lord of the manor, the provider, the head of the household. He beamed and with sudden alacrity sprung forward in his eagerness to greet his son-in-law. Swaying slightly, his stick over his arm as casually elegant as though it were a dress sword, his cigarette still unlit, Alfredo bowed graciously. "*Feliz Navidad, Señor!*"

Lady Hermione arrived next, exhausted from the journey, and staggering from their tiny car as though she'd been subjected to a day's journey in a pony and trap.

"Ugh, darlings," she said. "Ugh, ugh," before disappearing into the house. "Take me to my room," she said dramatically

One Flame Hour

looking around (in the absence of staff) for a willing person. Sophie was only too willing to oblige as Lady H was actually very good with children. She didn't hold with wearing dresses on any occasion and encouraged free living and art in all forms. When they couldn't find any paper, they'd once resorted to painting on Carla's newly hung linen wallpaper. It often struck Carla, that her own mother behaved more grandly and with more airs and graces than the bohemian Lady H. But then that's because Lady H could. One was a true aristocrat while the other aspired to be one.

"Glug, glug. Mad old thing," said Mungo crossly. "I now know why we divorced." He looked up at Carla's tense face. "Ah darling," he said kindly. Mungo said 'darling' just as many times as Lady H did, but with more feeling. Carla had always loved Mungo. In fact, she'd always got on better with the father than with the son. He moved towards her just as precariously as Alfredo had. Both seemed to have become rather bow-kneed with age and it took them a while to get going if they'd been sitting down. Alfredo had a head start on his *consuegro* and was fast gaining ground. He'd almost reached the front door with Mungo doing his utmost to keep up. Tom danced somewhere behind the two of them. As the lights went on in the best guest bedroom, Carla could see that Lady H had reached her destination. Eugenia was still by the fireplace, carefully draped across the hearth, waiting for the guests to enter. Only then would she shrug the mink from her shoulders.

But the putt putt of yet another car's engine caused everyone to stop and stare. It wasn't Christophe. Carla knew he was driving down some time after supper as he had to work late. And Roger, who had never learned to drive, hadn't yet, given any indication of an ETA. So, who was it? They all turned as the little Volkswagen beetle careered to a stop just short of Mungo's car.

One Flame Hour

Sophie pulled up the window in Lady H's bedroom. Carla caught her breath. The frame in that room was unusually low, on level with her daughter's thigh. While Sophie leaned out precariously, Lady H herself straddled the sill, more intent on trying to reach the overhanging ivy that framed the window than minding her granddaughter.

"We're going to paint it gold for decorations!" shouted Sophie.

Carla frowned. Would that she had showed as much enthusiasm for Carla's.

"Splendid idea!" she called back. "Just be careful!"

But Sophie's attention was already taken by the new arrival. "It's Uncle Roger!" she squealed.

Carla turned.

"But he doesn't drive," said Eugenia coming to the front door clearly tired of waiting for everyone to come in. The effect of appearing elegantly draped by the fireplace swathed in mink was already spoiled anyway as there was no one to see her.

"So it is," said Carla as Brother Roger stepped nimbly from the car.

"Hi fam," he said facing the gathering of octogenarians, drunks and assorted children.

"Roger!" greeted Carla but not before the driver had also stepped onto the snowy drive. A tall (taller than Roger at any rate and by first appearances older) woman, clad in crimson leather trousers clipped Roger at the back of his head as though he were a naughty schoolboy. Carla would be lying if she said red trousers was the only thing she noticed as images from *Guess Who's Coming to Dinner?* sprang to mind. And it wasn't Carla who would mind. The woman started laughing to herself with a contagious laugh that belied her years.

There was a stunned silence and Carla forced a smile doing a panicky mental inventory of her bedrooms. Well, this (Carla couldn't call her 'girl' exactly) *woman* would have to go in with Roger. It was just a shame that he was in one of the attic rooms but with her parents, Lady H and Mungo *all* having separate rooms there wasn't another one spare.

"Hello darling," called down Lady H from above. Everyone was 'darling' which helped when you were trying to untangle the who's who of family.

"Ah, Lady H," said Roger. "How *are* you?"

"Well, as you can see."

"Er…you might want to come down," said Roger who'd always retained a soft spot for the dippy, chronically eccentric, artist manqué.

"No, not that way!" giggled Sophie restraining her grandmother from leaping onto the snow.

"For god's sake Mummy!" shouted Angus concern clearly etched on his face. But then his mother was probably the only other human being (apart from himself) for whom he retained genuine affection. Carla had always thought it a little emasculating the way a grown man referred to his mother as 'Mummy.' Or perhaps it was just the way he said it.

"But who's the bleck?" said Lady H gaily.

One Flame Hour

Out of the mouths of babes... thought Carla.

There was a small silence as Alfredo and Mungo turned at that precise moment.

"Now Lady H," said Roger unperturbed. "This is Janette."

"Charmed, I'm sure," said Janette giggling and thankfully, equally untroubled by Lady H's remark.

"And this is my sister," said Roger.

Carla held out both hands in greeting.

"Welcome," she said her heart sinking. "Happy Christmas."

And that was only the beginning, reflected Carla as they whizzed past other snowy fields, all these years later. Seb's even snoring and the occasional tick of the car's indicators were oddly rhythmic. Christophe too was sleeping. Carla cast him a quizzical look. That Christmas hadn't just been all Roger, she thought. Alfredo had done his fair share in keeping Carla stretched to breaking point. But so, after a fashion had Christophe. She leaned her head against the leather seat. She supposed it was funny the way Lady H had then gone into overdrive, appalled at her Tourette's moment, trying to charm Janette at every opportunity.

"Oh, but we really do adore blecks," she'd repeated over and over until even Sophie had muttered, "Oh, do shut up Granny."

"But why?" Lady H had seemed genuinely affronted before going into a long family saga about the slave trade. "Well, I

One Flame Hour

don't know why you're being so tetchy," she'd said at last, tetchy herself. "After all, *all* our money came from sugar. And we *all* know who worked *those* plantations."

"Right," said Roger. "We're off to bed."

"Bed?" said Alfredo who'd been thankfully docile and oblivious, up to this point.

Carla, feeling pinpricks of anxiety break out over her entire body and carrying heavy plates from the dining room to the kitchen, resisted a strong urge just to drop them. She'd already served tea (rushing to find some vegan alternative to smoked salmon as Janette turned out not to eat fish and a cake without a trace of nuts as she also had a nut allergy which considerably reduced Carla's proposed menu), drinks (cocktails and canapés for the rest) and boiled eggs and toast (for the twins in the faint hope that they would be as tired as she was and go to bed). But then there'd come the argument about Midnight Mass - or more specifically whether the twins were old enough to stay up (Carla felt they were not and so did they) but Eugenia was insisting on being driven the thirty miles (each way) to a Catholic service as opposed to a three-minute walk to an Anglican one. Meanwhile, unbeknownst to Carla, Angus was in the drawing room happily unwrapping presents. The house was already looking post-Christmas tired as opposed to glorious pre-Christmas ready.

In the midst of this, Christophe had arrived.

"Have you eaten?" asked Carla wanly. He had not. Of course, he hadn't. "Oh, but don't worry about me," he'd thrown over his shoulder taking the stairs two at a time. "I'm in the usual room, I gather."

One Flame Hour

"Er...no you're not," said Carla racing after him. "Sorry, you *were* going to bunk up with Roger. But obviously now Janette is going to have to go in with him. So that means..." her voice drifted, and she hoped he would catch her meaning.

Christophe turned frowning. His beautiful cashmere car coat still buttoned to the chin. The fire in the hall had burned down and the house had reverted to being distinctly chilly.

"But Rache, is coming," he said. "Who's Janette?"

Carla shook her head.

"Who's Rache?"

"Oh, you'll like her," said Christophe reassuringly. "But." He retreated a step or two, still towering above her. She realised that she'd not removed her apron.

"But?" echoed Carla thinking that all she wanted to do was go to bed and wake up in February. Or May. *Any* date next year.

"Well," said Christophe thoughtfully. "We're not really a couple anymore."

"Oh good," breathed Carla thankfully. "That's the best news I've heard. In that case you can share with To-"

"Tricky," said Christophe making a face. "You see *I* don't think we are, but Rache does. No, we're going to have to have the green room. Don't want to upset her."

"Well, you can't," said Carla losing patience. "Lady H is in the green room. You're going to have to have Tom's -" and at his expression she added. "He can go in with ..." she frowned. She'd think of something.

Christophe leant down to kiss her cheek.

"Oh, and I might need your car boxing day. It's bigger than mine."

Carla was beginning to feel distinctly put upon.

"And why do you need bigger?"

"It's the boxing day hunt," said Christophe examining an immaculate nail which is more than she could say for her own. Carla had had her nails polished but they'd not survived loading the dishwasher several times already or stuffing the turkey or -

"Thing is, Rache doesn't hunt," continued Christophe having the grace to look a trifle shifty. "So, I'm taking Chloe."

"*Chloe!*" yelped Carla. Chloe was Christophe's ex. By the sounds of things soon to be ex, ex, after Rachel. They'd met in Japan, dated for a decade and then inexplicably - inexplicably to Carla that is - broken up. But they'd all remained close. That was the problem with her brothers' exes, they all became so fond of one another that it was doubly hard when they separated. Sophie particularly adored Chloe as they shared a love of horses.

"Yes, alright," said Christophe irritated. "And for god's sake don't tell -"

"Alfred?" volunteered Carla.

One Flame Hour

"I was going to say Rache," said Christophe. He shoved his hands in his pocket. "I could take Sophie. She'd enjoy a day out."

"Yes, she would," agreed Carla.

"Good," said Christophe. "So that's a yes to the car?"

Carla nodded reluctantly. What else could she do?

"Great. I'm turning in. I'm knackered."

"Oh, I'm sorry," said Carla untying her apron. "Er… um… Christophe." Carla felt herself flush. She was a people pleaser, wasn't she? Why couldn't she just say, no to the car? A simple no. Instead, she found herself saying, "But what about this Rache?"

Christophe supressed a yawn. "What about her?"

"Well, if you're hunting and she doesn't ride…"

"Oh, that's easy," he said breezily. "She'll love hanging out here with you. She's always said how she wants to get to know you."

"You mean me and the rest of the catastrophe."

22

"I'm not moving," said Sophie. She was doubled up, virtually hugging the bedhead, one leg pinioned under the covers, arms crossed, cuddling her pink teddy bear. If she had been physically chained, her body language could not have screamed defiance more.

"Please," pleaded Carla her arms full of clean bed linen. She'd blithely offered Christophe Tom's room when in fact Sophie's had the double bed, so it made sense for her brother and Rache (whoever she was and whenever she got there) to go into that, and to leave Tom in his attic room. Carla sank into an armchair for a moment's respite. She had yet to strip the bed (how many had she already changed that week?) and fetch more blankets. She cast a quick glance round the room appraising it for its suitability. It might be a bit girlie with its pink and white floral curtains and painted French furniture, its rosettes stuck on the pink gingham board and stuffed toys arranged carefully along the low window seat, but it commanded the best views of the park.

In her own nod to Christmas, Sophie had stuck a stencil of a tiny rain deer in a corner of the windowpane. On the sill below, were bits of broken china Carla recognised as having once belonged to Alfredo's mother, Carla's grandmother: white horses missing a hoof or a tail, a torn silk fan, a miniature set of ivory dominoes. Carla remembered her grandmother in another country, switching on the light in a display cabinet so that these treasured objects were beautifully illuminated. She also remembered how these prized possessions, so lovingly collected over the years, were dispersed amongst the family within hours after she died.

One Flame Hour

"But it's Christmas Eve!" said Sophie cutting into Carla's thoughts. "I want to wake up in my *own* bed on *Christmas* day. Besides how will Father Christmas know where to go if I've moved!"

"That's *if* he can get down a chimney," said Tom slyly, coming into the room, his hands in his pockets and rocking on his heels in the pose of a diminutive statesman.

"Why?" said Sophie a look of panic on her face. "Why wouldn't he?"

"Oh, I don't know," said Tom mysteriously.

"See," said Sophie tears catching in her throat. "I'm not moving! Father Christmas won't find me! And then I won't get my Furbie-"

"Your *what?*" panic furred up Carla's. This furry whatsit had not been on Sophie's Christmas list. There'd been a whole raft of toys for her rabbit and pony but there was nothing at all about a 'Furbie'. Carla frowned - unless of course that scribbled word at the very end of the letter had actually meant something.

"Get out!" screamed Sophie hurling a pillow in Tom's direction.

"Children!" said Carla wanly as the twins began a pillow fight in earnest and the room began to look as though they'd been playing shipwreck, a favourite game of theirs.

"I'M - NOT- MOVING!" said Sophie emphasising every word with a punch of the pillow and a bounce on the bed.

One Flame Hour

Carla watched mesmerised, fatigue pulling at her eyelids and all her good intentions flying in the face of this latest complication. It was simply impossible to locate a 'Furbie' in time. Sophie would have to be happy with her presents. A pillow hit Carla in the face. She threw it back. The twins squealed with delight.

"OK, OK," said Carla.

"So, I'm not moving?"

"No," said Carla. "I meant, settle down. You're getting too excited."

"Baby!" taunted Tom which evoked a war cry from Sophie. Carla retrieved a pillow and began changing its cover. She felt as frustrated as her children. In fact, Carla could have *howled* with frustration. After all, she'd organized the rooms, stocked them with fresh towels and flowers and the finishing touches for the women and now it didn't seem to matter who went where. Half of her wanted to get on the bed with her children and jump until she hit the ceiling, the other knew that she had to dig deep if she was going to pull this off, fight her hammering head with yet another Aspirin and somehow get the twins, if not to sleep, then at least to stay in one room so that 'Father Christmas' could at last get to work.

"It's only for one night," she began. "Just think of baby Jesus."

The twins made a face by which Carla was given to understand, they really couldn't care less. Christmas was commercial didn't she know.

"Or the Japanese hitchhiker," said Christophe coming into the room and dropping his bags on the floor.

One Flame Hour

"Uncle Chris!" shouted Sophie flinging herself on him. Her cheeks were flushed. She didn't look ready for sleep any time soon. Carla steeling herself for a very long night quietly began stripping the bed, hunkering down to pull the duvet from under Tom's feet.

"Who's the Japanese hitchhiker?" said her son stepping over her.

"Why don't you go and ask Avi," said Carla breathlessly, shaking out a clean duvet cover. Why was it that one corner always got stuck? The last time she'd changed Sophie's cover she'd found a table napkin wedged in the corner that had been missing for years. "At least see if he remembers."

"Avi doesn't remember anything!" Sophie volunteered cheerfully. She was now dancing around the room dropping things on the floor the minute she lost interest in them. She knocked over a small box of drawing pins and a book of sticky, multi-coloured stars.

"I do every job twice," Carla muttered under her breath, stooping to sweep them up.

"Oh, he'll remember the Japanese hitchhiker," said Christophe confidently. "I'm sure of it."

"Beat you to him!" said Tom turning on his heel and running out of the room.

"Oh, no you won't!" said Sophie tearing after him a bottle of glitter tumbling from her hands.

"And then it's bedtime!" called Carla. She could feel the veins in her throat straining.

One Flame Hour

"What? On Christmas Eve?" said Christophe.

"*Especially* on Christmas Eve," said Carla wearily. "Anyway, aren't you going to Mass? With Eugenia?"

Christophe adjusted his glasses. Carla didn't remember him wearing glasses before, but they suited him, giving him an air of gravitas that belied the chaos of his love life. He was fit, athletic, his clothes beautifully cut, his shoes expensive. He was certainly an eligible catch for someone. She wasn't so sure about Roger. Now, that she thought about it, where *was* Roger? She only hoped he was in the 'right' room.

"Thought I'd wait and go with the twins in the morning."

Morning... Morning seemed a year away with all Carla had yet to accomplish. For two pins she could have curled up between those lavender-scented sheets and...

Christophe began unpacking, hanging up his suit for Christmas day, his riding kit for the day after that. He dropped a couple of books on the bedside table, replacing Sophie's pony club favourite *Heartland* with *The Great Game*.

"I don't suppose you fancy a hot chocolate, do you?" But what Christophe really meant was 'I don't suppose *you* wouldn't mind making me a hot chocolate.' "It's so cold and frosty, it reminds me a little of Geneva."

Me too, sometimes. Carla wanted to say. *But without the staff.,.*

"Sure," said Carla bending down to pick up the bundle of Sophie's laundry. "I'll be right back."

One Flame Hour

"And some cookies? But just one." He patted his trim torso. "Don't want to get podgy."

"See what I can find," said Carla faintly thinking that her brother would never gain weight. He was far too disciplined for that.

"Sh!" he said suddenly. Carla halted, peering over her pile of laundry. "Listen!" Obediently, the owl began hooting again, a long, single sound penetrating the stillness, on that last cold Christmas night. "Oh, I love those," said Christophe contentedly.

"Yes," agreed Carla so do I. "Actually, so does Tom."

And there, as accurate and fine as an acupuncturist's needle, came the cameo of another memory. She remembered another house - where the master bedroom had had its own wide balcony - actually it was less of a balcony and more of a flat roof with a railing. One warm, summer's evening (they'd had a house full then too), Tom had volunteered to sleep under the stars. He'd been small enough not to mind a Lilo for a mattress and with his regular duvet and pillow had been snug enough. Someone had given him a whistle that made the sound of an owl and he'd spent a happy time calling to the birds.

Christophe went to the window, pulling back the curtains. "God, I love the country. Yeah, hot chocolate. And…"

"Yes?" Carla turned, one hand on the door handle.

"You wouldn't happen to have a hot water bottle?"

Carla blinked. "Coming up," she said.

One Flame Hour

*

Ecstatic to have the house to herself even if she knew it might only be for a few hours, Carla tip-toed down the stairs as quietly as she could. Few *minutes* as it turned out. She'd caught sight of herself on the landing mirror on the way down - smudged eyes (no matter how much makeup she removed the night before, there always seemed to be residual traces) and lank hair. She shook away disquieting thoughts about ageing and losing her sparkle. Now wasn't the time to think about her appearance, it was about catering to her guests. In the end, she'd not slept very much but it didn't matter. By working well into the early hours, the house was almost back to where it was before the guests had arrived.

Presents (at least the ones Angus hadn't unwrapped) were piled invitingly under the tree (Carla had double-checked to make sure there was exactly the same amount for each twin), fires were lit in the hall and drawing room, breakfast was laid out with all her prettiest Herend china and she'd remembered to leave a few crumbs on the dish the twins had left out for Father Christmas. She'd even rung a couple of bells under the twins' window when she knew they were still awake, just to confuse them. Imagining the expression on their doubting faces was worth the extra stress lines on hers. She carried the thought with her as she wandered through the rooms in her dressing gown, cup of tea in hand, inhaling all the delicious Christmas smells - eucalyptus and cinnamon and orange peel and tuberose. It was Christmas day in the morning. That was enough. It *should* be enough to keep joy safely berthed in her heart just a little while longer. The tree reflected in the long mirrors down the corridor leading from hall to reception room twinkled beautifully and outside, a new blanket of snow enveloped everything in a forgiving veil of white.

One Flame Hour

"Mummy!" there were squeals as the twins tumbled down the stairs, each one trying to be the first to reach her as she continued on her way to the kitchen.

"Happy Christmas!" breathed Carla. This was what it was all about and what it should be about. The children.

"Can we open our presents?" said Sophie.

"Mmmn?"

"Our presents!" shouted Sophie. "You're not listening!"

"Sophie!" said Carla her voice rising. "Don't shout! You'll wake everyone!"

"Good!" said Sophie, "They *should* be awake!"

"I know Uncle Roger is, we heard him," volunteered Tom. "Making funny sounds."

"Oh?" But Carla's thoughts were tumbling ahead. She would roll out the pain au chocolat while she made fresh coffee, or perhaps the twins could do that… just as long as they didn't quarrel over how much chocolate to put in each roll… Then she needed to get a handle on timings for cooking the turkey It was getting it all co-ordinated and just right that she found challenging. Maybe Janette would peel potatoes or was that wrong to expect her to help? Would she take it the wrong way? Better get Christophe - except he wasn't the kitchen type and forget asking Eugenia or her Lady H. Not that the latter would be adverse - she'd be more than willing just less than efficient. It helped that they wouldn't be eating until late. They'd go to Mass and come home to champagne and smoked salmon and as was a tradition in her family, they'd

One Flame Hour

sit down when it was beginning to get dark, and they could light candles. And more fires. Which would require more kindling. Her mind began to whirr. Preparations were far from over.

"So, if he's awake, can we open our presents?"

"Who?"

"Roger!"

"Uncle Roger, to you. No, we'll have breakfast first," said Carla firmly delaying the moment of the great reveal. Or not. When the 'Furbie' would not be unwrapped.

"Well, I don't see why we should have to wait. Avi's already up!" hissed Tom darting off to the kitchen and back again.

"Is he?" said Carla astonished.

Alfredo, was indeed seating at the breakfast table, shaved, dressed in his suit, leaning on his *baston* and frowning. The twins pirouetted around him, covering his faces in kisses, smoothing his hair, hiding his cigarettes, and generally making a nuisance of themselves.

"Avi, Avi, Avi," chirped Sophie. "Feel this." She produced her pet gerbil which happily Alfredo could only feel not see.

"*Oy yoy yoy yo,*" said Alfredo not unamused. "What is that?"

"That's Bond," said Tom. "Only Sophie calls him Blonde."

"No, I don't," contradicted Sophie. "Anyway, how can it be Bond when she's a 'she'?"

One Flame Hour

"Are you making coffee?" asked Alfredo. Carla who had already placed the kettle on the range, nodded. "Of course."

"Avi, Avi, Avi," began Sophie again.

"Sophie," said Carla warningly.

"Avi, Avi, Avi," echoed Tom joining in.

Carla closed her eyes turning back to the range. How was it that she could move from calm to irritated in seconds? *It's Christmas, Carla*, she warned herself. *It's Christmas.* Sophie was kneeling on her chair, the end of the tablecloth rucked up under her, a glass of juice precariously close to the edge. Carla resisted the urge to nag - what was it that Lady H had once said? That she mustn't mind about family life? But Carla did mind a lot of the time. She couldn't help wincing at the sight of her father's ashtray set in the middle of her pretty plate. Bond scampered through an obstacle race of Tom's Lego and the china bowls of jam and honey.

"Avi," said Sophie firmly taking her grandfather's face in her hands and squeezing his cheeks.

"*Qué pasa?*" asked Alfredo patiently, his unlit cigarette dangling from his lips.

"Enough," said Carla.

"But I have something to *say!*" protested Sophie.

"Then say it," said Carla sharply. Maybe if she turned on Classic FM, her Christmas feeling would return. Within seconds the apricot-smooth timbre of Aled Jones's voice flooded the kitchen and Carla felt momentarily soothed. *Good*

One Flame Hour

Christian Men Rejoice which came next, however, returned that agitated feeling.

"*I* know where Uncle Roger was sleeping," said Sophie.

"Yes?" said Alfredo only half paying attention, his eye on the chocolate rolls Carla had taken out of the oven. She brushed away a lock of hair from her face. The heat was making it frizz.

"Just wait," she said to her father reading his mind as she shifted the confectionary to a cooling rack.

"I do too!" chipped in Tom not to be outdone.

"One or two?"

"Beds?" said Sophie.

"Rolls," said Carla.

"Do you think," said Tom carefully. "That Uncle Roger *should* sleep in one or two beds?"

Carla paused her hand hovering over a pain au chocolat, sliding it from the baking tray to a plate.

"What do you mean?"

"Well, that girlfriend of his was in a tiny bed and Uncle Roger was on top of her! I know because I've just seen them and they were making these really odd sounds. Like she was hurt and -"

"OK, that's enough," said Carla slamming down the baking tray.

One Flame Hour

"I told you not to say!" hissed Sophie who sitting back down abruptly, had managed to pull the tablecloth - one of Carla's best white linen ones - from under the jug of orange juice with predictable results. Carla leapt forward with a kitchen roll.

"Now, look what you've done!" said Tom.

Alfredo lit his cigarette with a match then waved his hand in an exaggerated figure of eight, in the air to extinguish it rather than simply blow it out. But then he was losing his puff. In more ways than one.

"It doesn't matter," said Carla because by then it really didn't. She was beginning to accept that family life was exactly this - spillages and general chaos.

"You're right it doesn't matter," agreed Alfredo.

Carla shot him a grateful look. All at once she felt that Christmas feeling, that general 'good will to all' steel over her. At last. She chose the best chocolate roll and set it lovingly in front of him.

Alfredo inhaled deeply before blowing smoke not deliberately, in her face. He placed his cigarette carefully on a side plate. Carla flinched inwardly as it continued to burn, the paper curling and turning black, dropping ash on her starched linen tablecloth. But then she remembered a wonderful trick of his - one that could only be played if he was smoking with an ashtray to hand. She loved to watch him, the way he would set his cigarette on the edge of his ashtray, to take her hands in his beautiful ones, the fingers so long and straight and gentle. Barely touching her, he would ask her to clench her fists tight and choose a number from one to ten. He would then tap her hand and hey presto when she unclenched it there was, the dot of ash. Of course, it was an effective sleight of hand because what he was really doing was pressing ash into the palms of *both* her hands as he talked. "It doesn't matter because it's your mother's fault," he was saying now."

The twins, rolls halfway to their mouths, stopped as the temperature in the kitchen dropped a degree or two and electricity crackled all around them.

"*My* fault?" said Carla nonplussed. She scrunched up a paper napkin and fetched another. Her beautiful cloth was now puckered with a large yellow stain and cigarette ash. "How on earth is it my fault?"

Alfredo closed his eyes, taking a mouthful of chocolate, a moment's pleasure visible in his expression.

"This is your house," said Alfredo calmly. "Roger is with Janette under *your* roof. Your responsibility."

Carla shook her head in disbelief. "How can I …" she glanced in the twins' direction hoping Alfredo would follow her drift. But he wasn't giving her a bar. "How can I … *patrol* what people do…" again she cast a glance at her children but the twins, were riveted, eating with their mouths shut, elbows off the table, facing the table square on and hanging on every word. "Look, Roger is a grown man. I can't possibly control what he does at … at *night*."

"Yes, you can," said Alfredo firmly. He alternated taking a bite of pastry, with taking a puff his cigarette. Carla watched nervously as ash floated to the carpet. Already she'd noticed fresh burn marks on her Persian rug in the drawing room.

One Flame Hour

"It's up to you to set a standard. You can't allow that sort of thing in your house. And at Christmas."

"What sort of thing Avi?" said Sophie, wide eyed.

"Sex," said Tom knowledgably. "They're probably having sex."

"Oh," said Sophie. "That."

"See what I mean," said Alfredo in disgust shooting a Carla a withering look as though she were running a house of ill repute.

"But Avi?" said Sophie

"What is it?"

"How come married people don't share rooms and unmarried people who want to, aren't allowed?"

"Right," said Carla. "How about opening one present each, before the others wake up?"

"Yess!" said Tom leaping from his seat. "Beat you to the tree!" said Tom.

"Do you think," said Sophie extricating herself from the tangle of tablecloth, cushion and dressing gown. "Do you think Uncle Roger wants a baby? I mean he's never very keen on us, is he?"

With the last of the pastries cooling on the Aga, Carla slumped into a chair to contemplate her ravaged Christmas table. It was still only eight a.m. and yet it felt like the end of the day.

One Flame Hour

"The only baby you should be thinking about is the baby Jesus," said Alfredo tucking into another pastry. "Unless…" Alfredo's eyes narrowed. "Unless you're not having another?"

Not sure how, thought Carla, the words conception and immaculate, this being Christmas, springing to mind.

"Not *Mummy*, silly!" said Sophie delightedly- delightedly that is because she knew something the adults clearly did not.

"Sophie," said Carla wearily, "darling why don't you just go and open a present. Better still. Open as many as you like. Avi and I will come and sit with you in just a minute."

"It's Uncle *Roger!*"

"What do you mean Uncle Roger?" said Alfredo sharply as alert as he'd ever been.

"Don't you mean *Janette*," said Tom helpfully returning to the kitchen an unopened present in his hand. "Come on, I've been waiting."

"Tom," said Carla warningly.

The twins beamed. "Uncle Roger's having a baby! Uncle Roger's having a baby!" they sang.

Suddenly Sophie stopped as something occurred to her. She picked off a line of chocolate with her finger eating that first, before starting on the pastry. "What colour do you think it will be?" she asked. "And if they have twins like us, will there be one of each?"

"A boy and a girl would be nice," said Carla weakly having an inkling of where Sophie was going with this.

"No, I meant, will he have one black baby and one white baby? Or two black babies or two-"

"A disgrace," said Alfredo tottering to his feet and shooting Carla a withering look. "I simply can't understand how you could allow this to happen."

23

Come Boxing Day, Carla wondered not for the first time, why she had fretted about bedrooms - she should just have offered hers up too. Angus was virtually absent the entire holiday and the hours between her going to bed and waking were so few, she could have curled up on a window seat with a duvet. It almost came to that. Feeling faintly ill, shaking with fatigue, Carla was stoking the fire in the hall when Christophe strode downstairs looking magnificent in his riding clothes. Magnificent and rested. As were all the guests. With every twitch of her eyelid, they all by contrast, appeared healthier and bouncier.

"You couldn't help me with my stock?" he asked sheepishly. "Not sure what's the matter," he motioned to his collarless shirt. "Just can't seem to get it right."

"Of course." Carla got to her feet. "I'm so grateful that you're taking Sophie," she added.

"No problem," said Christophe. "Besides she loves Kirsty."

"*Kirsty?*" stuttered Carla. "As in *your* Kirsty?" If it was the Kirsty, Carla thought he meant, she was an ex from way before Chloe. "I thought you were taking Chloe. I mean last night -"

Christophe pulled away to admire himself in the little Regency mirror that hung behind the door.

"That's right."

One Flame Hour

"But last night…" Carla frowned. Was she just tired or confused or both? "I thought you said you'd asked Chloe?"

"Yes, I had." He wet his thumb and forefinger to smooth a lock of unruly hair, caught her eye in his reflection and smiled. "But you made me think. Probably not a good idea to an invite an ex-ex from way back, if you know what I mean."

"As opposed to a recent ex."

"Exactly."

Carla went back to plumping up cushions, emptying ash trays and sweeping the remains of kindling and dried leaves into the fire with the side of her foot.

"So, I thought I'd ask Tamsyn for …"

"Tamsyn?" she echoed faintly. "I can't keep up…" *Who the hell was Tamsyn?* "What ask out as in for a date? Or to a dinner in London?"

"Er… not exactly."

As if on cue, frozen gravel spluttered from beneath a Mini's wheels as it struggled through a gear change. The car skidded on a patch of ice before coming to an abrupt halt.

Carla watched dazed, hugging a cushion as a girl who was neither Chloe nor Kirsty, nor Rache, nor anyone she'd ever met before let alone heard of, got out of the car.

"Oka-ay," said Carla. "Does this mean that Rache and Chloe *aren't* coming, C?" she attempted to placate her brother with the name she'd called him when she was little.

One Flame Hour

"No, of course they're still coming. I hadn't the heart to put them off. After all it's Christmas, isn't it?"

"Yes," agreed Carla faintly. "It's just that I'm not sure where everyone will sleep."

Christophe cast her an astonished look.

"Oh, with me, of course. They'll all bung in with me."

For a moment she looked at him in disbelief but was too exhausted to even argue.

"So... is *this* Tamsyn, then?" she said limply nodding towards the beautiful blonde with an immaculate bobbed head, who was standing by her car. "And does she at least hunt?"

"Don't be silly," said Christophe. "Does she look as if she hunts?"

Carla threw down the cushion. Who cared about plump cushions anyway?

"Fine," she said tartly. "So, what is *she* going to do when you're out hunting with Kirsty and Sophie? And what about Rache? Oh God, and *Chloe*?" Carla's temples began to throb. This Tamsyn had pulled out a smart little Louis Vuitton holdall from the passenger seat and was sashaying towards the house, carefully picking her way through the snow. Her burgundy Gianvito Rossi boots were this season's costing almost as much as a car. Carla knew - she'd seen them on Mytheresa.com.

"I thought you'd get on," said Christoph watching her.

One Flame Hour

How did you figure that? thought Carla. *The only way I'd get on with anyone at this point is if I were on a desert island all by myself.*

*

And if Carla had known then that the exhaustion and exasperation of that Christmas would of course come to an end, as all things do, no matter how uncomfortable at the time, would she have done anything differently? By the new year, so much had changed anyway, and Christophe's coterie was the least of it. By the end of the Christmas week, he had ditched them all - Tamsyn included. Her beauty wasn't enough, after all, to hold his attention. The minute she entered through one door, Christophe would slip out of another, and Carla spent most of Boxing Day comforting a weeping Tamsyn, an irate Alfredo and a pregnant Janette while Roger moped in a chair by the fire drinking and bemoaning the end of his bachelor days. Needless to say, Rache, Chloe and Kirsty hadn't hung about very long either.

And yet despite its awfulness, it was funny how the sound of carols now as they entered the Moscow residence, could bring that Christmas straight back and Carla could think of it only with affection. Carla had been almost catatonic with exhaustion by the end of it and yet Alfredo had still been alive and the twins still little. And yes, she would give anything to have even an hour of that chaos back again, to grit her teeth in irritation when Alfredo flicked ash in her direction, or she picked up yet another towel off the bathroom floor.

Dropping their bags in this hall, Christophe waved them upstairs while he went to fetch drinks. They were all too wound up after the long drive back from Tula to turn in just yet and besides, it was their last evening in Russia. With England going into another lockdown and Moscow about to suspend flights to the UK, who knew when they'd be back in Russia again. Carla shrugged off her fur in a gesture worthy of her mother. The residence was deliciously warm, and she felt herself melt into its opulence, doubly warmed by her reminiscences. "Come on," said Seb. "Let's find some music."

"What now?"

"Why not? You're not going to go to bed and leave me on my own, are you?"

Carla shook her head.

"Well then."

She followed him through the dark, panelled rooms up to the first floor. Carla tried to commit every detail to memory. Somehow, if Carla could stay awake long enough, she could prolong this last night. Despite the constant pings coming from Seb's phone, Carla refused to look at hers. She knew if she did, she'd be sucked up in the general hysteria that the cancellation of Christmas plans was generating back home. She was certain Les Girls would have much to say about the matter, but she would indulge in this escapist fantasy a little bit longer. And in this beautiful house in Moscow, it was easily done.

They went through to the ballroom because Seb had seen a piano there. Decorated in the Empire style, the room had an exquisite parquet floor made up of different woods in the shape of a sundial. An enormous chandelier hung from the white and gold ceiling. In fact, everything in the room was white and gold. Each pane of wood was picked out in gold leaf and even the piano was white. Apparently both Chaliapin and Scriabin had given concerts in this very room, accompanied on that very piano. Not remotely intimidated, Seb lifted its lid to pick out a tune. He had perfect pitch as Alfredo had had and like her father, Seb had wanted to make a career of music. In both cases their parents had intervened. Carla curled up in one of the elegant Louis XV chairs by a window overlooking the Kremlin. She pulled back the heavy drapes to better see the illuminated onion domes: all pink and white swirls on green and yellow, orange and turquoise - like a giant ice cream with sprinkles. In comparative simplicity, the rectangular block of the palace itself, shone as a sheath of polished steel.

And as sparks flew upwards in the giant fireplace under the oversized painting of the queen, she thought of all the dignitaries, artists, musicians, and sportsmen who had passed through the Residence at some time or other. So many histories, so many personages who were truly extraordinary, others who were less so. All had lived and loved and were gone, some to be remembered across the millennia, some to be forgotten. She thought of the *'unhistoric acts'* that Elliot wrote about in *Middlemarch*, *'the lives faithfully lived who would rest in unvisited tombs…'* But they had existed. They had been given life. There were men like Tolstoy who left their written testament and then again there were those like her father who continued to live, for the duration of her memory at least, in her.

Carla's blurred reflection stared back at her. Who was she? Sometimes she felt she'd been caught unawares, slip sliding to becoming her mother - as if her mother had always been staring back at her, patiently waiting for this moment of recognition. Carla shuddered. Had she been resisting something for so long that was simply inevitable? Only a short time ago, before lockdown, Carla had felt positive, not invincible, never exactly that, but still youthful, still in control. But post the first lockdown and on the brink of another, she was becoming used to an unfamiliar and unsettling anxiety. It felt as though she were hurrying towards a finishing line that she'd not known existed a year ago.

Seb stopped mid bar - catching her expression. He moved away from the piano and pulled out his phone. Carla rolled her eyes before realising that he'd been searching for music as the strains of *Por Una Cabeza* filled the ballroom.

"No!" protested Carla.

"Yes," said Seb pulling her to her feet.

Despite her initial reluctance she felt Gardel's evocative music beat a delicious, irresistible tempo in her blood.

"Do you remember dancing in Palermo?" he said, circling her, taking her lightly in his arms. His hand rested just under her rib cage, her hand was on his shoulder, his knee parted hers.

"You know I can't dance without a chair," she muttered referring to the way the women had been taught to practise by making a figure of eight around a chair in order to get the right form. "And yes, yes I remember."

Carla had been embarrassed when Seb had grabbed her in the street in Buenos Aires after they'd had lunch at an outside café, only to realise that everyone including the waiters were all dancing tango, that tango was as essential as a shot of espresso. They began to promenade slowly - her body arching away from his, her back straight as he leaned into her. And then he stopped abruptly, extending his leg fully to block her foot which was the signal for her to step over and back again. This was the bit she liked best, when it felt (and looked) as though she were picking her way delicately over steppingstones. And then it was her turn to block him. She ran her leg up his, stalling his progress. He flipped her so that her back was against his front.

"Better?" he whispered in her ear, knowing that she wasn't.

"Yes," she sniffed.

"What is it?"

"It's just this blooming pandemic," she said, watching her feet, watching his. The truth was that the men in tango did all the work and all she had to do was relax. "I'm so bored of it. It's never ending. Do you think ...?"

Again, they slowly traversed the length of the room. "What? That at last, we're in a room big enough to tango?" Still holding her hand, he flung her away from him.

"No," she said against his chest as he pulled her close before holding her again at arm's length to form his own figure of eight.

"OK. I'm sorry. Go on."

"Do you think this is it? That we'll *never* revert to normal life? That we'll remember how it was, the way people in novels and films did before the war? I don't mind about me - well I do, but I mind most of all for Alfie. Not knowing what it's like to travel, socialise - hang out with his pals, do all the lovely things we used to."

One Flame Hour

"Well, he's already seen more of the world than I had at his age and as for socialising, he's catching up now as we speak and no doubt getting into all kinds of trouble as a result. Sh! Be calm." Seb turned her so that she was facing him again, his steering her shoulder blade. "You're forgetting that the world has been here before. There've been other plagues and pandemics. You don't have to look further than this residence and the changes of governments it has witnessed. And endured. Each generation thinks it's so important but really what are we in the scheme of things? Nothing at all. A drop in the ocean, a wrinkle in time. One flame hour. That's all."

Carla gave a final sniff reassured as she always was by Seb's mere presence, the white linen smell of him, his physical strength. He rested his forehead against hers and for a moment they rocked in one place before once again setting the pace and walking off. But while the music was passionate and intensely romantic, their movements were utterly controlled and measured.

"I like that," she said slipping her hand in his, twirling away from him. "One flame hour. I like that."

They moved around the whole dance floor until still holding on to her hand, he pushed open the balcony doors. "Come outside," he said. "Let's take a look at the city."

"But it's freezing!" she protested.

"It's only for a minute."

The cold took her breath away but was exhilarating too. She remembered having her breath drawn out of her by the beauty of other panoramas, Rio would always and foremost spring to mind. She would always, always remember climbing to the top of the hill and standing with the statue of

One Flame Hour

Christ the Redeemer behind her. In the early morning, before the crowds gathered and in the rainbow light of dawn, there was nothing but sea and sky and undulating hills. *Yes, I get this*, she'd thought to herself. *This* is a city - *this* is beauty. There were cities like Rome or Paris, or London revealed in snippets, with nothing from the air at least, to suggest an impressive history, or timeline. And then there was this. Before them the river was glassy and slick with the lights from Red Square dancing through it.

"See there's life," said Seb letting go of her hand and turning her so that she was leaning against him but facing the Kremlin. "Nothing can stop this surge. It's bigger than us. This too will pass, you do believe it really, so let's make the time count. Like we did last summer after the first lockdown. Do you remember? We were actually quite happy despite everything." His breath was warm on her cheek as he enveloped her.

Carla felt anxiety fall away, the pain of bereavement lessened, the funnel of nostalgia filled in, so that in their place was kindness and humour and hope. Above all there was hope.

"But-" she began out of habit. She was used to questioning, to overthinking, to finding problems where there weren't any.

"No," said Seb firmly. "No buts. One flame hour. That is all."

Printed in Great Britain
by Amazon

66497894R00173